Casting Giant Shadows—Copyright 2017 © by F. Bradley Reaume

This is a work of fiction. Any resemblance between actual events and those herein described is purely co-incidental.

Penshurst Publishing   First Edition—June 2017

ISBN   978-0-9959906-0-9

Front and back cover photo—A photograph of a real American Army unit in Biarritz, France in 1919 after a baseball game. The photo includes the author's Great Uncle Hubert Rodway, who served in the Great War. Unfortunately no other details of the photo are available.

Casting Giant Shadows

By F. Bradley Reaume

For

Leila Matilda (Rodway) Harris

1898—1993

Prologue

The sun was very high in the sky, beating down on the parade of carriages making their way along a track towards a small village in the near distance.

Rural France was lovely this time of year, trees in full leaf, the fields pregnant with the promise of a bountiful harvest, and cool nights which normally made for peaceful, deep sleep.

However, this day was very hot even for August.

The heavy horses were too lethargic to pull their carriages with any determination and moved slowly enough along the rural track that they raised only a light trail of dust. As the dust rose, the drivers in the second and third carriages let their vehicles lag back and steered them off a straight line, staggered one behind the other, to minimize the effect of the dust kicking up and dirtying their Sunday finest. The procession plodded along with the occupants very conscious of their slow progress.

Pierre sat in the first carriage, holding the reins, and wearing his finest suit. Typically French, he was of average height, dark haired and like others in the north, blue eyed. His suit chafed at him more than a little. He was unused to wearing such clothes, especially in this kind of heat. With him was his niece Molly, a young girl about seven or eight years old, dressed up for the day with additional ribbons and flourishes for the big event. She had a supporting role.

An older couple rode in the carriage behind them. The lady sat facing away from the direction they were going. Dressed in her finest, she sat very straight, her head covered with a stylish kerchief and enough layers of clothing to be very warm and uncomfortable. She did not smile.

She looked like she might bolt at any moment and appeared to remain stoic only by sheer force of will. A look of contemplation appeared to have her considering the speed of the carriage and its movement and the relative level of success she might have if she leaping from it. Her husband was also guarded and his eyes moved back and forth to the horses, their seats, their destination and the distant horizon. He could hear occasional deep percussive thumps in the distance.

"I hear it too," said the lady who could see the worry in her husband's eyes and the tension in his shoulders.

"They are distant still. We have time to get this done," he said. "We are ready to go from the farm. Everything is packed and we can leave by simply hitching up the horses and going."

"I know. I hope you are right. It appears we have some time but will it be enough to get far from here?"

An additional carriage, much larger than the first, had been hired. It joined the procession part way along its route. It contained a group similarly attired people, they waved happily at the rest of the procession as they swung into line behind Pierre and Molly and in front of the older couple. As the carriages reached the cobbled street of the village the dust tail dropped away, exchanged for the increased noise of the wheels on the stone.

The last horse drawn carriage, the most ornate, contained only a few people. Eustache Dumont, ran the small general store in the village. His wife Audrey had accompanied him out to the farm to pick up the third occupant of the carriage and form up for the procession to the church.

Marianne Dumont was in her wedding finery. Not a traditional wedding dress however as she had been living with her husband at his family farm for eight years after a civil service, as they struggled for independence while raising their daughter Molly. Today she would be formally married to Charles Augure and they would complete their promises to family and themselves and make their little family complete in the eyes of God.

Marianne sat in the carriage trying to enjoy the moment. She looked at the ring she wore. An engagement ring, Charles had said, a little unusual it had a center square setting filled with a medium sized diamond. Marianne would receive a complimentary ring during the wedding ceremony. She gazed at her ring, thinking of the promise behind it, and how Charles had done what he said he would do and by arranging this church wedding. Their unusual betrothal was familiar to their families and friends. At the end of the day, many wedding arrangements followed unusual paths and theirs was no less normal than most.

The deep percussions were now preceded by a different noise. The German Army was advancing in a staggered manner. They had put extra troops into the area to try to push the front forward to avoid a salient that could be attacked easily on its flank. The artillery shells were distant as the big guns were slow to move. Though the Dumont's did not know it, the German troops had advanced rapidly and were only just out of sight on the far side of a wooded area to the north east of the village. The villagers had all fled the little settlement in the last day or two while the Dumont's had remained hopeful and determined that their plans would not be derailed again. They had moved it forward a week earlier than planned, forcing a smaller and quicker event than they had wanted.

"We cannot linger Marianne," said her mother, Audrey. "The priest and guests have remained in this place for you and particularly Molly. We must complete the ceremony quickly and give them the peace of distance from this place."

"I know mother. I offered to move the ceremony and even wait for a better time, but everyone insisted we keep the date and move ahead. I am here, just trying to do what everyone wants of me."

The carriages bumped along the cobbles and the first one turned into the church yard to deposit the occupants at the door where they could move quickly into position in the church. Pierre stopped and looked back to wave the carriages quickly into position. The noises coming from beyond the wood were ominous.

The booms had been echoing softly, distantly, for the entire journey from the farm, like a far away thunderstorm, except the sky was a cloudless blue. Looking to the north or east provided no indication of any movement as the village was shaded in those directions by a significant forested area. And yet, the persistent deep thump, like a bass drum being struck in a nearby basement would not cease. Added to it was the background sound of rattling, something was jangling but nothing could be seen.

The thumping and soft rattling set everyone on edge. Things were not quiet to the east as the Germans were advancing. In some areas they moved miles at a time. In others it was mere meters.

There was already a carriage at the church. Marianne's husband and father of her child was already inside awaiting the arrival of the small party. He had collected the priest for a return to the village church.

The sound of the following carriages approaching the church was interrupted by a loud whine. Everyone instinctively looked up as the shell exploded on the village street they had just passed. Cobbles were kicked up splattering the buildings on the far side of the street. Windows were broken but there was no sound of shattered glass above the explosive percussion. Then another whine and another and two more explosions rocked the village.

Those in the carriages were panicking trying to steady the horses who stamped and moved and pulled in two different directions making control of the carriages difficult. Dust raised by the explosions rose in the village street.

Pierre leaped into his carriage and had just about gotten control of it beginning to turn it around the church drive, when another whine, short and very highly pitched, caused him to duck his head as bits of wood and slime and God knows what, were thrown in his direction.

"Oh, no," was all he could squeak out, as he looked up and saw a crater and small bits of wheel, where once had stood the fourth carriage.

There were only three carriages on the church green now. Pierre ran back to the edge of the crater. There was a wagon wheel still stuck on its axle. There were two of the legs of one of the horses near the wheel. There was little else that could be identified. He looked wildly around. Marianne and her parents had simply disappeared like the rest of the carriage after the direct shell hit.

Pierre ran one way and then the other looking for some evidence of a body or someone being thrown clear of the explosion. More shells whined and then exploded but he ignored them. A strong hand grabbed his arm.

"Go, get the carriages out of here, back to the farm and pick up our vans and leave. Go south, west anyway away from here. Keep Molly safe. I will find you." It was Charles, tears streaming down his face. "Get everyone to safety. I will collect the priest and take my carriage away."

Pierre simply looked at Charles. At first uncomprehending. Then his words sunk in. He nodded and moved back to his own carriage, as he passed the second carriage he saw his mother curled up into his father's shoulder. Molly sat alone in the first carriage, cowering in the wake of the explosions, her eyes glazed. Charles urged them away and ducked back inside the church. A shell hit the uppermost clerestory and exploded throwing large chunks of masonry out the sides of the building. Fortunately, with the carriages on the west side of the building they were mostly shielded from the explosion.

Pierre climbed back into the carriage, grabbed the reins and quickly guided the carriage around the drive, slowly skirting the crater where the fourth carriage had been destroyed, and then speeding up as they emerged on the village street, turning towards the farm. Another shell hit the church, and then another. Damage was extensive. The second carriage had followed Pierre but upon emerging from the churchyard it turned the other way into the village, the quickest way away from the shelling. It was soon out of the line of fire, south of the settlement, and moving further from the fighting every moment. The older couple had moved most of their things from the village and simply turned to leave as quickly as possible.

The shelling continued as it appeared the German guns had settled on the stone building as the most likely place for resistance to collect.

By this time some French troops had fallen back to the village area, occupying buildings, barns and sheds for cover. Charles realized he could never get his carriage out - he was too late.

The priest waved to him and several of the guests who were in the church to follow him. They had all been oblivious to the sounds of the advancing army until the shelling hit the church. The thumps and rattles had never really penetrated the thick stone walls of the church.

Charles took the priest's direction and waved along the few guests that had been inside. They moved toward the back of the church, where the priest grabbed an iron ring in the floor and heaved up a door that led down underneath the small nave.

They scrambled to safety and as another shell blasted a hole in the ceiling of the building, Charles as the last man in closed the door behind him as he descended the steps into the crypt. As the door closed his eyes needed to adjust to the dim light cast from a few oil lamps already lit. One of the guests, charged with lighting a lamp, made to light them all, around the perimeter of the underground chamber.

"No my son, don't light them all," said the priest. "We don't need that much light and we may need light for a bit longer than the usual visit down here."

The man nodded his assent and moved to snuff out two of the lamps he had already lit, leaving two more, one near the staircase and the other under the main altar as far back from the stair as he could get.

In the dim light the group took stock. There were still noises of explosions above, but they were muffled, even if they were frequent. A few came with significant rumbles, like they had taken place very close. Charles worried that a direct hit might open their hiding place and leave them very vulnerable.

He counted all his friends among him. The small group was less than a dozen. They began to find comfortable places to sit among the stone monuments. Two chairs that were available were filled and the men found low stone caps with headstone backs as the most comfortable places to sit, if they could stand the proximity to the dead.

"Listen to the sounds of the battle," said one. "I'm thinking that once we cannot hear it anymore we should wait a while before trying to escape."

"Who knows if anyone will remain in the village or which side will control it."

The deep thumps and rumbles continued unabated for hours. Some of the people sat quietly. Others chatted in low voices. One of the oil lamps had snuffed itself out. The priest motioned for another to be lit.

The subject came around to the approaching carriages.

"Did Marianne and your families get away before the shelling?" Someone asked Charles. His thinning hair still held in place despite the frantic actions in which he was engaged.

"At least one of the carriages was damaged and I helped Pierre turn around his carriage with my Molly aboard. His parents were behind him and they were following him last I saw. I saw them turn out of the church yard before I came back inside."

Charles did not want to upset the women or scare them more than they were already scared. But he knew the extent of it. Marianne's carriage had been completely destroyed. He hoped she had been thrown clear but in his heart he knew he was clutching at anything he could. The carriage had experienced a direct hit. He was numb and also fearful of Molly's escape and that of his parents and in-laws.

He had long been a married man, having lived with Marianne and having a child with her. The civil service years before had confirmed that. Today was only the completion of a formal promise he had made to her. She already wore a ring he had given her after they had said their vows in a quick civil ceremony just before Molly had been born. Their parents knew of it, the village priest knew of it, but Marianne largely dismissed it in her mind as the church ceremony felt more official. Of course the civil procedure had regularized their social standing, but Marianne was never entirely comfortable with it and he stood by her determination to complete the church service. However with other financial concerns the wedding had often been put off, until finally finances could be squeezed and Marianne could wait no longer.

Charles wondered if her sudden lack of patience had anything to do with the Great War and the thrust of German armies into French territory. He had volunteered for local service but had been spared due to his farm responsibilities. Hungry soldiers needed sustenance, and so did the folk of France. His other skills as a handy man were also prized around the village.

The thumping continued. After more time another one of the oil lamps flickered and went out. The priest moved to light another of the lamps near the stair, lingering for a time, listening intently near the door.

"I haven't heard anything for a while. Do we wait or do we try to get a look at what might be out there?"

There was a general discussion on how to proceed before it was decided that they should open the door only a little to see if anything could be seen to help their decision to flee.

The priest moved up the stair and pushed gently on the door.

It would not budge.

"Mon Du, I don't recall it being this heavy. Of course it is many years since we closed the door behind us when we entered the crypt. It is usually only closed from the aisle for processions and Sunday Mass."

Charles moved up the stair to push on the door. "It's bit awkward reaching above your head like this."

With two of them pushing the door slid upward providing a sliver of light to the top of the stair. Charles looked out at a sea of German soldiers wandering about. The church had been turned into a field hospital. Then there was an explosion and some bricks fell. Charles let the door close quietly hoping the movement in the floor had not been noticed.

"There are Germans everywhere up there. But I heard an explosion. I think the French are fighting back. The Germans won't stay in the church long if it is falling down on them. If they remain under attack they will leave it and then we might escape. Listen carefully for more shelling."

Sure enough there was the sound of shells and the rumble of movement above them. They returned to their vigil. There were plenty of oil lamps around the perimeter of the crypt. The priest assured them that there was even a small supply of oil in a small utility room if they needed it.

The group was silent save for a few whispers. They were listening to what was happening above hoping for a sign to suggest action and escape.

18

Chapter One   New Jersey—1982

The ceiling sloped hard on both sides completing the A-frame of the central section of the large old house. It had been added to on several occasions making it almost castle-like with two turrets and a large addition at the back and one side. Most of the ceiling in the attic was covered with insulation but it was old, tattered and not very thick.

Once the home on a substantial farm, acres had been sold over the decades leaving a gentleman's rural farm property, a few acres of fruit trees, a market garden usually filled with tomatoes and in some years strawberries, an acre of corn, and a couple of old but well kept greenhouses. The old farms nearby had similarly been transformed with the rural road the last bastion of the agricultural community that proceeded the suburban agglomeration that now filled the once productive fields.

Framed by the slope of the roof, light filtered through the small, streaked window and caught a thick stream of dust specks floating in the air. The light through the window cast long shadows on the floor and back wall of the attic. A string of bare bulb lights had been installed temporarily in the ceiling to help mitigate the dark areas by casting a little light in the nooks and crannies between the piles of books, boxes and bits of furniture all around. They did a wonderful job of heightening the contrast between the lit spaces and those denied light by objects, angles and clutter. Seeing the streaming dust exposed by the light from the window he held his breath for only a second, before realizing he'd been breathing in the dust for a least an hour.

The window did not open. He made a mental calculation regarding an air filter or a fan, or maybe just a filter mask.

He reached up and grabbed a cardboard box emblazoned with the Budweiser logo, but looking a bit old fashioned. He wondered if he should keep the box, a souvenir maybe or something he could sell at the auction. He held his breath against the inevitable cloud of dust and swung the box down to the unfinished wooden floor. The puff of dust was largely unseen before being stirred, but the swirl of particles illuminated in the air gave a pretty strong suggestion it was everywhere.

The attic was large enough for an adult to stand up through the central run of the roof, maybe 15 feet wide with enough ceiling height and another 10 feet on each side of rapidly diminishing usable space. Cleared out of all the crumble and piles of stuff, this was a significantly large room, about 50 feet long. Lower sections where the A-frame walls were nearby would work well for a bed, a couch, some shelving or even three sides of a table. It was the perfect place to gain a lot of space in the old house. The usable width was perhaps as much as 25 feet with about five feet on either side of the crest too low to walk in but not too low for other uses.

The house had been a gift to his parents from his paternal grandparents when they had first married - oversized at the time - and they slowly filled it up. First with children and then with the inevitable detritus of life. And then the leftover bits of other people's lives, the possessions of dead relatives, furniture, clothes, photos, collections of stuff. Stuff that was at one time too valuable to throw away and now too much trouble to excise, possessing just enough hold on his memory to cement it in place. And now the house was officially being passed to him though he and his younger family had lived there for years.

With his mother moving out, his first job was to sift through boxes and boxes of collected stuff. Some of it from relatives he barely remembered, some from ones he never knew. Bits and pieces of things from people his mother knew, and she was standing at the bottom of the stair making the cleaning job a bit more difficult. Mixed in was years and years of all the items that his parents couldn't bear to throw out but didn't really want. Some of it went back generations to the origins of the family and their claim on this part of New Jersey.

He had reflected on this issue in the planning of the clean-up. There were all the useful things people couldn't throw away because inevitably they would need them one day. Of course, when they were required it was impossible to remember where they were or it turned out that what you had was the wrong size. Then there were the things that family had stored, memories of lives lived. Unfortunately these things usually had little impact on anyone else, no matter how direct the relationship. Now that more than two generations had passed, the real people that lived those lives were gone and largely forgotten, save maybe a detail or two that might relate to the present day. What was more likely left was organic; a turn of phrase, common traits, a certain similarity in the look of emotion.

Some of the material items might one day be worth considerable money as collectables, as historic bits and pieces but it was impossible to ascertain which things to keep and which to toss. Those concerned for the future kept everything and those who lived in ignorance of the past kept nothing.

He decided early to separate things into those he would keep, those destined for the garbage and those offered to family or for sale. Keeping some of the items was good; especially if he wasn't charged with keeping them all. He liked to have a tangible connection to the past close at hand. It kept him grounded - sure of who he was, in a world that made it easy to forget sometimes. Even he could remember this part of the world was much different than when he was a boy and so much of it seemed fixed and immutable. Anything that had been build since was new, transitory and a little bit unreal.

It had taken him only a few minutes to string up the pair of bare bulbs hanging from temporary light fixtures strung from the peak in the ceiling. That, with the light from the front window gave enough light to work by even though the space was large. He figured he could move the bulbs as he worked his way along the ribs of the attic.

"That's one more box shifted. What the hell are we going to do with all of this stuff? I've got to get rid of it to make more space. Shifting it around isn't going to work," he yelled down the stairs. "It's time to get brutal up here."

"Bring it all down here dear, and I'll go through it and keep only the more important stuff. The rest goes into bags and into the garbage."

"Mom, I have to move it all if we are going to build a living space up here," he stood with his hands on his hips and looked around. "Now that some of it's gone you can start to see just how much space there is."

His mother had decided to move out of the old house to a nice beachfront condominium in Florida. She had sold the home to her youngest son who was going to take the opportunity to renovate. His wife was insistent that they were going to upgrade the old place entirely. The first job was to get his mother's old things out to facilitate her move and to empty the home for the builders.

His father had died a protracted death from lung cancer two years before. His mother had been reluctant to move to Florida but several of her contemporaries had already taken the plunge. They raved about the weather and the lifestyle. They had been persuasive.

"How much more is there Rodney?"

"Mom, I've hardly scraped the surface. Didn't you put the stuff up here? Haven't you seen it?"

"No, your father put it all up there. Most of it came from my mother when she passed and some from your father's father when he died. Be careful there are some valuable things up there."

"It can't be all that valuable if they've been sitting here for 30 years."

"For some things, that's what makes it valuable. But it's really more like 20, your grandmother passed when you were away at school. And, some things of high value are not worth much money."

He grabbed a load of envelopes, probably old financial records, and as he swung the folders toward the cardboard box a black and white photo slipped out. "Ahhh," he said inadvertently, anxious to catch the picture and recognizing it at the same time.

He quickly tossed his load into the box and snagged the photo as it glided to the floor. He was careful not to damage it. There was a puff of dust as the envelopes crashed abruptly into the box, but he didn't even notice it.

"I remember this," he said out loud, holding it closer to his face to try to pick out the detail.

"What do you remember Rodney? I remember you saying that we couldn't get caught up reminiscing about every little thing or we'd never get done," his mother yelled up the stair to him.

"It's that photo of Uncle whatever, you know your brother who we didn't see much, the photo from World War One."

"Put it aside, of course we want to keep it. Let's get a move on. I will sift everything to make sure we toss only junk. The truck is coming day after tomorrow."

"Maybe we should toss the obvious stuff and if there is enough stuff that's questionable we can put it in a storage locker and you can sift through it before you go south."

Rodney looked again at the picture, he was familiar with it. The job before him seemed infinite as every little thing needed to be scanned, considered and processed.

He shook off the thought and brought his attention to bear on the photo. His uncle was in the center, sort of, right there; he looked hard at the picture, trying to see a family resemblance or a hint of who his uncle was. The man looked a lot like one of his cousins. He certainly had the air of a man who knew himself and who was supremely confident in that knowledge. Not arrogant, not the possessor of super human powers, just a man who knew things. He looked to be in his early 20s. The photo stared back at him, full of secrets, but giving none of them up.

"So far I'm doing nothing as I'm waiting for you to bring something down," his mother's voice drifted up the narrow staircase.

He focussed his eyes on the center of the photo where his uncle crouched, among a score of men standing in two rough groups, many of the front line of people down on a knee or crouched like his uncle was. Along the front line three men were each holding a stick, one was his uncle, Uncle Herb he suddenly remembered. He was in the middle with two others. One man held on his left hand a large glove. Another in the back looked like he had a protective vest on. It was two baseball teams. They were kind of together for the photograph but not chummy enough to mix altogether. Along the bottom of the print was the hand written caption, apparently carved onto the photo plate - the first word was unreadable but the rest said "8F Baseball - Biarritz France 5-19-18.

Uncle Herb seemed out of synch with the rest, in the center on one knee beside a much older gentleman who was dressed a bit more formally, and on the other side of him a man carrying a satchel. There was one guy who was hugely tall. He had to be nearly a foot taller than many of the others in the photo.

Uncle Herb had his arm over his raised knee showing his left hand so the unusual angle gave life to a ring or something on his finger which glinted into the camera. Was it a ring or only a spot on the photo plate? Or was it just a trick of light?

There was a gap behind him as if the two groups were distinct. Perhaps they had naturally lined up in the teams they had formed to play. He was clearly in the center with the older man sharing that spotlight. Rodney thought, here was a man he had never met who had died without any fanfare. And yet his grandmother had spoken softly and fondly of him, with more than a hint of sadness.

His mother had met him once or twice that he knew of and he remembered him as a nice man, very much interested in the doings of his newfound nieces and nephews, even though they never really crossed paths again. Rodney knew his mother had idolized her older brother, and tried hard to get him to reverse his vow to remain aloof after a family rift forced him to exile himself. His mother was too young to side with her brother then, and she always wished she had. He had died of cancer in the late 1970s, comfortable and wealthy from a successful business career.

Rodney's grandparents were dead now, of old age. Ancient family battles forgotten, the cares of that generation reduced to rumours of explanations, not even important enough for history books; the shadows of those actions still there, remaining in temperaments, reactions to drama, odd sayings and patterns of speech picked up by their children and passed down to their grandchildren.

This house he was cleaning had been the family pile. An old farmhouse, it had been enlarged, rebuilt, added on to and remodeled several times before his grandmother had willed it to his mother, and his mother had passed it on to him.

And now the next generation was about to put their mark on the continuum. Rodney's daughter was planning to be married and needed a space to live while she and her husband finished their graduate degrees. Her husband-to-be had accepted a posting as Associate Professor of Medical Imaging at a large new hospital in Texas, but had to finish his obligations at the local school of Medicine before moving to Texas with his bride to begin the job. That was expected to take at least six months, perhaps longer.

They needed enough space to live. But it was a temporary life and did not require extravagances. Rodney's wife had hit on the idea of using the attic, cleaning it out and renovating at the same time. Sometimes life's streams have a funny way of meeting perfectly.

Rodney looked at the photo again. What of all the men in that picture? Unusual it was, taken at Biarritz in south western France in 1918. Hundreds of miles from the battlefields. What were they doing there? Battle was still raging in Flanders. He stared at his uncle, the promise of his life in front of him, the rift with his family unknown. Or, was it? Was that glint a wedding ring? But, he thought, wasn't it supposed to be the wedding that caused the rift?

The young man exuded a certain charm in the photo, centered as he was. Did that charm come from the photo and the young man's expression? Was it pasted in Rodney's mind because he knew something of the subject and had a connection to him, however tenuous? Certainly he looked like a Hathaway. Rodney had Hathaway cousins that looked very similar to the young man in the photo.

He stared longer trying to puzzle out the picture. Were they about to play the game? Had they just finished it? Was this two teams? Who was the older man? Why was the man carrying a satchel. Why his Uncle centered out so? How did they play? How was baseball different so many years ago?

"Rodney, are you bringing anything down, dear?"

He mumbled something and looked more closely at the photo, moving his attention down the line of people in the front row. Looking for something tangible to ponder over. Except for the grins, the poor quality of the photo revealed little. They were all in some form of leisure dress, but it appeared to be military issue clothing. Similarly he scanned the back row and found nothing unusual. Only one man had a glove but then they didn't play with gloves back then, except the catcher and first baseman. A closer look and there was a lump or two that may have been a mitt lying on the ground between the legs of the men.

"Hummhh, I wonder what became of all these guys, returning to the States after the horrors of war? Heck, I barely even know what happened to my own uncle, let alone the others."

"Hurry up Rodney. I thought you said there was loads of stuff to move."

He put the photo into an envelope and placed that in a large wooden box he had cleaned out so he had a place to put the stuff that was saved. Then he turned around, lifted another armload of paper and tossed it into the cardboard box for trash. Then he moved to the bulkier items that would clear out the space faster, a suspended rod which held a large number of old coats, a few chairs and a table.

"Some of this stuff could be sold or donated," he yelled down. "These old clothes are probably garbage."

He tossed a pile of clothes down the stairs to buy him some time to ponder his next move. Those dusty old coats and dresses should keep his mother busy for a bit.

"And some of it, like this table, Larissa might want to keep, at least while she needs it. Setting up an new house costs a lot of money."

Rodney continued to throw clothes off several racks down the steep staircase. That left the racks themselves to be taken down. At least they could be piled closer together to make some space. Once that was complete he took a second look at the crowded attic trying to discern his next angle of attack. Moving the larger items gave him a better feeling of accomplishment.

"We are going to have to clean the whole house after tracking this lot through the halls," said Rodney's mother. "Isn't there a window up there? Can we not just toss things out of there? It would be quicker and cleaner."

"I would if I could but it is stuck and very small. Not much would fit through it. Much of what we might throw that way would flutter about the yard and make the clean up even more extensive."

Actually, there were some things that could be salvaged, used for a while or even longer. A few had a nice antique look to them - a bit formal perhaps but very functional. In fact he took a fancy to a small table thinking it would look nice in the stairway alcove, and not take up too much space. The longer he worked the more he came to the conclusion that they would be storing some of these things in a rental unit, hopefully to be cleared out by his mother after the renovation was done and the important things she needed safely moved to Florida.

He decided to move out the easiest things that were not likely to be kept or even agonized over. He turned to another pile and gingerly moved some dusty linens and towels hoping not to stir the dust too much, and he revealed a smallish wooden box underneath. He tossed the linens down the stair.

The container was a bit larger than a jewelry box and maybe twice as deep. It had a clasp but was not locked. He opened the lid.

There were a number of items immediately recognizable, a old passport, an envelope, a 50 Franc note and two Swiss Franc 20s and some smaller things - pins, a bit of wood, some odd coins. Rodney rooted down a bit, after looking at the passport - his uncle's which expired in 1981, after he did. It was stamped with an entry into France in December, 1969. Switzerland too, a few days later.

Below much of the paper and hidden under it, Rodney pulled an old baseball out of the box. It was discoloured with age and bore a few light repairs to the seams. On it was written - Biarritz France 1918 and a few barely legible signatures.

"Hey, that's cool."

Beside the box he saw an old baseball bat partly buried under other bits of stuff that had spilled out of a nearby box, probably old financial records. He grabbed the large cardboard box and moved down the staircase to deposit it on the floor.

"Mom, this is likely garbage but take a quick look and make sure there's nothing important there. There are a number of boxes of papers up there. I'm sure it's all garbage but it's probably important to make sure there is nothing important. Hey, maybe there are some old stock certificates or property deeds."

He made several trips up and down the staircase with boxes of papers, leaving his mother with a lot to look at. He trotted back up to the attic and picked up the bat. It was crude by modern standards, likely it was milled but it's handle was much thicker than a modern baseball bat and it had only a trademark burned into the barrel. He moved the ball and bat to the same keeper box in which he had placed the photo.

There was still much work to do. He was going to have to pick up the pace.

Chapter Two   Biarritz, France— May, 1918

There was a bright poof of powder and light, before the residual smoke drifted off to one side.

"Several of you 'gentlemen' moved. We will have to do it again."

"I thought you said you were going to take three shots. That's what we paid for."

"I remind you 'gentlemen' this photo was requested by your Commanding Officer, Colonel Hart. You have paid nothing but your time, and for that you are ably compensated by Uncle Sam and the United States Expeditionary Force."

"Damn it Pete, quit talking and face the camera. You guys have the bats in place? Hey shutter boy, give us a few seconds notice before you fire off that flash, so we can get settled and be ready."

This time the scowling photographer gave them a signal, they settled in, some smiling, some serious, all facing the camera - the powder flash went and they were sent on their way, the put upon photographer unwilling or uninterested in taking a third shot.

As the photographer packed up his equipment the men wandered about, collecting in small groups to decide how best to get fed. They had been pulled back from the front after their first serious action. It was a chance to regroup and stay away from the influenza which plagued the front lines. And a chance to move new units to the front and get them some experience. There was talk of peace. The Germans wanted the war to end but the British and French saw their peace overtures as weakness. The Germans realized that their best chance to end the fighting was a major offensive before the Americans reached the front in large numbers. They planned a large stab towards Paris followed by a sweep to the Channel. Success would stem the flow of Americans and perhaps convince the British and French to come to the peace table. Of course the Franco-Brits wanted to keep the war simmering to push their American advantage, and to extract significant penalties from the Germans in the final peace.

Unfortunately for Diamond Company spring was not the best time for a beach holiday, and though accommodations were plentiful as the summer season had not started, Uncle Sam and likely Uncle Pierre insisted they pitch a camp away from civilians.

They had followed orders, set up a camp outside of town and took their rest time cleaning, repairing and generally getting everything shipshape, a colloquialism that more than one of them found odd given they were an infantry unit.

"Hey Cap, where do you want me to put the bats?"

"Here, give them to me, I've got the balls and I'd better store them together," he held out his hand.

Dick Shawcross, his wave of sandy brown hair his only distinguishing feature, handed him the bat. "That one is really head-heavy. Good for hitting the long ball."

"Not a percentage play Dickie," said Allen LaRue. "You're just going to fly out. Better to top it slightly and use the bumpy ground to your advantage. Four for four today, bud."

"I guess, if you count errors as hits."

"Tough plays; you can't count 'em as errors when I tried specifically to get the ball down."

"So you talked to the official scorer?"

LaRue gave Shawcross a disappointed look.

"It's not about you Allen, it's about the team," countered Shawcross.

"But we won."

"How many runs did you score?"

"None."

"How many runs did you hit in?"

"None. But I was in the middle of a few rallies. Moving guys from first to third."

"Ok, rallies that you neither scored a run nor hit one in. I think I've made my point."

"I think you made mine too, we won and my hits helped us win."

They continued to jaw as they wandered to the mess tent, ready to fill up on whatever their camp could muster.

"Nice catch there Duff," said a burly Hughie Coleman, as he scrambled to catch up to the group. Duff, turned his head and made like he couldn't remember.

"The one in the middle of the game," said Coleman. "You might remember it. It was the only catch you made."

"Yeah, well it was the only catch that anyone made," said Duff with a grin, "being that it was in the air and not affected by the bumpy ground. Grounders were tough today."

"Like I said," chirped LaRue. "I wouldn't have tried so hard to get the ball down if the field was good."

"If we play here long enough we'll beat down the bumps."

"Don't count on it. I hear we are moving back north soon. CO says they want us for our arm flashes. Wanna give the Krauts a look at a whole new army coming on side. It's supposed to make them want to try harder at the peace talks."

"You mean no more ball games?"

"Not unless you want to teach the Limeys how to play. I don't think the Krauts are up to it."

"Wonder where they are going to put us? I'm not sure I like the whole armband thing. That means we have to get real close up so the Germans can see us."

"Hate to tell you Pete but they will be shooting at us and likely need to see some of us up close - as in dead, just to be sure we aren't a mirage."

"Here's hoping they don't pull the plug on all this before we get a shot at them."

"Oh, I don't know. Just talking to some of those Frenchies who were at Verdun, it sounds like strong and smart foreign policy on our part to have waited so long to get involved. They are funny guys some of them; happy we are here and somewhat 'perplexed' that we took so long getting here. Some of those battlefields sound like massacres far worse than Manassas or Bull Run. And that was a civil war - this one is decidedly uncivil. Word is the tactics are better now - but they kept trying for the big breakthrough, the big knockout blow but it never comes as trench defence far outweighs offence."

"Not sure where we are going but its sure to be hot. The Russians are out of the war and the Germans are moving troops to their western front - that would be us. We have to do our share of suffering if we want to have any credibility at the peace talks."

"That's not comforting."

"It's not supposed to be."

"So what we've done so far doesn't count?

"Oh it counts. Brass sees the casualties, the Germans get wind of us and our numbers. New units are piling in fast. If we want a piece of the peace talks then we have to have some skin in the game. Word is Wilson wants his view of the future to be the basis for peace. He's a bit of a dreamer though."

"Hey Cap," yelled a voice from across the compound. "Delivery for you from Screaming Eagles, down the road, "It's on your cot. Sergeant who delivered it said, thanks for the bat from him and the

CO. He said he'd be back for it in two days, they have a game scheduled."

Duff looked at his Captain sharply.

"You loaned 'em one of our bats?"

"Had to, the CO over there is a Major - didn't want him ordering me to give it to them. Anyway, we still have these three. And with only one bat they are much more likely to take care of it," he laughed.

As all the men headed for the mess tent, Captain Herbert Hathaway veered away from the group, promising to join them after he deposited the bats and balls in his tent. He was a bit shorter than average, but not noticeably so. Wiry, quick and strong, he had used his physical prowess when called upon, leaping on a moving truck as it trundled by or quickly disassembling a tent and packing it double quick. His men took note of his physical co-ordination and dexterity.

He put the three wooden bats in his kit and picked up the bat that lay on his cot. In the box were several changes of clothes, his dress uniform, his shaving and hygiene kit and some personal effects, a watch, a bundle of letters from home, a St. Christopher's medal from his mother, and six baseballs - four of which were brand new, white like pearls. He liked to turn one of them over in his hand and feel the stitching and the perfect leather for a minute each time he saw them. A brand new baseball was so full of promise and insurance that there would be another game.

On this mid-May day the sun was shining like June, the air crisp and clear like late April and the camp virtually empty with everyone in the mess tent. Captain Hathaway, lifted the fourth bat off the cot, sat down and placed the heavy end on the floor. He pressed his palm into the knob on the handle and began to work the knob back and forth, feeling a tiny bit of give. It was so subtle that he was never sure if the knob moved or if it was his skin giving in to the pressure.

"Left, left, down, right, down, left, down, right," he said in a whisper to himself. He felt the knob pop up with the last click and he quickly unscrewed the knob. The handle of the bat was hollowed out, leaving a cylindrical hole about six inches deep and a bit more than a quarter inch across. Not much could fit in there, but not much had to.

He stood up walked out of his tent and did a casual look about. Back in his tent he tipped the bat and out slipped a tightly rolled bit of paper. He reached into his kit and took a small piece of paper out and slid it into the hole. He replaced the cap, screwed it on and reversed the combination, feeling it click back into place. He reached over to the bare floor and scraped up a pinch of dirt which he applied to the base of the knob to fill in the tiny crack that had appeared.

Hathaway scanned the paper he had received. Then he stood up to make his way to the mess taking the paper with him.

Chapter Three   France, 1918

Hathaway mentally ran through the battle his men had participated in some days before they had been assigned to Biarritz and some R 'n R. It seemed a world away, like it had happened to other people, many months ago. There was enough carnage that brass had sent his unit and several others for a little R 'n R, a bit ahead of their scheduled time and many more miles away than usual for units taken off the line. They were trying to break the influenza that plagued many units. Northern France was clogging up with new arrivals and displaced Picards, Alsatians and the like.

Hathaway mentally walked himself through the whole battle event. It had started according to plan when it was still dark out, as they moved into place there was only the slightest hint of a sunrise creasing the horizon.

Most of the prep work had been done the night before. The men were nervous, doing their last minute tasks by rote. The trench was remarkably quiet even as it began to fill up. There was a click, and other click, a soft exhale of breath and a sharp exclamation of pain, but quickly muted, even though it didn't matter anymore.

The first group went over the top quietly. The German lines were only 50-75 yards away in this sector, due to the terrain and trees. It wasn't easy digging trenches through eight inch thick roots.

They had exactly 10 minutes to slip into German trenches before the artillery barrage began. This time the shells were aimed behind the lines, isolating the front trenches and providing the Allies a real shot of capturing them and making some progress. As the commanders explained, trench war had stalled and required new tactics, and they were willing to give anything a shot, as nothing had worked terribly well in the past. The grunts in the trench weren't quite so willing to be the experiment.

This time it was different. The first German casualties never knew they were about to die. Knifed, bayoneted and shot at close range they were dead in the moments before the shelling started. Normally a sneak attack like this would be quickly reversed as troops from further back would step up and kill the invaders.

However this time the second wave of German resistance tried to stand up to the sneak attack and their cries and the rattle of their movements could be heard up and down the line. The attackers knew they would be all alone without support from the rear so they pushed their advantage. The German defenders could never get organized enough to put up much of a fight and were soon casualties.

"Now why wouldn't they have been doing this sneaky stuff before now," asked one of the Americans.

"Because the Krauts in the back would get wind of it, charge up through the support trenches and wipe out our boys. The trenches are supplied from behind. If you win the front edge you have to be prepared to fight the whole network. That's why we are trying this new tactic today."

"So it never dawned on them until now? Oh, yeah, this is the army. I forgot for a moment."

After 30 minutes of continuous artillery barrage, the rest of the infantrymen leaped over the top and ran to the German trenches without encountering a shot. The initial invaders had fanned out through the trench network and killed as many Krauts as they could find, only taking defensive positions once the precisely timed artillery barrage began.

After half an hour they emerged to join their fellows and leaped out of the most forward trenches to attack those that had been shelled. The return fire rattled across the small valley.

"Mother of God, that is loud," screamed one soldier, with his knuckles jammed into his ears and his head buried in his chest. "What happens if they shoot back?"

The soldier next to him, an Englishman, wondered at how green his compatriot could be, and then saw the US Army pin on his shoulder, before nodding grimly.

"Laddie, I'm glad you are here but I need you to be some help now that you've joined us."

The American lifted his eyes to him looking for some direction.

"If they shoot back we are all full of holes, some of them big enough holes that it doesn't matter anymore. The whole thing here is to not have them shoot back. I've noticed lately that they shoot back less and for a shorter period. Still, when they decide to put up a fight they can be awfully bloody."

"I hear some shooting. Are we going to die?"

The British soldier smiled wanly, "That's us doing the shooting. When they shoot it sounds different. I'll let you know when I hear it."

"What do we do next?"

"We move out. Stay down, and stay to the right, the machine guns are designed to spray but they don't cover their left, our right, as well as they do to their right. And most guys are right handed and so they prefer shooting to the center and the right. Shooting left is awkward and the guns make it more difficult."

"What if we just run into another gun?"

"Then we are dead. I'm still here though, and I've done this more times than I care to remember."

The two joined the mass of men heaving out of the trench and moving toward the German lines. With the addition of the American troops the Allies were getting bolder and this time moved their artillery up past the first captured German trench looking for likely positions up the hill, in the trees at the top of the valley ridge. Knowing the Germans were bringing troops from the eastern front, now that Russia had collapsed in civil war, the time was ripe for major offensives on the western front.

Rudimentary air reconnaissance gave them a pretty good idea what was behind the wooded area - it was a large German tent encampment, five rows of tents with maybe 15 tents in each row. There could be no mistake as the tents were precisely aligned and spaced, almost as if they were placed by strict measurements. Intelligence suggested the base supplied much of this area of the front - perhaps 15 miles in both directions. A punch through here would be monumental and would put the Germans on the run. At least that was the plan. These plans had a way of going awry.

As the artillery pieces were heaved into place up the hill the infantry had secured the forward German trench and moved to attack the second set of trench and gun emplacements back from the top of the hill.

Dawn had fully broken revealing the devastation. Where some of the trees in the wood were in full leaf many others looked like the remnants of a forest fire, burned, black and without many remaining limbs, they formed a weak, staggered palisade at the top of the ridge.

Reaching a deep trench the Brit and green American jumped in, eager for a few moments respite. Catching his breath the Brit laughed grimly and pointed to a tree.

"I thought so," he said, and buried his bayonet into the trunk. "I'll just mark my passage again. This old foxhole is practically home."

The American looked at him quizzically. He finished carving the crude notch in the tree beside their hole.

"See, now two times coming and one going," he pointed to the notches, two of which pointed forward and one, in the middle of the others, pointing back to the floor of the valley.

"So far no real resistance. In fact pretty few Germans. It's almost as if they'd scarpered. Maybe the end is nearer than we think."

They were joined by a few more infantrymen and pretty soon the trench was filled and everyone was taking a bit of time to have a little nibble and drink.

A flare exploded above them, and then another further down the line. The sun was up now but it was still very early.

"That's the signal to move out boys. We are headed for the German supply camp about a mile back of the last of the trees. If you look carefully, you can just see the tops of the tents through the trees."

The soldiers gathered themselves and moved ahead, this time walking briskly inviting resistance. Artillery pieces were still being moved into place. The troops moved easily through the wooded area and formed a thick and staggered line across the open field on the other side. They began moving north east. They had encountered no resistance - though there was some indication of movement in the tent encampment.

A shot rang out. "Don't shoot now, you'll just alert them that we are coming," somebody said.

"Alert them? Are you stupid? Don't you remember the loud shelling from about an hour ago. I'm guessing they are plenty alert. They are just waiting for us to get close enough to not waste ammunition on."

The line moved closer and the more experienced soldiers began to feel uneasy. Resistance had always stiffened when they approached valued targets. The Americans in the front of the charge and inexperienced at the methods of warfare started to whoop, and many of them broke into a run toward the tents, still more than a quarter-mile away.

A boom and then another momentarily stopped them from running. The artillery pieces had made it up the ravine hill behind them and been set up just inside the tree line, and were beginning to loft shells at the camp, but no hits appeared. The gunners were still calibrating, and had orders to shell some of the tent area but move quickly beyond the tents to halt any reinforcements from arriving.

"Hold up laddie," said the Brit holding out his arm to partly restrain his new American friend. He went down on one knee. "Let the shells do their work before we get there."

The main body of Americans had resumed their run, once they realized that the shelling was their own. They were closing the gap to the tents rapidly and would arrive within a minute. Heavily laden soldiers could run, but they were no sprinters, especially across the soft, wet ground. The artillery gunners realized they had better shift their aim beyond the camp to avoid hitting their own men who would soon arrive at the front edge of the tent camp.

The Brit and his contingent picked up and angled to the right, away from the direct line to the German base. They walked toward the south end of the tent city. Every step forward they took seemed a bit slower.

"This doesn't seem natural," said a concerned voice just behind them.

"Aye, I can't put my finger on it but there should have been some resistance by now. Did all the Krauts simply pick up and leave?"

Then, when no shells had whined, one did. And it exploded just behind the front group of running, whooping, greenhorn Americans. Three of four of them were tossed up in the air. Suddenly the advancing rank appeared much smaller than it had.

It wasn't immediately apparent if the shell had been fired from the east or if it had merely been a bad case of friendly fire - a poorly aimed or a defective shell. The more cautious, experienced British stopped moving toward the tents. They were perhaps 200 yards from the edge of the camp. They waited, tense and ready to hit the dirt. There was no second shell.

In the quiet they started to move forward, almost as one determining that the danger was from their own gunners. Then the front wall of tents erupted.

Four, five, ten men fell in quick succession. The Brit dropped to his belly almost landing on top of the American who went down just a little slower with a little cry of surprise.

He moved his rifle into position, propping it on top of his kit bag, and started to shoot. He heard a ping, of metal on metal. Then he heard the thundering of the machine gun emplacements, dug into the ground and hidden under the westernmost tents.

Was it a plan? Was it simply a perfect bit of luck or a timely defence. It didn't really matter as thousands of Allied troops, more than half of them facing their first experience of battle, were caught out in the open in broad daylight on flat ground with nothing more than their uniforms and rifles to defend themselves. The artillery had better begin to knock out some of those machine guns or it would be all over - a rout of the British and Americans.

Soon one of the nests exploded, victim of a particularly good grenade throw. There were Americans who could loft a grenade 75 yards. The Brits and the French had been amazed at the American ability to throw for distance and accuracy. Still the bulk of the troops were outside that range and only a few could hit the tents. Then another nest all but disappeared as a shell hit it dead on.

The resistance from the tents slowed considerably but it didn't stop. It appeared the Germans were pulling back into a town which was perhaps a mile or a bit more through another shattered wood off in the distance.

The Brit rose and began a crouched run toward the south-east.

"We might be able to outflank those guns. Pray our boys knock a few more off, or we might not make it."

He rose and swung his arm to beckon the men around him. The American rose, a few others too.

"I'm with you, Tommy. Right behind you . . . " his voice trailed off.

Many men remained on the ground, the rest took the same crouched stance and moved as quickly as they could off the main field to the south of the tent city and found a small hill to hide behind. The dirt was fresh and had likely been dumped there from the machine gun nests dug in secret along the western edge of the camp. Dirt piles beside every tent would have given their secret away. Now that dirt shielded the Allied attackers from the tent city defenders.

"Okay there's 22 of us," said the Brit trying to hide his disappointment. He pointed at a few Americans. "You gentlemen get some defensive positions on this hill and cover the rest of us as we move into the middle of the camp. We'll try to get them from behind, if they haven't already left to regroup. Don't stop moving until you reach the far side of the tents, then hit the dirt. Remember your grenades. Save nothing. Better to knock out one of their guns twice just to make sure. Unused ammunition is of no value to a dead man. Let's move."

A small group of 14 men skirted the hill to the east and fanned out running through the first two rows of tents. They shot at each one as they approached hoping to flush out anybody hiding inside. The Brit looked into the second tent he passed in the second row, behind the hidden machine guns. Empty. Even the supplies had been cleaned out.

He tried the next. It too was empty save for a single box. He kicked it softly and it spilled a load of spoons and forks. He sent his men toward the machine gun tents and they systematically took out the four remaining nests from behind with a couple of grenades. He looked in the other tents - all were empty, save for a box here or a bit of furniture there. They bore the marks of a hasty but orderly retreat.

"Don't know if this was planned or if it was put together after they realized we were attacking this weak sector."

As the tents were being investigated the last of the hidden resistance was neutralized. The Americans' skill at throwing grenades for distance and accuracy proved useful in the advance through the tents.

"Either way, we need to start building defences. If they are in that town they will be dug in pretty good."

The Brit ordered several men to start connecting the machine gun nests into a continuous trench. With luck they could get it big enough and deep enough to resist any shelling from the town.

"From here, that town looks like it has survived the war remarkably well. Or are we just finally making enough progress to see places that haven't been obliterated and overrun multiple times?"

Several of the more experienced men took to the trench building with gusto. They knew the next issue of command was the toughest.

"Okay, the rest of you, go and collect up the dead. Take them to that open area just south of the tents. Use the last two tents on the south side as hospitals for the wounded."

The American greenhorn, had stopped paying attention. His head was bowed and he rested up against the stock of his rifle, using it like a cane to prop himself up. Then he couldn't hold his own balance anymore and he fell, sideways towards his gun first, and with a final effort to use it as a prop, finally spinning and dropping to the ground away from the weapon which fell across his body.

"Your first customer gentlemen. It is remarkable he lasted this long, I expect significant loss of blood. Yes, there, in the leg, his britches are red. He was hit at the start of the machine gun barrage but valiantly stayed with us until it was decided and secured.

Quickly now, get a tourniquet on his leg. It isn't that bad or he'd be dead already."

American casualties were horrific in the action. Of the 8,000 US troops engaged, 986 lost their lives, and more than 4,900 were injured. Many, most, were quickly patched up, others lost limbs or eyes or were otherwise disfigured. At least there had been no gas or flame.

The battle gained the Allies an insignificant patch of ground - moving the front about one and a half miles to the east, but it severely disrupted German lines and supplies. And the tactics on both sides signalled a new kind of war - attrition was finally catching up to the Germans. Now they would adjust and dig into new defensive works and they would wait, trying like never before to bleed the Allies for every inch of ground they covered. They knew their countrymen who had been fighting in the east would soon join them.

However, the battle story quickly ran up the Allied chain of command. The tent defense and the chess -like offence within a defence were new tactics. There were those in Allied command who clearly saw these tactics and this battle as an indication the German resistance was crumbling. Their supply lines were shorter but the supplies more precious and rare. They did not expend unnecessary ordnance. They were acting in a completely defensive mode, merely trying to take as many enemy soldiers as they could for every inch of ground they gave. It never crossed their minds that the Germans were willing to draw the British and American troops to the east in advance of a major offensive where they would try to encircle their enemies.

American exuberance was noted and with US command deeply desiring battle, plans were drawn up to use the Americans to bleed the Germans into the final phase of the war.

The battle story quickly found its way by word of mouth to virtually every American in Europe. The conversion of the American greenhorn from a scared, inexperienced cog, into a fighting man, a battle presence and a hero of determination was played up by the French and British retelling of the story.

Pretty soon, the use of American troops in front line actions was dramatically increased, and when some units were disbanded when too heavily infected with influenza, the American units remained together, despite the fears of disease, so they could gloriously take part in the rapidly ending battle presence of the Germans who were determined to defend their nation but knew there was no way to kill enough of the Allies to make them wish for peace. Thousands of American troops were entering the war making the German task more difficult by the day. They needed a big offensive to either push the Allies back and out of the war or to force a peace on reasonable terms.

Almost 1,000 Americans killed in one battle action, itself a suicide run at an enemy determined to kill more than they were killed, was disheartening among the American military brass, especially those who had battle command and who directly interacted with the troops.

The top brass, the political brass, they could see that their use of fresh American troops was necessary to get them a seat at the peace table and to get their country and President a voice in the post-war world.

President Wilson had been touting his 14 point plan, a way forward to a peaceful world. He desperately wanted the European powers to grasp his approach and to form a League of Nations, which, from a war President who did not want to fight a war, would be his legacy, and in his eyes, make the war worthwhile.

Those who would be made to pay the price in blood were not consulted. Many were not blind to the tactics and the approach of their officers to the war.

Chapter Four

"Hey Captain, a word please."

The two regiments had come together for a bit of respite from the front. It was an opportunity to realign the units which had been decimated in the last offensive push. Hathaway had been walking through the camp to the CO's office when he was waylaid. The CO was expecting him.

"I already spoke to him. They want us to go in again. Same kind of attack. It worked once, they figure it can work again."

"It didn't work. There were hundreds of dead Americans on the field."

"Luck, they figure. The Germans managed a lucky strike in the field when they were on the verge of panicking in a virtual rout. I told you I already spoke to the CO. Talk to him and then we can talk. I'll have something for you."

Hathaway nodded and continued his walk through the camp, between tents and supply areas, past the motor pool and through the horse stables - the smell of the horses and the odour of the grease and gasoline meaning the same thing.

He rapped on the door of the CO's large field tent. Hearing a muffled voice he ventured inside.

"Ah, Captain Hathaway. I hear you had a bit of a rough time recently. One of your corporals was shot in the leg but I'm told he will be fine, in fact he should be back on duty by now."

"Yes, sir. He told me what happened and what he learned from the British. Valuable intelligence for the boys on the ground. It is amazing to me how quickly the battle plan breaks down in actual combat. My corporal was apparently lucky, the bullet that hit him missed the vital artery and his bleed was fairly slow."

"The battle plan was perfectly executed. It's only a shame that the Krauts managed to dig in - we are convinced it was a last minute response to our overwhelming victory. A battlefield tactic under fire - they are Prussians after all - tough as nails. All our intelligence suggests they are worn down past the breaking point and all we need to do is keep up the pressure and they will collapse."

"Respectfully Colonel sir, expect them to act a bit more desperate as we appear to be able to push the war into Germany proper. Defending their home soil and all that. Especially if a stiff defence buys them better terms at the armistice talks. And don't forget the additional troops coming in from the east. They might try a last push before we get our boys here in numbers."

"Not your problem Captain. General Pershing has ordered me to ready our forces for a series of minor pushes, testing the front for weakness. He wants to find the right spot to make a huge push perhaps in the summer but more likely in the early and later autumn, before it gets too cold. His thinking is that we can hold any gains through the winter and shore up our positions."

"Just let me know what you want us to do Colonel. I trust we'll receive orders soon."

"Right now in fact," he reached to a small table and picked off a rolled scroll. Please read these, commit them to memory and burn them. Regimental commanders and platoon commanders will meet tomorrow at 0700 to go over the plan. It's not too complicated, very similar to the last one, except we play it a bit safer when we encounter a tent encampment," he laughed.

Hathaway cringed inside. "Yes sir, 0-700."

He left the tent and immediately sought out the officer he had spoken to.

"Major Ewing, hello," he tapped him on the shoulder. "Can we have a private word?"

"Absolutely, let's review the situation in the stables. I understand we are having trouble getting sufficient feed."

The two officers walked slowly through the camp, exchanging information and nodding and saluting other officers they encountered while moving ever so slowly towards an understanding of each other's concerns about the battle plans and the leadership. They appeared to have much the same feelings about the way troops had been used and were likely to be used in the future.

"Bluntly and off the record Captain, I think we see this similarly. Our CO Colonel Hart and the brass have more political interests at heart, including their own advancement. We have the welfare of our men at heart and simply want to return home to live our lives."

"Aye, Major. That about sums it up. And yet we have answered the call and done what is required of us."

"Captain, a number of us at the platoon level, and I want to be delicate here, will continue to take some of these matters into our own hands, as we react to the demands of the battlefield. We will do our duty but we will continue to collaborate on how best to do that duty and survive the political plans of our . . . betters."

"Yes, your insight has been helpful, Major. You don't propose to move beyond that do you?"

"Quite. There are a number of us, in fact I don't know how many as for the sake of anonymity and necessary deniability, we each have only one or two contacts, but I know there are several others involved. I only speak to my direct contact, the belief is that the Armistice is imminent and many don't want to sacrifice ourselves for nothing. The war is over, essentially, there just isn't an agreement to stop shooting yet. Such a position is delicate in any army and could cause some personal difficulties should it be discovered. As the war is obviously winding down we want to be more aggressive in ensuring our men survive the final pushes. You need to know our situation if you want your platoon to continue to take advantage of our collective . . . . approach."

Hathaway thought for a few moments. "Okay, but I see that there is a fine line between doing our duty and suggestions of cowardice. I refuse to place myself or my men in that pile of horse manure.

We will require continued co-ordination with other proximate regiments."

"Just like we've been doing, but we are not holding back any tricks at this point, it might all be over soon. Maybe any day. Any battle we engage in might well be the last of the war. If it's not, then we will have exhausted our options to keep this manageable. I will receive a message from my contact, which I expect about a day after the battle plans have been reviewed by all commanders, sometime after that 0700 meeting tomorrow morning. I will relay what I know to you. As always, we still do our duty Captain, we just do it with the knowledge of what others are doing to improve their chances. I don't even know who is the instigator, by the time the plans get to me there are multiple units involved and co-ordinated. For example, how many American regiments moved aggressively to that tent camp? How many Brits? Suffice to say, not all. Some were prepared to sacrifice a full breakthrough, for survivability of their fellow soldiers, despite that fact they were half expecting the ambush."

The Captain and Major had wandered through the stables and were doubling back to inspect the quartermaster's supply areas. The hospital section was quiet as many of the most egregiously wounded and sick had been moved well back of the front to traditional hospital settings.

"Thank you Major, I will follow whatever protocol this operation requires."

"We want what the US Army and the President wants. We also want to survive the war. We've heard the stories of early battles, The Somme and Verdun and the way the troops were cannon fodder, forgotten as human beings. Too many of us have seen the despicable way some of the Allied commanders have treated their troops, as totally expendable and infinitely replaceable. We are Americans, not the subjects of any King and we act as free men. I am not expendable and neither are you! Co-ordination of our activities gives us the best chance to be successful on the battlefield and to return safely from it. Good day."

He saluted and moved on.

Two days later as the regiment was preparing to move out to its battle location, Hathaway received a tap on the shoulder and a quick word from the Major.

"Here, take this for your R 'n R after the battle," he said handing Hathaway an old baseball bat. You can give it back to me for use by my troops. It's your lucky charm but it's cracked and unusable for baseball." He left.

A few of Hathaway's platoon saw the exchange and thought it odd on the precipice of battle that such a talisman would change hands.

"If it's cracked why does he want it back," said one of the soldiers nearby.

"It can't really be used, but the crack is slight and he likes having a back up when they play," said Hathaway.

"Why not wait to give it to you after the battle?"

Hathaway was just then engaged by the quartermaster inquiring after ammunition supplies.

Some commanders carried a lucky charm, a walking stick, a hat, something that gave them and those under their command a bit of comfort and helped to identify them at a distance. Hathaway had been carrying the bat with him as they moved out. Only when they had found their places at the front did he have time and privacy enough to scrutinize the bat and eventually the piece of paper that was concealed within.

Hathaway knew the basic battle plan but the paper told him that several American platoons would approach the German lines more slowly than ordered. In addition, instead of a full charge, two platoons would act as covering agents for those who were advancing. Two more would circle the north flank of the village that was targeted in the battle plan and engage German resistance there in an effort to draw off defensive capabilities - they would make no effort to advance into the town as long as resistance was in place.

That was contrary to the official plan which called for a steady advance from the west. Those platoons which took the offensive initiative this time would be rotated into a defensive support role in the next offensive push. Hathaway's platoon was one of those expected to flank the village. The attack was set to commence in a few days time, giving Hathaway an opportunity to ascertain his best approach. He noted that his men had been assigned a spot just north of the middle of the offensive group exiting the trenches. He would have to manoeuvre his men to the left and behind the advancing allies, in order to gain a small rise on the northern side of the village.

He decided the best approach was to simply have his platoon follow his lead and he could move left of the line towards the flanking spot he was supposed to handle. That way he wouldn't have to explain his actions and with luck they would just seem like the choices of battle under fire.

Rain. Days of rain. The attack was scrubbed and the date reset.

During the delay Hathaway saw Major Ewing as he passed him in the trench. "All set Captain, we go in two days?"

"Hathaway nodded in the affirmative and added, "Yes sir Major, we are ready to go once we dry out a bit. It will actually be a pleasure leaving the soggy trench."

"Don't be so sure of that Captain. Even soggy trenches reduce the chances of getting killed."

"But not dying. I see many of our soldiers are succumbing to the influenza which seems to come easier and with more force to those in soggy trenches."

The bombardment commenced as soon as the first wave had dropped into position. The attack was precisely timed so the infantry attack would follow so closely on the heels of the artillery barrage that the defenders would have no time, theoretically, to defend themselves.

Hathaway moved his platoon to the left and toward the north side of the village. There was a little hill there between a wooded area and a small creek which skirted the town to the north. The creek joined a larger one to the west of the town. That water course went right through the middle of the village, it's main water source. However, being downstream the British and Americans couldn't stop up the stream or otherwise affect it in any meaningful way.

"Okay boys take up positions on this rise and get ready to charge those two buildings on my command," said Hathaway.

"Okay, Cap, hope nobody is in there."

"That's the plan Charlie, we don't move until we see that the way is clear."

"And what if it isn't?"

"Then we don't go. We are not charging into a firefight, we are charging into a breach. Hopefully one created by the frontal charge of the regiment."

The artillery ceased and the infantry, already close up to the village, made its move. The Germans had moved their machine guns to the western edge of the village and poured fire into the attacking army.

Once the Germans commenced firing, the entire southern side of the advancing troop hit the dirt, content to draw the German fire without being too much exposed, other than lying down on flat ground perhaps 75 yards from German firing positions.

One of the two units assigned to the north flank of the village began to move. They encountered no resistance. Still Hathaway held back. His unit was closer to the western edge of the village and an attack by the platoon would be noticed by the western defenders. It seemed odd that there was no defense on the north side of the settled area.

He watched the other unit advance. There was no response from the Germans.

Hathaway motioned his troops to follow him. He moved up and away from the village to the north and swung through a small wooded area. They used the trees to camouflage their movements, leaped a narrow stream, and emerged from the wood to the extreme north east of the village, staying low behind the last stand of trees. They were perhaps 100 yards from the edge of the village where a road exited it and carried on back east. There were a steady stream of soldiers moving out of the village, and a few leading supply trucks moving in. There were no refugees or villagers in sight.

The German resistance had stopped. Americans and British troops started to move back into the village from the west. Hathaway watched the scene unfold, as the other American platoon moved into the village from the north and appeared to fan out, moving building to building. The main battle group to the west of the village had reached the edge of the village and begun to move among the buildings as the initial resistance had at first slowed to a trickle and then stopped completely, inviting their advance.

The sounds of resistance were muted, and it appeared there was smoke coming from several of the buildings nearest the western edge of the settlement. He held back, unwilling to attack soldiers leaving the fight, concerned that an attack would expose their position, and that their numbers were too small to sustain any firefight.

Then events moved rapidly. Two more huge supply wagons swung into view through the trees as they were being pulled westwards into the village. A large number of well armed soldiers moved out to the east, pulling wagons and artillery pieces and supplies. Hathaway realised the situation in a flash.

"Shit, it's a trap. It's a trap." He looked wildly about. He considered shooting at the soldiers leaving. But that wouldn't be a warning of the trap. He considered running madly forward shouting a warning, but realized the only people who would hear him were those setting the trap.

He grabbed Charlie Hauser by the forearm. "Chuck, run back as fast as possible to the western side of the village and tell them it's a trap, the village is being loaded with explosives. Get the men out. Go, as quickly as possible."

Hauser, looked at him, and then back to the activity on the road exiting the town. "How do you . . . . yes sir." He took off running back through the wood as fast as he could. Hathaway watched him and realized that Hauser was retracing the serpentine route they took from the hill on the northern edge of the village. That way back would take too long.

"Tom .... Billings, come here; and Larry come here," Hathaway barked. "Boys the town is wired. Run straight to the western edge of the attack. Quickly, don't get too close to the shooting but don't take too long getting there. Tell the commanders that the town is wired and to get their guys out. Leave your packs and rifles here we need speed. Go now, fast."

He clapped Billings on the back. Billing's eyes widened, "Okay," he turned to survey the lay of the land and plan out a route. "Let's go Larry."

The two took a couple of walking steps and then broke into a run along the front edge of the wood, hopped the stream where it emerged from the forest and ran as fast as sprinters across the open fields only moving toward the town as they approached the edge of the fighting front.

A shot and then another thudded into the earth around them. Neither stopped running. With Larry a bit faster he pulled slightly ahead of Tom as they skirted the village in front of the wood and approached the hill they had originally set up on, slightly to the north of the village. Tom strained to catch up.

Just as the two men approached the hill the troop had hid behind earlier, Larry slowed and then stumbled. Tom tried to catch him and ran behind the hill the platoon had originally set up on. Larry was down. Tom emerged from behind the small rise and he was running alone. He turned briefly but could not see Larry anymore. Now the message was his alone to deliver.

He dove behind a low rise of earth. He caught his breath scanning back through the field for any sign of Larry.

He picked himself up and started running again, the sounds of shots still in the air. Then they were no more. He ran quickly and found a small group of British soldiers near the edge of town.

"It's a trap, it's a trap. Get out of the village. Call everyone back."

The Brits were slow to understand. "Now how would you know that son. We've just managed to silence most of their resistance. Think we got the last one, eh Alfie?"

"That's just it, they are leaving from the other side of town. You didn't kill them, they are drawing us in and getting out of Dodge."

"Dodge? What?"

"They are leaving in droves to the east. Getting out of town while it's still safe. Before they blow it up."

The British captain realized in a flash. He yelled to his guys to retreat and the call flashed down the line. Tom could hear it more and more faintly as it moved away from him. From his position at the northern end of the line he could see the message getting to the troops and the mass of men hesitating and some being called back as they approached the edge of town. Others emerged from between the buildings, crouched low and running, ready to fling themselves down at the slightest sign.

He puffed out a mission accomplished breath trying to remain calm and decide whether to follow his warning or let word of mouth carry it along. He sat down behind a small supply wagon that had been drawn into place.

A minute went by. Another. Still no plan had formed in Tom's mind. Then the village exploded. In a flash there was nothing but a roaring sound and a hurricane of smoke and debris. Soon the red flash of fire could be seen as the smoke thinned. Then another thump of explosion and another. Charges were planted all through the village and were exploding, intent on removing the settlement from any future map.

Hathaway literally counted the seconds since he had sent Billings and Schilling around to the western edge of the village. It was perhaps a half a mile, maybe a bit more to the main concentration of the Allied infantry. He figured they could cover it in less than three minutes.

He heard the firing from the village stop less than a minute after they had left. He heard the whoop of a charge from the Allies to the west. Then he heard it all stop and then it exploded.

The German stream out of the village grew wildly for a few moments and even though Germans were still streaming out of the town, the village exploded, first with a gigantic blast on the western side of town and then quickly, several more blasts as buildings, filled with explosives, were detonated.

Once the smoke cleared there was fire everywhere. And then another explosion as the fire reached another dynamite cache.

With the explosions concentrated in the western half of the village, Hathaway's remaining troop suffered no casualties, especially since they were still among the trees when the explosion occurred. The troop which had first moved into the town from the middle of the northern flank - simply disappeared. There was nobody left to tell their tale.

Hathaway ordered his men to start shooting at anyone on the road. There were still a few Germans trying to escape the carnage. A few went down. They made no attempt to shoot back and only tried to move away east as quickly as they could. Hathaway considered charging after them but his small group would not have inflicted enough damage to take the risk. He did have half a dozen men charge towards the road and loft grenades at the retreating wagons. Two were hit and a few of the locals killed.

Anyone in the village was decimated. Many of the attacking Allied infantry were killed and many, many more were wounded by flying debris and shrapnel that appeared too widespread to have been accidental or incidental to the explosion. Days later Allied command surmised that some of the shrapnel had been laced with the explosives to inflict as much damage to Allied personnel as possible.

Hathaway carefully worded his report. He needed to justify his actions prior to the warning as decisions made under fire in a combat zone to support the objectives of the battle plan. he said he had moved his unit to the east to find another place they could easily enter the village, hopefully unopposed, but the stream had slowed their advance and made for a gap that could not easily be breached. So they had moved even further east and paused in the wood to regroup when he had noticed the telltale signs of the booby trap.

In the days after the battle, he managed to meet up with the Major he had befriended. They each took a long look at the other.

"Vicious stuff, eh Captain? I heard you saw it coming and tried to give warning."

"Yes, it all happened so fast. I realized what they were up to and sent three men. One did not make it."

"Many Americans are dead and more are scarred and wounded grievously. We are lucky that it was not more. I hope even more for the armistice to take hold. I think your platoon and many other American forces are being reassigned to the north, to a quiet sector north of Arras. At least that's what I heard from the Colonel's adjutant. We will likely get our specific orders in a few days. I think the brass is concerned that there may not be much war left to fight."

"A quiet sector is a good idea for us. We have lost too many men, and yet they still pour into the ranks. Washington is determined to have its say in what all comes out of this. From what I hear, it is as much about politics as it is about peace."

"Hopefully politicking will lead to a lengthy peace. Permanent peace is a pipe dream. And if the Allies stick it to the Germans then peace will be very elusive."

"Will we continue to play baseball sir?"

"Yes, we will, as the boys need an outlet. Why don't you come by my tent after mess and we can try to plan something out. Give the locale a bit of a look see for a suitable field. One that isn't too shot up. It's never fun to field grounders in a minefield or over bits of exploded village. I'm told that through this sector there are dozens of villages that no longer exist. Some of them you can see the foundations and perhaps a wall or two of previous buildings. Most are nothing more than a particularly flat field, or the occasional unpleasant find in the mud. A doll here, a broken plate there. Who knows when these fields will ever go back to the farmers. They are probably all dead anyway, or scattered to the four winds. How would they ever be able to identify their farms - there are no buildings, no trees, and barely anything recognizable at all."

Chapter Five

They were lounging at some rough wooden tables. Having an after supper tea, removed from the front, they were getting a bit of rest and resupply before being moved forward for the autumn push. There were the usual bits that went into a camp, but here the tents circled an old farmhouse that had been repaired enough for use as a general area headquarters.

"What are you going to do after the war Duff?"

"Sitting on a chair with a back. This squatting on boxes is uncomfortable. After the war? Serve out my enlistment I guess. After that . . . ." he shrugged, and rearranged his body to try and make it more comfortable.

"I'm going home to Troy, New York and getting a job with General Electric. It's all arranged, my dad's friend works there and they are looking for electricians and engineers. They even put you through school to get the specialty training," said Hughie, with a grin. "What about you Charlie?"

Charlie Hauser had slid in beside them, plunking his tray of grub on the table. He was a tall, tall lanky blond in his early 20s.

"You like that stuff; machines, electricity? It's all a bit hocus-pocus to me," he said. "Me, I'll go back to the farm. Hadn't really thought about it too much. I just finished a few years learning to be a dairy farmer - so's I could help my dad. There are a lot of new things you can do to improve productivity on the old farm and my dad wanted me to find out about them - so I went to Penn State to find out."

"Where's the farm Charlie?"

"In southern Pennsylvania, pretty close to the Maryland state line."

"Hey there's a lot of Amish in that area," said Dick Shawcross who was sitting across the table from Charlie. "I'm from Philly. Not too far south of there. You Amish or something?"

"Not me, nor my dad anymore. Well, he was, but he split with them before I was born. My grandparents were Amish but even they had their doubts and my dad couldn't abide by the old ways. He didn't mind the church-going but he couldn't understand the determination to remain ignorant of new technology. He has been upgrading the farm for years. That's why he sent me to school."

"My dad is a printer by trade," said Shawcross. "We have a small family farm but it's impossible to feed a family on the size of property we have. Original farm has been divided through the years, my two uncles own property beside us. I've been apprenticing with a welder for a couple of years. Saw the army as a good break from welding. Not that I don't like it, but change is always good. Whether you find something better or you realize you were happy where you were. There is no down side to trying new things. Unless of course it's the food around here," he snorted a laugh.

Shawcross was brown haired, which he wore short with a little wave above his eyes. He was tallish, but not tall, with square shoulders, big hands and a helpful face.

The boys started in on the army cooking and moved into reminiscences of their mother's cooking back home.

After a while they began to try to outdo each other's story of a great meal or great dish, to the point they all began laughing at the outlandish stories. More than a few stomachs were rumbling despite the army grub on the tables.

"Well, my mother is a baker. And she's taught me some pretty fine tricks when it comes to cakes and bread," said Frank Eisenrick, who up until then had been silent.

"Well you should try them here. We could use a decent loaf or two."

"Yeah Frank, you been holding out on us. We're your buddies, bake us some nice, edible bread. I'm sure Clancy over there wouldn't mind the help, even if it's just for one day."

"I don't want him to think we don't appreciate his efforts," said Frank with a shake of his head.

"Frank, we don't appreciate his efforts. He's good on stew, and potatoes and slabs of beef and pork, but the bread around here is . . . . is . . . is, well it's not really bread, in the truest sense of the word. It's more like moulded boxboard. Sometimes its moldy boxboard. Help us out, and if you really are as good as all that, pass on a trick or two to Clancy. You'll have his and our eternal gratitude."

Clancy had looked up at the sound of his name. When it came a second time he yelled over to them, "Hey, I'm doing my best. I didn't want to be the cook. Blame the US Army, they made me the cook after I told them I worked the coke ovens in Pittsburgh."

"Oh the irony," someone yelled. "It takes a lot of mettle to eat your cooking."

A few of them smiled and some just winced. Despite the complaints nobody was wasting away.

"Watch it. I'm doing my best. Any more complaints and I'll get the Cap to assign you to peeling potatoes for a week or two. Maybe onions. Anybody else have anything to say?"

The boys went silent on Clancy but continued to push Frank to help Clancy bake. A little jawing and some well placed complements and it was worked out with Clancy that the next morning Frank would get up early and take over the bread making for one day. He told Clancy what he needed and Clancy promised to get it for him.

The next morning at Reveille everyone had just about forgotten the bread making plan as they had been told to prepare to tear down the camp and get ready to move out by the end of the day. It was going to be busy. Talk was thick about where they might be going and how they were going to get there. Plans were laid for collecting up the camp and loading it all on a train headed north. Of course the tents and personal effects came last.

As the platoon moved into the mess tent after roll call but before the work of packing up the camp began. They had all gotten their assignments from the CO and were thinking about more than breakfast.

They lined up to receive orders on the camp move and as they reached the front of the line, they were handed a paper by the CO and then moved into the mess tent, in twos and threes. They all stopped. Each one, to a man, looked like he'd hit an invisible wall. He stopped, took a deep breath, and appeared stunned by something completely unexpected. A slight delirium swept across each face in turn and everyone who was in the tent already, lined up at their tables and watching silently, grinning before they laughed out loud.

"I always knew you guys smelled," said a rival sergeant, already sitting down, to the amusement of his men seated around him. "I've put in for a transfer for Eisenrick, I think we need him more than you."

"Is that what that is . . . . the smell of fresh bread. I think I'm going to cry," said Duff.

A very strong smell of fresh bread and melted butter permeated the tent, knocking down all the other camp smells only to remind the men how bad the rest of the camp smelled and how they had gotten used to it.

Frank, held up a tray of freshly sliced bread on one side and a pile of croissant buns on the other.

Duff reached out for a croissant, his hand shaking.

"Hurry up, we want to eat too," said a few in the growing line of men behind him.

He looked down the line, and again at the tray, and quickly grabbed a thick slice of fresh bread, and then reached back for another croissant as well, before loading up on the eggs and bacon also on offer.

"Am I still alive. Is this heaven?" he said.

"It's not heaven," said Pete Delaney with a deliberate shake of his head. "It's the US Army."

"If the US Army is heaven then you are in a bad way my friend," said one of the men already sitting down.

Duff couldn't resist and took a bite of the croissant before he even sat down. The flakey crust, the buttery dough, the subtle flavours. Duffy nearly melted. He started to shake. "It is heaven, this is as light as a cloud. It's food that actually has a flavor. I think I'm going to re-enlist."

They all laughed, a little giddy from the experience.

Frank sat down once his entire platoon had gotten its rations.

One by one his mates looked at him with gratitude and a new found respect.

"If you told me you could fly to the moon, Frank, I'd believe you. This is the best bread I've ever eaten," said Martin Wilson. "It tastes just like the bread they have at the Waldorf Astoria in New York City. Where did you learn to make this?"

"I told you, my mother is a baker. She knows how to make bread."

"Where are you from?"

"New York City, New York. My dad runs the shop. My mother does the cooking, I do the deliveries. Every morning I stop by the Waldorf Astoria." Eisenrick's stone face broke into a big grin.

Wilson, pursed his lips. "Well, who knew? My dad is in real estate development in New York. I help him out and sometimes join him at his morning meetings with clients. He likes to meet with them for breakfast at the Waldorf."

"Army asked what I did when I enlisted. I told them I made deliveries in New York. They assigned me to drive an ammo wagon," said Frank.

"Well from now on, you are loading us up on bread," said the platoon CO, Captain Hathaway. The rest of the men cheered. "I assume you'd prefer that to delivering ammunition by horse drawn wagon?"

"I could get used to this," said Duff as they finished off their breakfast the next morning. "It might even get me to reenlist."

"That was funny the first time, let's not get crazy now Duff."

"No, I'm serious. If the food was a bit better and the roofs a bit warmer, life in the US Army wouldn't be so bad, especially if you are looking to learn a skill and you don't have a strong career path already set. It's a changing world. Think about it, technical skills are valuable and the army pays you to learn them."

"Back in the States there's not a lot of call for living rough and shooting people."

The tents came down and the platoon shipped out, catching a train for Paris where they would receive their sector assignment.

"We are being moved into the line," said Hathaway. "Good news is brass finally figured out that the mass charges into machine guns were not working. We are there mostly as mop up troops, there to secure areas recently taken after the big push back from the German summer offensive. We need to clean out minefields and booby traps that might have been planted in the Somme salient."

"I certainly don't mind letting the more experienced guys do the tough sledding. We've only had the most minimal training."

"Yeah, well, everybody has just had minimal training. With two actions under our belts we are among the more experienced troops. At least as far as Americans go. A lot of our guys have already bought it. Brass oversold our experience and training to the Brits. They are using us a bit more judiciously now I'm told. Still, we have to wave the flag."

"Yes, we are being moved into support roles as some of the front line units have been decimated by that horrible deep cough and influenza which spreads quickly and can affect 90 per cent of the men. They are moving whole units out because adding men to the units simply means the new guys get sick too."

"So we get a couple of days in Paris and then move back east to the front?"

"Yes. I'm hopeful that we can escape the worst of it. But I think there will be another big push to convince the Krauts they can't win. They want to get this done before winter sets in."

The train from Alsace moved slowly northwest and then found the broad Loire valley before turning north at Tours for Paris. The US Army held camp at a few moderate sized hotels just north of the Arc de Triomphe for use of troops taking a short rest in the city. Troops were rotated in and out continuously on a three day turn. They had been careful to not allow any units into the city which had exhibited any signs of the influenza. Those groups were sent south into the better weather. The poor conditions in the field had already contributed to a large number of non-combat deaths in all Armies, but the US Army seemed to be taking the worst of it.

Chapter Six

"So that's the Arc - it doesn't look like it would float."

"That might be the worst joke I have ever heard."

"You gotta work on that LaRue, puns are the lowest form of humor," said the burly cook Clancy.

"What are you Clance, a literary critic?"

"No, not at all. I think that is the point I was trying to make," said Clancy. "Dealing with subtleties is not the strongest point in this unit. I wonder if the Screaming Eagles are more understanding?"

"Well, when it came to it, they understood you couldn't bake bread," said LaRue. "But I don't think that required a lot of subtlety - just taste buds."

"Much better LaRue, much better. Comedy might not be your thing, but keep at it and you might get a bit part as one of the Keystone Kops. They love people who fall flat on their faces."

"Gentlemen, enough," said Hathaway. Clancy gave a broad grin to LaRue, having just achieved the last word. "We have to plan for our attack on Paris - our time is short."

"We do have our orders. Stay out of trouble. Don't annoy the locals," said Hathaway.

"We need to put some meat on those orders. May I Captain?" asked Martin Wilson. Hathaway waved him on.

"I see Paris for us as a multipronged attack. We don't have enough time to do everything so we must split up and take on those tasks for which we are best suited and most desire."

"I'm not baking bread in Paris. Get to the point Marty."

"Some guys might want to go on a museum tour. Some might want a landmarks tour - I hear Notre Dame is very impressive. Some might want to go out on the town and see a little nightlife."

"Notre Dame? What's that?"

"It's Our Lady."

"We have our own lady? Now you are talking."

"Don't be stupid, it's a church. A huge gothic cathedral with flying buttresses."

"Sounds like a lady I know back home, runs the local lunch counter."

"Let's get back on track here. Wilson makes an excellent point," said Hathaway. "Men, line up - museums here, landmarks there, and nightlife over there. I'll assign an NCO to go with each group and hope we do not get ourselves kicked out of France or the Army. While it might seem a good idea sometimes, I remind you that the stockade is never very pleasant, nor is dishonourable discharge. Uncle Sam wants no trouble between us and the locals, and sometimes they and us are looking for it."

The three lines were formed, each headed by a non-commissioned officer. However, all the men lined up as one. The nightlife line was exclusive so Hathaway changed gears.

"Okay, here's the plan, everybody will hit the town tonight, so the guys in the nightlife line pick one of the other lines to take in some of the sights."

Hathaway assigned himself to the nightlife group to chaperone. In the end they all went out together, with smaller groups of men deciding to visit this church or that landmark or museum on the way to regrouping and meeting at a dance hall frequented by American soldiers. Management had been induced to host the Americans thanks largely to several francs changing hands, a guarantee of large beer sales and the subtle ring of military police which surrounded the place.

The day passed quickly. Sunshine and cooler, early autumn temperatures were perfect for touring the capital. Once inside the dance hall and comfortably seated at tables of four, the boys exchanged stories of their impressions of Paris sights.

"Notre Dame is very old and dark."

"The view is nice from the top of the Arc."

"The streets are so narrow."

"The lingo is a bit tough to pick up. 'Allo' is Hello, 'mercy' is thank you, and 'parlez' is talking."

" 'Est' is east, and 'ouest' is west and never Mark Twain shall meet."

"Saw some nice pictures, some weird ones too."

"That tower is pretty Eiffel."

"What does Eiffel mean?"

"Tall."

"No, it's the guy's name who built it."

"Oh. Well it's the onliest Eiffel Tower I've seen."

"Anybody take a river cruise?"

"No need, there are plenty of bridges."

"One might come in handy tonight."

Pretty soon they had all managed to find the place and settled at tables and ordered drinks. Though they received some distasteful looks, most locals knew the place as a haunt of the US Army and stayed away. Those that came, knew why they were there.

"This place is full of French girls."

"I thought that's why we came here."

"Of course, maybe you were expecting frauleins?"

The band struck up the music and for most of the rest of the night the boys conducted themselves with the locals through gestures and smiles. The girls were used to the quick turnaround of Americans moving through Paris and came to the dancehall to dance, to flirt and perhaps to get a drink or bit of conversation about the wider world. The Army chaperones and the cordon of MPs made sure there was little else going on.

Hathaway sat a bit apart from the main group. As chaperone he was determined to look for any signs of trouble before it happened. He took a long look at each man in his charge. He was proud of them. They had conducted themselves well. Taken on the tasks they were assigned, completed their missions and been the picture of hale and hearty Americans in comparison to their European brothers, who were smaller and less bright-eyed having been beaten down by the length and ferocity of the war.

Hathaway gazed at his company and let trickles of his secret plan soak through his thoughts. They all looked sharp in their dress uniforms. He was protecting them. He was protecting himself from the fear of a mistake that cost one or more of them their lives. He was still acting in compliance with the battle plan, just changing it to recognize changing situations on the ground. All these ideas rattled around his head, save the idea that he was undermining the effort of the United States Army, that he was laying down and refusing to fight as his country wanted him to.

All this swirled in his head, but he was never quite able to face the basic facts, as rationales and complications always managed to snip off any thoughts that moved in that direction.

The boys laughed with each other while checking out the French girls who were subtly gazing at them. Bernie Smith was talking to Andy Endicott. Endicott was a talker but this time he listened intently to what Smith was saying. Probably describing the best way to approach the girls to dance. Hathaway smiled.

Allan LaRue, Freddie Allen and Hugh Coleman sat together silently sipping their beer and looking around the dance hall. He had tapped Coleman to help him keep an eye on the proceedings as one of the company corporals but promised him he could enjoy himself as long as he remained sober. Apparently Coleman has a different idea of sobriety than I do, Hathaway thought.

LaRue leaned in to Allen and nodded toward a phalanx of French girls across the room. Allen nodded at whatever LaRue said, and pushed his seat back an inch. Likely they were going to make an approach once the music started up.

Pete Delaney took a sip of beer and caught Hathaway's eye. He grinned at him and tipped his head toward Duff Richardson, Dick Shawcross and Clancy McDonald who each tapped their beer glasses to the table and proceeded to drain their entire drink with Clancy slamming his empty glass back down before the others. Shawcross made a face and finished his beer then tipped the empty glass over his head before putting it down on the table.

The three leaned in a bit and jawed over the rules before Richardson rose to get another round of beer.

Eisenrick and Wilson were speaking to each other and gesturing expansively, with Wilson almost knocking Jocko Rollins in the head while he was drinking. Jocko exclaimed loudly and angrily, but Wilson immediately apologised and rose to buy them all another round of beer. The placated Rollins took a deep drink, knowing another one was on its way.

Tom Billings brought a drink to Hathaway and sat down beside him.

"I see you eyeballing everybody Cap," he said. "Must be tough always having to be the responsible one."

"You know Tom, I don't mind. I never was much of a drinker and having a bit of responsibility sits well on me. I'm used to it I guess. What about you, why aren't you sitting with the other guys?"

"Same as you I guess, never took to a lot of small talk and such. I like listening to what everyone has to say. The whole world is a lot smarter than me. Listen to them and you get a pretty good education on all the important stuff. You can learn a lot from other people's mistakes," he gave a crooked grin.

"So that's why you're sitting with me?"

Billings opened his mouth and closed it. His grin faded. "Aww Cap, I didn't mean that." Hathaway gave him a broad grin. Billings was relieved and grinned back.

"What you going to do when this is over Tom?"

"Oh, I don't know. Learn a trade probably. Get a job. Listen to people and see what happens. I guess I haven't got it rightly figured out yet. And you, Cap?"

"Oh, I have some business to take care of back home. Spent a few years in university and I'll see where that goes. I hear from brass they want to keep officers above sergeant here for a time after the war to try to understand the best way to build an effective military, seeing as how we don't have one."

"Effective or military?"

Hathaway thought for only a second, "Both."

"Given the state of military intelligence that could take many years," laughed Billings.

Hathaway chuckled. "Or no time at all if they figure they have it all figured out and are just paying lip service to Pershing and President Wilson who want some paper report they can point at."

"Well, tell them that charging into the line is foolish. They likely know that but can't seem to help themselves. Sometimes conditions on the battlefield change quickly and officers need to be able to adapt with it. As long as the objective is kept in mind commanders should have more leeway to react."

"You get that from listening?"

"Yeah, I suppose. Mostly to you. You haven't been afraid of adapting and its kept us whole. Larry just got caught by the odds, you know. Larry should have run with me behind that hill, it was no shorter to cut in front of it and there was plenty of room for both of us behind it. Why did he do that Cap?"

Hathaway shook his head, "I don't know Tom, I don't know. In the heat of the moment he just made a quick decision that probably didn't seem terribly important at the time. It was."

"You guys got the message through and saved some lives. That was what was important. And you got your Distinguished Service Crosses to prove it. That was a nice presentation Colonel Hart made.

Sending Larry's family the medal is a nice touch. He spoke well of Larry's sacrifice. You two saved a lot of guys."

"Don't forget your Distinguished Service Medal. You were able to put all the clues together and get the warning where it was needed quickly."

"Thanks, Tom. I wasn't expecting any recognition on that. I guess Colonel Hart must have put in for it after reading my report. I did recommend you and Larry for your citations, and Colonel Hart agreed entirely."

"Nice to know brass is willing to take your recommendations. So why haven't brass taken your suggestion and used our aeroplanes to scout around a bit more?" asked Tom. "The balloons are wonderful but they are sitting ducks. At least the planes move around."

"They make a lot of noise. And once they know that you've seen them, they move, making the scouting information old as soon as it's gathered. At least that's what Colonel Hart said to me."

"There goes LaRue with Coleman right behind him. Figures the French guy would make the first move."

"LaRue is about as French as me. I don't think he knows any French unless it's from high school."

"Well, his French is good, it seems . . . . and so is Coleman's . . . . there they go up to the dance floor with a couple of mademoiselles."

"I'm guessing it doesn't take much to get the girls to dance. That's what they are here for. Some of them probably know a bit of English, especially if they've spoken to American soldiers before."

"Go ahead Cap, I'll spot you the chaperone duty at least for one dance."

"Thanks Tom, but no, I'm not much of a dancer. Fancy footwork usually gets me in trouble. I like to keep it simple. I'll stick to my knitting tonight."

"Hey there goes Jimmy, up to that gaggle of girls. Now I didn't see that coming. He's pretty shy usually and not one to burst off on his own. Mind you he's been steadily sipping courage for an hour."

"Look at the grin on his face."

Jimmy was leading a lovely young lady behind him as they made their way to the dance floor. He had a huge smile on his face that he was trying to suppress and making a major effort to not look at his mates. As soon as he did, the grin doubled in size and he looked away for a moment before saying something to the young lady.

"Now why doesn't the military name its citations more creatively? The two our unit got sound like the same thing. You gotta like the Brits with the Victoria Cross. That's got a little cache and a bit of a back story. At least Uncle Sam should call the medals something different to distinguish them," said Billings.

"A very good point Tom. I'll mention it to brass. The distinguished service medals are not distinguished enough from each other . . . right, got it." Hathaway smiled.

Billings started to say something and then just conceded with a nod as the music rose.

Watching his men enjoy themselves Hathaway thought back to several paintings he had seen that day in a gallery while they were walking down a Paris street. The paintings were different somehow, not very detailed, and brightly coloured. It was a new style of painting, he had overheard someone in the gallery say. The paintings showed some Parisian street scenes, with well dressed people enjoying themselves, not unlike the scene which unfolded in front of him in the dance hall. Quite a different thing than the more usual morose religious pictures or historical realism that was more common in the galleries and museums.

He noticed that as the light went down in the dance hall, and his eyes became more tired, the bright colours and sharp distinctions of dress became more noticeable while at the same time the details of the people and musicians and what they were doing became less important - just the way the artists had painted the pictures he remembered from the galleries. They had seemed sloppy to his afternoon eyes. They seemed deeply realistic now.

Chapter Seven

The train jerked to a stop. It was still dark but every man aboard was now awake or at least had their eyes open even if their brains hadn't registered wakefulness. A cursory glance from the windows revealed they were not at a station. Speculation was in every voice. But the men knew indignation was not an option as the army moved its assets like chessmen. Eventually word of mouth spread back through each car. Their train was waiting for other trains to disembark as thousands of new American troops were moving into front line positions.

Arras, taken by the Canadians in their Spring offensive the previous year was the natural gathering point. There wasn't much left of the small city. It's prewar population of 50,000 had dwindled to under 500 at one point but since the Canadian offensive the year before, people had trickled back to Arras and were rebuilding. It had become a natural jumping off point as offensives were planned both north and south of the ruined town in an attempt to push back the Germans and give the Allies more leverage in the peace talks.

It was all about speed and leverage now as the peace seemed imminent. The German spring offensive a few months before had been successful to a point, pushing the front forward but not achieving the demand for peace they had hoped. It could not be sustained and now the Americans were pushing the Germans back and re-establishing the front. Trench warfare had given way to the more usual movement of armies and battles usually for a town or a piece of landscape, a highland or a river crossing. The technology had helped as the new tanks and more refined tank tactics were rendering the trenches less hospitable to defence.

Thousands of new American troops coming every day bolstered the morale of the British and French already on the ground. Notwithstanding the US troops' poor training and general inexperience, they were a welcome sight for the battle weary Europeans.

The American troops were at the mercy of their commander Blackjack Pershing who wanted some glory for his command. Even though he had seen the results first hand he wasn't entirely against the over-the-top suicide charge that had been so spectacularly ineffective in the first few years of the war. What he wanted was an entirely American operation.

A few battle deaths would also help with American leverage in any peace talks. Without sacrifice, the desire for influence in international affairs would be ignored by the traditional great powers, diminished though they were. They wore their national sacrifices on their sleeves. There was a sense of payback in the air. Blame was everywhere. American troops were moved both north and south of Arras. They got the action they desired in the south, but less so as part of the northern offensive where they were used mostly to fill in behind the lines and support the more experienced British and Canadians.

By the summer of 1918 the Allies were prepared to push hard against the Germans to force peace. A last gasp of an offensive by the Germans that spring and summer had been spectacularly successful, driving a huge wedge into the front lines, but the Germans lacked the ability to capitalize. The long war of attrition had finally bled the Germans dry. Civil unrest at home and defections in the army were taking their toll. The Germans wanted peace. With the addition of thousands of American troops, the balance had shifted. The peace would not be amiable. The Allies wanted their pound of German flesh.

"Okay boys, we are moving out. We're going north to Belgium."

The platoon moved with an American contingent into position outside of Ypres to the south.

It wasn't long before they were engaged. Artillery began in the evening of their second day there, almost as soon as they were in place. There was the blast of the big guns and the distant whoomp of the shells landing. First there was one, then two, then a few in succession, and then the sounds of a continuous barrage of shells for several hours. Infantry moved forward with the artillery continuing to pound German positions, and gradually moving the landing points deeper into what had been German-held territory.

The first wave of Canadians, British and Belgians moved out. They were joined by several slow moving armoured vehicles. Soldiers had their gas-masks in place and crouched low against the drifting fog, the watery sun hanging low in the sky. It always felt as if the sun would burn off the fog but the lateness of the year, and correspondingly low temps, even if they were pleasant enough, were not sufficient to heat up the ground enough to clear the mists.

The push succeeded as the Germans fell back continuously for four days, taking the time to fight back at bridges, in villages and at any defensible position. Soon the Allied offensive stalled as there were not enough troops to follow up and the artillery could not be moved fast enough to support the advance. However by early October 1918 the tone had been set. The Germans were aware of the large American presence and simply could not fight any longer in an offensive capacity.

"They found him. He's dead. Drowned in a shell crater after the truck he was driving crashed."

"Dead . . . Jimmy's dead? Oh no, it can't be. We didn't even see the Krauts."

"Yeah, it's a funny thing, war. So many people moving around doing so many things, accidents happen amongst the intentional carnage. The guys who found him said it looked as if he was tossed into the crater, probably bumped his head in the crash and drowned, never knowing what hit him."

"Something hit him?"

"No, there was no local shelling. He likely was driving too fast and saw the crater at the last minute, jammed on the breaks and was tossed out. The truck had its front wheels in a deep hole. Would have stopped him rather quickly I'm guessing."

Jocko dropped his chin to his chest, and expelled a large breath. "What a way to go."

"It's a combat death, Jocko. He was doing his duty. I'm guessing that without the war going on the shell crater might not have been there. He'd definitely not been driving at speed through the area. We all have to be aware of more than just German bullets. Like several of the boys have that influenza that's dropping a lot of our guys. They've been moved back to hospitals behind the front. I'm hearing that many of the British and French have actually died because of it. Gets in your chest and you can't breathe."

Jocko nodded. He moved off and found a little spot to sit. He rummaged through his kit and found a pen and paper. He started to write a letter to his mother and father.

Dear Mother and Father:

We have arrived back at the front and our boys have just completed a victory at Ypres, pushing the Germans back about 6 miles. I was in a supporting role in the battle, which seemed to be fought mostly with artillery pieces and something called a tank, an armoured vehicle that allows men to be protected inside while they move smaller guns deep into enemy territory.

I didn't see any Germans, at least none that were alive. Some of the other guys did say they saw Germans moving backward where they have dug into trenches that were likely there before.

One of our guys, Jimmy Albright was killed in a truck accident during the battle. He was delivering ammunition and food to the front line.

Our platoon simply moved up behind the attackers after the Krauts retreated. Now I'm told we need to move our artillery up quickly if we are to advance more. If we wait too long, the Germans will be able to move to the offensive as our gains are not yet secure.

Several members of the platoon are sick with a bad pneumonia that has cut down a number of Allied troops. I am fine and have learned much about front line trench living from the Brits and Frenchies that have been here a while.

There are lots of rumours of peace, as the Germans don't seem to want to win anymore, they are just content with not losing too fast. Some of the guys want to get more of the action quickly as they are afraid the window is closing. I'm just content to stay alive and do my duty.

I have seen some of France in our mustering and travels. Paris is a lovely city - but we were only there for a few days. I would like to see some more before I come home.

I hope everyone there is well.

Your Jack

He sealed the letter and took it to the company post. It would take several months to find its way to St. Louis and by then the war would be over.

He took out a second sheet and penned a letter to Jimmy's family.

Dear Mr. and Mrs. Albright:

By now I expect you have had the sad news of Jimmy's passing. Official channels are much quicker than the slow mail they provide for us. I was proud to be a friend of Jimmy here in France and since basic training in New Jersey.

I was surprised by the unexpected nature of Jimmy's passing, but want you to know he was a true friend, a loyal soldier and died doing a difficult and dangerous job that most men did not want.

I am truly sorry for you and share your grief as I am sorry too that I will not see him anymore, nor hear his voice, nor look for his presence. We shared some good times and passed the time, where he spoke fondly of you and the good times of his youth.

In Biarritz, in the south of France, our platoon spent a week training and muster-ing for our assignment in Flanders. During our down time we played baseball. Jimmy mentioned that he played for a local team in Detroit, and while he never bragged, it was obvious that Jimmy must have played for a very good team, as he was clearly the best player on the field, making outs and hitting the ball hard on every occasion. It is his grace and ability in those games I think I will remember most - like his passing, quite unexpected.

Sincerely, Jack Rollins, Corporal US Army

Jocko folded the letter and again made his way to the company post.

The scent of fresh bread caught his nose. Ah, yes, dinner. He turned to go to the mess tent.

"Jocko? I need a volunteer. Don't look so stricken. It's just a driver to take me to Sector HQ. We can go after mess."

Jocko's guarded look melted into a smile, "Sure Cap. You know how to get there?"

"Yeah, I think. Unless the directions are bad. I guarantee nothing. Just bring a compass to make sure we stay on our side of the lines. Just have to have a word with brass."

Jocko managed to get a staff car and took the directions Hathaway gave him. Within 45 minutes they pulled up to a partly collapsed church near Bapaume, headquarters of the sector command of the American Expeditionary Force. Two marine sentries guarded the driveway approach.

"Gentlemen. I'm Captain Herbert Hathaway of the Fighting 49th, this is my platoon Corporal Jack Rollins. We are with Diamond Company. I have an appointment to see Colonel Douglas Hart."

The shorter of the two sentries took out a clipboard and flipped a few pages. Hathaway? Yes, right here. Drive up to the side door. Up the stairs there is a desk. They will get you to Colonel Hart."

99

The other sentry had been eye-balling the two Diamond Company men and the contents of their jeep.

"What's in the bag gentlemen?"

"Oh, feel free to take a gander, or I can get it if you want," said Hathaway. "It's some papers for Colonel Hart and a bit of our company's recreational equipment. Your Colonel said he wanted an idea of the condition of our supplies to ascertain if we needed more."

The sentry paused a moment. He took a step back. Then he requested Hathaway exit the vehicle and remove the bag before opening it.

Hathaway shrugged. He took out the bag and opened it. The sentry looked in and saw a sheaf of papers bound with a leather strap and the knob end attached to a worn and battered baseball bat. There were a few dirty baseballs in the bottom of the bag. He waved them through.

"Can't take any chances Captain. There are spies everywhere, and some nasty French as well."

"I understand Sergeant. Nothing to hide here."

Jocko stayed with the car and Hathaway made his way up the fancy steps and through the portico and into the building. It had once been a very beautiful church. Some gothic stained glass windows had survived and Hathaway couldn't help but notice the multiple stone casings and tracery in the windows. He looked around to see it had once been a fairly large building. Signs of battle were all around, but some extensive work had been done recently to enclose what was left of the building and shore it up. Battle had raged around it at one time, but now it was miles behind the main line east of Arras.

Hathaway was shown into a large office space and the door was left open as adjutants and office comings and goings continued. Rollins stayed back with the car. He had the hood up to give the innards a gander.

"Colonel, nice to see you again."

Hathaway saluted and then rummaged through the bag. "Here is the baseball bat you wanted to see. It isn't too bad but I think it is beginning to crack and as you can see it's pretty old and battered. The balls too are a bit past old. They've been repaired many times. And here is the report you requested about our strength, wounded, experience level and mission success. As you might know we had a casualty yesterday. James Albright of Detroit, Michigan was killed in a traffic accident while on duty making a delivery. He is only the second man I've lost so far though several have been taken behind the lines with the influenza and battle injury. I also have a number of minor injuries among the men, a few stitches was the worst and a couple of twisted ankles. Jack Rollins, my corporal and driver today, was shot in the leg a while back but the medics patched him up in no time."

The Colonel nodded sagely. "I see, Captain." He turned the baseball bat over in his hand. "I will show this to company quartermaster and see if we can get you some more equipment. A happy regiment is a successful regiment I always say."

A British attaché entered the room and approached the desk, "Colonel, my Commanding Officer, General Sir Lewellyn Bridge is requesting your attendance at the staff meeting which began on time 10 minutes ago."

"Ah, yes, Sir Bridge . . . . please tell the General I will proceed with all speed, once my business with my front line commander is complete."

The attaché barely tried to hide a sneer while he saluted and turned on his heel.

Colonel Hart waited until he had left the room. "Nasty sort, that man. The General, for all his insistence on social graces, is not a bad sort. Aristocratic for certain, but at least a soldier when called upon."

"Captain, would you be so kind as to close the door so we can conclude our business quickly."

As the Colonel spoke he placed the bat between his knees, just behind the desk, and placed his palm on the knob, giving a short burst of exertion before a soft pop signalled him to twist the knob off. He raised his head to make sure Hathaway had closed the door, before he tipped the barrel up high, letting a few papers slide out. He quickly replaced the knob and lay the bat on his desk.

"Excellent, I will pass this along the chain of command. We have several of them. They are all notched at the top, broken from a playing standpoint but useful as a bludgeon weapon for self-defence. Carry it with you as a sort of talisman. We can exchange them when we meet."

"And what about the upgraded equipment for the boys?"

"Ah, yes, come back in four days and I'll have it for you. We don't want the bat to be used in games anymore."

"What about the balls?"

"New balls? Of course . . . "

"No, well, yes, that too, but I tried unscrewing the balls but I couldn't get them open."

"A fine thing, very secure. Although that's because the balls are just that . . . baseballs. No secret to them, well, nothing more than Christy Mathewson knows, or Big Walter. Hathaway.....?"

"Yes, Colonel."

"The balls don't open."

"Oh, but the instruction I was given - take the balls and bat and open as per instructions. I tried for at least two hours."

"It must have been rather comical. I will endeavor to ensure that future instructions are very much more clear. Good grammar and all, you know?" the colonel said with a smile.

Hathaway saluted and held out his left hand, open palm face up. The Colonel dropped the handle of the bat into his grasp. Hathaway saluted again with his right hand and placed the bat alongside his left leg. The Colonel returned the salute and Hathaway turned to leave. He exited the office and found his driver in conversation with a young woman at the front desk at the top of the entrance steps. He looked around what had once been the nave to give him a few moments to complete his discussion.

"Young lady, thank you for entertaining my Corporal. We will return in a few days and he can entertain you with comic tales of our derring-do, or at least let you know what it's like to sit in a wet, cold trench for days on end."

Hathaway strode out of the building and down the steps with Jocko at his side.

"She was nice. Had all kinds of questions about trench life and the lulls between battle actions. Rosalie, I think she said, wanted to know if I was scared before and during the battles?"

"That's the first woman I've seen in any army position outside of Paris or London. How'd you start talking to her?"

"I wandered in looking for you. As she was at the desk she was just a natural to talk to. Told me you'd be along presently. We chatted. Her father is somebody or other and her mother is dead. So he put her to work for the army."

"We're back in a few days, Jocko. You can strike up another conversation. We're getting new stuff. In the mean time I think I'll keep this old bat as a souvenir and a bit of close combat insurance, if you know what I mean," he slapped the barrel into his palm before he climbed into the jeep and slid the bat down aside his left leg. "You never know what's going to jump out at you."

Chapter Eight

"Colonel, how's everything with our experiment?"

"General Sir, the Diamond Company are using the knowledge we provide them to their advantage. So far, Captain Hathaway has not passed that information on to any of his men or any other unit, as far as we know. He appears to have a reticence about the whole project but he is putting the survivability of his men first."

"Colonel I can't help thinking we need more units in our study as the reactions appear more various than we imagined. Given all the trouble we are going to we want to have a comprehensive set of data to work from. Holes in our study work to invalidate the results."

"As we have previously determined General, the short timelines and the rapid deployment of troops into the battle theatre have made expansion of the project difficult. We currently have enough units operating under the knowledge of battle plans and with the suggestions that superior officers tacitly approve their subtle alterations to plans for keeping the troops alive that we should get a fairly comprehensive data set. Unfortunately expanding the program at this time might inflict as much damage as having too small a sample group. With the experiment running on its own and in real time we have just enough resources to maintain our watch and insure that any reactions by commanders, should they be detrimental to the war effort, can be co-opted quickly."

"Ms. Robert were you able to ascertain any understanding of the experiment from the adjutant?"

"No sir," said the young woman who had controlled the unit commander's reception desk. I did not have enough time to probe his thoughts too deeply. He did not give me any indication of foreknowledge."

"The collection of this data is imperative to future army operations. This project has the backing of the highest authorities and beyond them is known only to us in this room. We are charged with keeping it that way for fear of impacting the integrity of the project."

"Captain Hathaway seemed reluctant to you?"

"Yes, General he still appears to be content receiving the information and deciding on how best to utilize it. He has asked for no additional units to be brought on board, nor has he appeared to have included any of his men in the plan."

"What messages has he returned in the hidden compartment?"

"He has included a rationale for his actions and tried to defend them as battle decisions that are actually beneficial to the army's effort. His diversion at the small village recently, actually may have saved lives, as he was able to see the trap being set because he moved to a different position from his original orders."

"And that is precisely the moving parts of this experiment that cannot be controlled," said the General. "We want to know what his pure reaction would be but it is clouded by real events."

"And the other unit commanders?" asked the Colonel.

"We have seen a range of actions that appear to be within a narrow band," said Ms. Roberts. "All commanders take the rationale at face value. All commanders make some attempt to protect their men, within a range of actions from avoiding the front line engagements entirely to unilaterally changing their assignments. At least one has taken his subordinate officers into his confidence."

"I expect the war will conclude soon," said the General with a sigh. "I am told by Pershing that the Germans are near collapse and cannot carry hostilities much further without a potential social collapse which would be catastrophic not only to their war effort but also to the fiction of a fair decision on their part and a shared peace."

"If that's the case we may not get the Diamond Company into combat again before it's over. They are about six weeks away from combat readiness given supplies, manpower adjustments and in-theatre strategy."

"We need to retain the Captain in France with the US Army as a consultant or some other job you can find for him or drum up if necessary. I would like to interview him in depth regarding his war experiences and attitudes."

"Yes, sir General."

"And Colonel Hart? Let's get a chat set up with the other unit commanders that are included in the project. This thing may be wrapping up quickly and we want our accounts to take place like Captain Hathaway's; while hostilities, and potential subversive actions, are still possible."

Bridgewater made a formal salute and strode from the room, followed by his adjutant who gave a cursory salute and a wink at Ms. Roberts who appeared not to have seen it, as she was peering at her notes.

"I believe some pattern is emerging sir," she said, once the General and his adjutant had left the room.

"Now, now, Ms. Roberts you know better than that. Science is impartial. Don't form any opinions yet as they may poison the data you collect and the ultimate conclusions you draw. You don't want to be biased in your note taking by only noting things which appear to support your pre-determination."

She looked pensive for a moment. "Of course Colonel, you are right. Data collection first. A detailed report second and potential conclusions only then."

Chapter Nine

"Come on boys, it's time."

Pete Delaney, grabbed his rifle and moved out with the rest of the platoon. He realized that being hyper-aware was not confined to his first mission. Every time he went out with the unit he found himself acutely aware of his surroundings, almost down to any unusual movements of grass or leaves, or birds or clouds in the sky. It wasn't colours he remembered it was movement.

This time there was still a light fog which a weak sun tried valiantly to break through. An early autumn chill was in the air, sure to lift with the fog given enough chance. Pete figured it was the large amount of uncovered earth which gave rise to the fog, earth devoid of vegetation, of buildings and of wetlands and small ponds which are common in farming country. That bare earth allowed the temperature change to take moisture out of the soil unimpeded by pavement, buildings, crops or much else.

The platoon was charged with checking out a ruined village, really just a collection of what were once farmhouses near enough to each other that it seemed like a small settlement. The remnants of a cross roads, passed though the fractured landscape but only hinted at the crossing as the road petered out in all directions.

The place had been overrun in the last German offensive and the eventual Allied counter-offensive. In fact it had been overrun more than that as battles raged back and forth in five years of fighting. It was St. Giscard on the map, a couple dozen homes and shops, a church and some workshops and storage buildings. In reality there wasn't much left. The platoon was charged with clearing it of any unlikely Germans who might be lurking about and identifying potential minefields and other booby traps. The latter was a far more likely prospect.

While other platoons moved out to cover their assignments Hathaway and the Diamond Company began their march down what was left of a country road, so battered with pot holes and shell craters that the going was very slow.

When the going was good they might make a hundred yards advance before being forced to circle round large holes or find a fairly flat way to traverse the destruction. The remains of the village were a mile or more from their camp position. The front was several miles forward and the platoon expected no difficulties, save any unpleasant surprises in the ground, in getting to and from St. Giscard and discharging their mission.

There were plenty of tracks in the dried and partly dried mud, giving evidence that this path had been trod many times by men, horses and even gas-powered vehicles, making it safe to travel.

They walked single file until they reached the ruins of a building. It might have been a house, or a substantial shed, but it was difficult to tell.

"Okay boys, lets break up into four groups. Coleman, Hauser, Shawcross and Eisenrick you guys take the northern quadrant, from here to that tree over there," Hathaway pointed to a shattered trunk, all that remained of a large hardwood, to the east of where they stood, some distance north, off what was likely the eastern road. Then he swept his arm northward, "From that tree trunk all the way around to what's left of this northern road; check out any structure and the spaces in between for mines. It should be pretty obvious where the settlement ends and the farm fields, or what's left of them begin. Leave the fields to the corps of engineers, just worry about what used to be the settled areas. Move out."

"Got you Cap."

" 'Yes, sir', works a whole lot better, especially if there is any brass around. Here, when it's just us, I'll take what I can get," said Hathaway with a grin. "Be careful boys, use the long poles to poke anything that looks suspicious. Don't get blown up. Take no chances. I'm guessing that we will find nothing, but don't take that for granted. I want everyone back here whole and happy when you've finished your assigned area."

"Jocko, you take Wilson, Delaney, and Waterly and cover the area south of that tree trunk to what's left of the road. Same thing, be careful and mark off any spaces you want the minesweepers to come in and check. Use the little flags I gave you. Meet back here."

"Got you Sir Cap," said Wilson with a big grin. He shook his pike, fitted out with a sharp steel end. "Yes, sir. Going to poke everything with my 10 foot pole."

"Duff, you take Smith, Endicott, LaRue and the ever vigilant Allen," he shook his head, as Allen had sat down among the gear and fallen asleep with his head on his chest. Duff reached over with his pike and gave Allen as slight poke on the leg. He woke with a start.

"As I said, the ever vigilant Allen, the soldier's soldier, catching 40 winks where ever and whenever he can. You can lead the way south of the road to that stone building. You guys check out the stone building - and be extra careful, it looks like the most substantial building in the area, if anything will be booby trapped, that's what it will be."

Hathaway spun around. And the rest of you guys follow me. We'll swing south immediately and take the area south of that stone building. In fact, Duff, let's join forces at that stone building, looks like a church, and we can take it on as a group. Let's move out."

There was a whole chorus of "Got you Cap," as the men picked up their gear and prepared to move.

Jocko and his group moved towards the first ruined building facing the road, just east of their position. There were the remains of foundations for several buildings along the roadway and it appeared that each property might have had an outbuilding. Anything else north of the roadway fell north of the tree trunk marker.

As they approached the remains of the first building, Jocko waved Wilson and Delaney around back while he and Shawcross took up spaces about 20 feet apart and surveyed the ruin. It consisted of a loose stone foundation firmed up by mortar of maybe two feet in height, now mostly lower than that without much of anything else to be seen save a bit of wood flooring and tile.

"There isn't much left to sift through. It looks as if this was a small home and it was hit directly by at least one shell."

"At least one, or at least one big one," said Shawcross. "The foundation was stone, and look over there, that rock appears to have been blown out of the foundation." Even the wood is either burned, buried or simply blown to bits, splintered beyond recognition as a building material."

"Reminds me of when our shed at home was hit by lightning. It was at the back of the yard. My dad used it as a workshop. He's an engineer and liked to build gadgets for the house. During a thunder storm he came running in from the shed saying the hair was standing up on his head. Not two seconds after he said that a lightning bolt just destroyed the shed. It was all wood and it was there one minute and gone in a flash of lightning the next. Boom!"

"You could feel the tingle in the air. There were bits of wood around the yard and most of the stuff inside was scattered by the concussion. The wood was in pieces big enough to clean up but so shredded and battered and burned that the pieces were nothing but kindling."

Jocko started to poke at the remains with his pike. "There is virtually nothing left. It's not much more than a collection of rocks that appear to have been laid out according to a plan. Let's look for evidence of a basement."

The four men sifted their way through the ruin, poking the ground here and there, noting the one wall of the foundation that seemed the only section that might be reusable. They found no evidence of a basement. Though they did see bits of things that had once been in the house, a shattered pot, a spoon, a picture frame.

"I'm not afraid of finding bodies," said Shawcross, "but I'm afraid it might take a while to realize what they are."

"This place has been pummelled back and forth. Anyone here is long gone, either ground into the earth by successive bombard-ments or rotted away from five years of war. I'd say pretty much anyone here was long gone before the shooting started. The bom-bardments were not a surprise," said Duff. "They knew the Ger-mans were coming."

The men worked their way through the ruins with very little to show for their efforts. They did find a few unexploded shells, which they marked with little flags for the bomb disposal unit to identify and secure later. They also marked two areas as potential mine-fields. In both cases the vegetation in the areas was growing oddly. In one it appeared to be significantly behind the new growth in adjacent areas and in the other there appeared to be a number of areas where soil had been irregularly overturned. Not conclusive evidence but enough of what they had been trained to look for, that they marked it as suspicious.

The two northern groups had nearly finished their job when the two groups south of the road met up at the stone building. It was obviously the village church as one stone wall remained partly standing, featuring a nicely carved gothic window with a cross carved into the key stone.

"You guys find anything interesting? Hathaway asked.

"If nothing is interesting, and I mean the complete and utter destruction of the village, then yes, that a village could be virtually removed from existence is our interesting find. It reminds me of some of those long abandoned pioneer settlements back home. Who knew that ignoring something or blowing it to kingdom come had the same effect in the long term?"

"This building seems to have sustained the least amount of damage, though that seems like a poor way to describe it. There is a wall, some of the interior floor and bits of the building strewn around. It's hard to describe it as even being a ruin. There is really nothing left to ruin."

Hathaway's group took what had been the inside, while the rest of the men circled outside the building's floor plan. Again, as they circled around there was nothing of significance to see, save some larger sections of masonry which fell or were thrown from their original positions.

Those surveying the floor plan looked around as large chunks of intact masonry, sections of 20 or more bricks still clinging together were strewn around the floor of the modest sized church. Much of the floor was covered with even smaller bits of one or two or three bricks mortared together. Then Hathaway saw it. A thick iron ring, perhaps three of four inches in diameter, attached to a wooden door in the floor of the church. There was a heavy piece of masonry, larger than most, still intact, sitting on the door. It had fallen from God knows where during one of the bombings, thought Hathaway, but failed to have been pulverized further in additional explosions.

"Now look at that. I wonder if we can push that off." He called in the group and together with a few levered boards and a lot of sweat they managed to push the large mortared section off the door.

Hathaway, grabbed at the iron ring but the door wouldn't budge, it appeared to be wedged into its bent metal frame by the force of the fallen stone. He took one of the pikes and threaded it through the ring, wedging the end on the ground and trying to heave up the other end to lift open the door. It moved a bit. He motioned one of the other men to help and tried again. It screamed as the metal door edge, scrapped slowly on the metal frame imbedded in the ground. He took a second pike and was able to get it through the same ring so there were now two wooden poles to lever up the door. Another man was conscripted to help. The poles strained and bent but did not crack as the door moved slowly, with a painful scraping noise, giving up its hold on the frame.

They kept up the pressure as the door moved up slowly. They jammed bits of brick under the pikes to maintain their progress while taking a moment to rest. And then it popped, jumping up to meet the levers as the pressure was relieved and the levers straightened.

They extracted the wooden poles and flipped the door open. It revealed a stone stair going down into blackness. No bottom was visible, even in the growing sunlight. Hathaway moved to the front of the group staring down the dark hole.

"Anyone fancy a look," he said. Most of the men said nothing. A few inadvertently said no. Only Endicott stepped up.

"Let's go Cap. Anyone got a torch?"

The two men descended the steps, Hathaway first, holding a makeshift torch.

The steps went down and then wound back upon themselves. Halfway down it was evident they were in a crypt. At the bottom of the stair, surrounded by memorials and raised coffins, there were two pillars each with an oil lamp just above head height. Hathaway touched his flame to the tip of each lamp and they lit and threw a weak light.

"Quick, scamper back up and grab a few more torches so we can look around a bit. There is sure to be a few more oil lamps down here somewhere."

Once Endicott returned they placed a bit of burning wood in the oil lamps to stoke the flame and proceeded to move away from the stair.

Moving directly out from the stair, all they found were more stone coffins and memorials covered in thick dust. Even the floor was covered in carved memorials, suggesting there were more dead buried beneath the crypt.

"It's a bit creepy down here Cap."

"Yes, it is. I've heard of these places but I've never been in one. We have no need to save space when we bury people back home."

"Not sure it's entirely about saving space. Usually these places were purchased by the local nobility. They were safer, closer to God and all that. I guess they also reminded people of who was important," said Endicott. "I saw some of this in England, when I travelled there a few years ago with my mother and father. Took the tour at St. Paul's in London."

"I've heard of that. Christopher Wren - If you seek his monument look around you. I wonder who's monument this is?"

"God's I'd guess."

They doubled back to the stair and started to explore behind it, back toward to front of the church, under the high altar. The smoke from their torches swirled above them and exited through the staircase entrance.

As they moved past the stair, Hathaway yelled up, "It's just a crypt boys, nothing to see here ...... oohhh!"

"What is it Cap?"

Hathaway pointed ahead to the right, and looked at Endicott, who winced. "I think they may have been trapped down here after seeking shelter from the shelling."

"Looks like more than a few."

There was a group of people, who appeared to be lounging around a group of monuments.

Endicott and Hathaway made their way up to the remains, some on the floor, others propped up against monuments. Some looked like they were preparing to pose for photos. The corpses appeared as if they had died recently but Hathaway knew the seal on the inadvertent tomb must have been good, as there were only small telltale signs of decay. It was that seal that likely contributed to their deaths. They had obviously only descended into the crypt for what they thought would be a short time, there were no supplies nor really anything other than their bodies and the clothes they wore and the things they carried with them.

"You know, it almost looks like a wedding party," said Endicott. "I'm not sure about French customs but everyone looks like they are in their Sunday best."

"Maybe it was Sunday."

"Look, Cap, right here, the ladies are wearing their finest pins and broaches and the gentlemen are quite well dressed. This guy here has a fancy walking stick and that one, sitting on the floor, has shoes on that have no wear on the bottom."

"What are you, Sherlock Holmes?"

Endicott broke a wan smile. "Elementary my dear Captain."

He moved cautiously toward the gathering of people to get a better look. Sure enough, everyone was well dressed and seemed to be in possession of a bit of finery, be it a hairpin, a broach, jewellery, or a walking stick.

"I've seen enough," said Hathaway before turning and hopped up the step. He emerged into a circle of Diamond Company, or at least the familiar faces of such a group. Alone for a moment, Endicott spied a small box sitting on top of a stone memorial. He grabbed it and put it in his pocket, a souvenir of war. Then followed Hathaway, giving a heavy sigh upon reaching the light.

"Looks like a crypt with a few additional inhabitants; some locals trapped after sheltering from the shelling. They've been there a while. We'll report our find and have civil authorities come by."

"Close the door boys. I'll let the command know so they can be properly buried. Strange, they and the previously dead are about the only recognizable things left in this place."

With the village cleared, the two groups started back down the road to meet the rest of the group who had almost reached them, after waiting at the crossroads for a time. As the two groups came together their relief of a mission completed was broken by the whine of an incoming shell. It burst, throwing dirt and stone chips around. Then another.

"Shit, find some shelter," Hathaway yelled, "this way." He waved and ran to a low stone wall, where he jumped and crouched behind it. "Don't go in the crypt. The last time that happened it didn't work out too well."

The men followed, with some finding an equally dismal place to try to stay clear of any explosions or shrapnel. The stone chips were especially dangerous.

The shells came in one, then two and then several at a time, pounding what was left of the village.

"Krauts must have seen us from the heights over there. Either that or they are on the offensive. Anyone got a field glass. One was quickly passed to Hathaway who scanned the wooded rise about two miles to the east. He saw some artillery emplacements and a few troops scurrying around like rats. He looked across the plain but couldn't see any advancing troops.

"Either they are preparing an advance or they are practicing their aim. I'm guessing the latter, but I don't get to make the call. We will see what the brass wants to do when we return. The shells still whined by, but the effort slowed and seemed haphazard. A few minutes went by without an explosion.

"It's not enough of a barrage to be fronting a charge. The shells appear to be aimed at the few remaining stands of stone and remains of buildings that are visible from that rise," said Hathaway. "And we happen to be at that same place."

"We can circle south of here and then west and we should avoid any unpleasantness getting back to camp," said Hathaway, who gave the command to move out. He left the position last, making sure he had a count of his platoon.

Then he circled back through some ruined foundations trying to time his movements between the shell bursts, diving behind low stone walls when he heard the telltale whine. He could see the serpentine line of men in front of him, snaking through the riven fields in twos and threes, circling bomb craters and moving slowly south and west. Slower perhaps but less likely to take a hit.

Then a higher pitched whine sounded sharply in the air. He yelled and hit the dirt. The shell went over and past him and landed with a thud before waiting a split second and exploding in the side of an existing crater. Endicott and Larue were closest to the point of impact, but hit the dirt beyond the point of the explosion, so the sound was muffled by the hole it occurred in. The resulting throw of dirt was tossed on top of them in their repose.

"God, I hate that," yelled LaRue, jumping up and brushing the dirt off him. "You never know what kind of slime is going to land on you. It's bad enough being here and getting that crap all day and night, but when it flies through the air and lands on you indiscriminately, that's the worst."

"How would you know. We've never done this before. They shelled behind the lines in our last two actions."

"Maybe you haven't, I have. I was making a run to the tent city in our action before Biarritz and got caught up in a shelling action. I think most of us got it when we preshelled the trenches we took at the beginning of that attack."

"Well I agree with you," yelled Endicott as if the noise of the explosion hung in the air. There was another of the strange whiny noises and the men ran forward a few steps and then hit the dirt again in anticipation. Again the shell landed in a crater before exploding, and again the dirt was simply shuffled and the cratered surface was shifted into a new and indifferent view.

The whole platoon was down. They shook off the shock and noise and began to rise to continue their escape. Delany opened his eyes. "That one was pretty close," he thought. He put his hand down on the moist earth that had been tossed around him to brace himself as he rose. Getting away from the ruined village was paramount to avoid becoming a statistic.

His left hand felt something cold and hard as he pressed down to take his weight. He curled his hand around it grabbing a handful of loose earth in the process. He looked down into his hand as he rose. There was a notched white stick threaded through with something shiny among the handful of dirt he grasped. He heard another whine and he ran still clutching the clump of dirt. The shell exploded well behind him. He dove forward with the sound. He clawed his way to his knees and then rose and saw his platoon do the same and they continued to move west away from the village and the shelling which now slowed considerably.

He opened his hand and brushed away the dirt. Most of the stick crumbled and fell away.

A golden ring remained in his hand. The band was narrow, a lady's ring, with a single diamond, maybe half a carat in a square setting anchored into the band point to point, angled like a diamond. Delany brushed more dirt from the band. His attention went to the ground, and he cried out and leaped back a step. It was no stick - it was a finger bone, which crumbled at the joints when he brushed at the dirt. He looked around for a moment, and the blood drained from his face. The rounded, stones, the shattered ground, pummelled, tossed and sifted more than once as battles raged back and forth. This was a cemetery, a graveyard.

He vomited. Wretching, his breakfast, his drink rations came up. Then dropping to all fours he continued convulsing with nothing to show for it. Momentarily he wondered if more nasty surprises awaited him and if more treasures were kicked up by the explosion, before remembering he had run a distance from the first explosion to this place. He looked back to where he had come from hoping for a glint of gold, but only fractured earth and a few ragged but hardy weeds were visible.

He was almost relieved that nothing caught his eye. He saw a man running toward him. He returned his attention briefly to his hand, removed whatever grit he could and slipped the ring into his pocket.

LaRue caught up to him. "You okay Pete. You look a bit dazed."

"Yeah, I'm okay, just wondering about this godforsaken village. Not much left. Wonder who lived here?"

"Might ask the skeleton's back in the church. I'm guessing they all fled when it became obvious they were in no-mans-land. Took anything of value and high-tailed it to Paris."

"Yeah, let's get going. It's likely not the first burned out village we'll see before this one's over." He tapped the ring in his side pocket, a little souvenir of his combat action. He was still unnerved by the conditions of the find but unwilling to just toss a bit of gold and the smallish diamond away. He'd sell it for some cash at the first opportunity, he thought, and be done with any memory of the find or curse that might follow it.

"We will be back at camp soon and Eisenrick said he'd bake up some croissants for us tonight, something about some big brass coming through. He's hoping for a field promotion, maybe a move up to the general's staff. He wants to be Keeper of the Bread. I told him he could be 'flour boy' but he wasn't too happy with that title," LaRue laughed.

The whole platoon made it back to camp and while tension was high for fear of an attack after the shelling, none came, and the boys settled into their evening grub.

Back in his tent, Endicott, took the ring out of his pocket. He had quietly cleaned it when he washed his hands for dinner and wanted to inspect it before putting it away in his kit.

It definitely looked like a wedding ring, but an unusual setting in the band with what appeared to be a half carat diamond in the center. the setting was a square of gold attached to the ring portion of the band at opposite corners which seemed odd in a wedding or engagement ring. Endicott shrugged.

He studied it further, looking on the inside edge of the band for any identifying marks. It was shiny yellow gold, and then he saw a faint mark - 18K - and the word - 'toujours' - always. It appeared to have been worn for some time, with a large number of nicks and light scratches.

An interesting souvenir and potentially worth a bit of money when I get home he thought. He quickly dismissed any claim on the ring as it would be impossible to identify the owner and with the owner likely dead, no one was likely to appear with a claim. With visions of ghosts with their hands out, he almost laughed at the thought, but he kept the ring to himself just the same, wrapped in some paper and placed among his few important papers and his pictures of home in a leather sleeve in the bottom of his kit bag.

Ammunition was being shipped in everyday, coming as it was with thousands of fresh new troops from the United States. Most were keen to get their first action in before the war ended, as talk of armistice was everywhere. The battle hardened French and British troops couldn't even muster a smile at the Americans' youthful lust for battle. They just shook their heads. Some wished for their American friends to get a little taste of it so they would understand what had been happening for the five years they had not been there. Others wished the Americans no harm.

The weather was cooling noticeably from the crisp mornings of early autumn to the crisp complete days of late October.

Word flashed through the trenches and camps. The armistice was close. Battle hardened troops barely took notice as such news flashes had come and gone on several occasions without so much as a cease fire.

A few weeks passed, and rumours swirled. Then, after days of false hopes and renewed tensions, only a few minutes before the appointed hour word reached most of the fighting men. The guns would go silent at 11 am on this day, November 11, 1918. Many commanders were determined to keep the pressure on until the last, firing artillery shells timed to explode right up until the last minute. And if they shot them they wouldn't have to carry them to where ever they would go next.

The Germans had some of the same ideas, and shot indiscriminately, almost as if their munitions were fireworks. Who wants to carry around a bunch of dangerous stuff right when you found out your life had been spared. Lighter travel, easier movements translated to quicker way home. That was the prevailing wisdom.

There had been a ragged cheer in most companies as the men were officially informed in small groups. They were pleased to be sure but wary of the peace, knowing of the false starts, rumours of peace and not wanting to be too sure of taking a premature sigh of relief.

And then the armistice - peace came to the silent trenches. There was dancing in the streets of Paris and London while the war-weary in the trenches finally got a peaceful sleep from which they knew they would wake up. They had little to celebrate with - an extra bit of rations, a handshake among friends. In some areas the Germans presented themselves in full view of Allied lines, and causing no little tension, before retreating back into German territory leaving the Allies alone for a time with the front lines and trenches all to themselves.

As the days of armistice passed, assignments of duty changed and into the boredom crept the uncertainty of peacetime as the men contemplated their immediate futures. There were several extensions of the armistice but slowly the surplus of men and armaments began to disappear from the front and the Hathaway platoon received orders to move backward and then eventually to embark for home. They were kept in reserve for a short time in case tensions boiled over during the lengthy peace talks. By the late spring, units were being removed from service. Return to the States was imminent.

It was now left to the politicians and government officials to forge with honour the world they believed to be just in the wake of unimaginable carnage. French and English ideas of armistice and peace did not mesh with German thoughts of honour and sacrifice. All European parties thought the American ideals of Wilson to be propaganda and dreamy rubbish. It all made for a prolonged and difficult peace negotiation which took more than a year to conclude. And even in the completeness of the discussions and agreements were the obvious seeds of the next conflict - there, clearly visible for all who wished to look.

First the Diamond Company were held in place. Then they were used as military police as order was restored in contentious areas along the German - French and Belgian borders. Then they were shipped to Paris where they were cleaned up, fed, provided with dress uniforms and paraded around for several weeks. Then came their orders to entrain and head for Calais. Hathaway was to remain in Paris and be debriefed about his unit's experiences.

Hathaway bid farewell to his men at Gare-Du Nord. As they approached the train they would board, they gathered around their Captain. He stepped up on a pair of kit boxes so everyone could see him.

"Boys, I'm proud of every one of you. We made it through without much of a scratch, except for Larry who died a hero and Jimmy who died doing his duty. We should all remember them. Any one of us could have been Larry or Jimmy. We saw some combat, but most of it was us being shot at rather than us dying, and for that I am grateful. We were engaged enough to know it and wear that badge of courage and honour, and enough that we can all still talk about it and take home memories rather than disfigurement and terrible wounds. I know that some of us will feel the battles forever, we are not the same as we were when we were thrown together at basic training in Jersey. Some of us have pain, some have a record of their wounds imprinted on them and all of us are hurt for life with the memory of what we have seen. Talk around HQ is that we carry on the soldiers code. I think you all know it already. We have already begun to live it. That we bear our wounds both physical and mental without complaint and without acknowledgement. We will not speak of the horrors of war to anyone who was not there, who cannot know the detail of what we experienced in order to fully understand of what we speak and the language we use to describe it. But amongst ourselves, in our own company, we can talk freely, we can reminisce and we can help each other bear the burdens of service to our great nation and the freedoms it stands for. Others carry sorrows and visions of things only we know about. I know we will see each other in twos and threes. When we do, when you do, please offer a toast or a benediction on the welfare of us all. I propose we get together again in 10 years and talk of old times and new times. Here is my address, please forward your address and any changes to me, I will make arrangements for a reunion. Mine is an old family home not far from Philadelphia on the New Jersey side of the Delaware and unlikely to change. I will make formal invitations to the addresses you provide when the time comes."

The men had gathered around and nodded with Hathaway's words. A call went up and they sang a round of "For He's a Jolly Good Fellow." As they began to board the train, shaking hands with Hathaway at the foot of the stair someone started to whistle Auld Lang Syne, it was taken up by the soldiers on the train, hanging out of the windows, until at least one full verse was sung by Diamond Company, to their general amusement.

Hathaway bid them farewell insisting they travel together in a train car he had arranged. No sooner had the last strains of melody finished, the laughter died down and final waves completed, when the train jerked to a start and slowly rolled out of the station. Immediately waiters trundled through with trays of French cheese, meat and luscious fruits fresh from harvest in the south - a gift from Hathaway to his men.

As the train pulled out of the station, Captain Herbert Hathaway stood saluting his platoon as the cars passed. And as it passed and the train began to pick up speed, once it left the station a smile creased his face, then a grin and then outright joy as he had completed his command without significant incident - save Larry's and Jimmy's tragedies.

Sotto Voce

Conventional wisdom says the Great War was touched off on June 28, 1914 when Gavrilo Princip shot Austrian Archduke, and heir to the Austria-Hungarian throne, Franz Ferdinand and his Duchess to death in Sarajevo, Serbia.

The tides of history had set up that moment to be the spark where the tinderbox containing decades of decisions, events and concerns leapt into an uncontrolled conflagration.

Europe had been engaged in centuries of constant adjustments to the balance of power often breaking into smaller wars. This time the confluence of events, alliances, technological obsolescence which rendered stockpiled weapons useless and put everyone on the same page, and a generational desire to set things "right" piled up into a many layered determination to fight.

As the chips fell and the decision to go to war was made it became an irreversible choice. Battles until then were smaller affairs, and battles once won forced concessions on the losers. This time however, new weapons could kill more efficiently, defensive oriented battles were never really won or lost, but the dead piled up, and up and up.

The United States took a neutral view as President Wilson asked Americans to be "impartial in thought as well as action."

This was of course impossible as millions of hyphenated Americans took the sides of their heritage homelands.

American banks loaned money to the French government. Attempts to stop arms sales were repudiated by the Wilson administration. Industrial interests, seeing an opportunity for wartime profits, protested any attempts to restrict trade with the belligerents. Wilson the pacifist was crumbling in the face of national, business and political interests.

The British were likely guilty of using flags of neutral nations on their ships to break a German blockade on the British Isles. And then the passenger liner Lusitania was sunk by U-boats in early May, 1915 and 1,198 lives were lost. The cry for war was deafening. It mattered little that the liner was carrying some armaments.

Perhaps the final straw for the United States was the revelation, today somewhat discredited as a potential British straw man, that the Germans had discussions with Mexico about joining the Germans should the United States enter the war on the British - French side. Remembering that the War With Mexico had occurred only about 60 years before, and resulted in the Mexican loss to claims of huge territories - this was not as far-fetched as it seems to later generations.

On April 6, 1917 the United States declared War on Germany. Armistice was declared on November 11, 1918, only a scant 19 months later. In between, an unprepared United States mobilized and took part in several important battles to establish its credibility as a world power.

The United States instituted conscription, a draft, with many Americans violently opposed saying there was little difference between a conscript and a convict - a difficult comparison for a nation founded on freedom of choice. By June more than nine million men had registered for military service. The United States had leapt headlong into the modern world, seeding the future with taxes, the military-industrial economy, and a place in international affairs that could not easily be rescinded.

The Germans realized they needed to push their efforts in battle before the US could become fully engaged. The newest belligerent faced a standing start with almost no modern military equipment. By October 1917 American units found their way to the front and by the end of the year there were about 250,000 Americans in the field, with most still in training. That number doubled by March 1918. That same month Russian revolutionaries took their country out of the war freeing German troops to come to the western front and allowing a final huge push prior to the expected increase in American involvement. It was the result of this push that the Americans had to retake areas and battle Germans determined not to lose while not attempting to win in the final months of the war. Even though the German push gained them territory, it failed to provide the knockout blow which would force peace.

Active American participation lasted only a few months but 50,000 men were killed in battle, enough to stamp the American ticket into the peace talks and into the corridors of power.

Gas attacks started early in the war as a strategy against the defensive nature of the trenches. As many as one-third of American casualties are attributable to poison gas. Often this gas would drift into civilian areas killing or causing permanent injuries to hundreds of thousands of innocents. Despite the gas attacks being in open violation of existing treaties, the use of gas continued on both sides.

Wilson, French Premier Clemenceau and British Prime Minister David Lloyd George headed up the group of allied nations in fashioning the peace. It was a laborious process, with the French and British, who had fought for so long and sustained such losses, determined to gain their pound of flesh from the Germans at the negotiation tables. It was this process and the punishing treaty that was eventually signed that led directly to the Second World War. Future historians will likely pull the two wars together into a single protracted event as they are very much interconnected.

Wilson's desire for a league of nations was his biggest prize. Concerns in the United States Senate in particular with the idea that the League would tie US hands in foreign affairs because of their membership in the League, ultimately forced a rejection of the entire Treaty of Versailles. The US closed its war participation with a resolution dissolving the original declaration of war. And while a League of Nations was formed American participation was slight.

But for the veterans of the war, it never really ended. Surely the fighting and active participation in events were concluded but the war never really left the experiences of those who participated. For some it was a great adventure, as they retired to their homes and farms. For others it colored their perceptions, affected their lives in many ways. Those who nursed injuries and disfigurement were constantly reminded of their days as soldiers.

Others would have it affect their judgements and decisions often in subtle ways. And still others would have jarring memory flashes triggered by car accidents, booming sounds like artillery or even the smell of grease, gas, or burning flesh. Collectively these 'shell shocks' as they came to be known, could strike at almost any time, even among those with no apparent effects. For some the affects were so profound that they found it difficult to function in a day to day way affected by shaking, nerves and mental stress. To those who never experienced the cause of these afflictions, it seemed weak and unnerving that they could occur.

After the Great War, in spite of only cursory participation, the United States was never again the same. Industrial capacity had grown exponentially. The government's desire to maintain military preparedness, and the revelation that taxes would be tolerated by the people for worthy uses seeped into every corner of American life. In the great cycle of empires, the United States had just woken up to its potential and as great cycles of history demonstrate, they were almost powerless to avoid the events that such an awakening produces.

Chapter Ten

Hathaway had an appointment to keep. He was to meet with a young woman he had come to know while the paperwork on repatriation for his platoon was being completed. He was expected to provide intelligence to Army brass on the conduct of the war, as the slight US involvement was going to be picked clean to understand the deficiencies of the US military and the lessons of the war.

Hathaway could see that warfare and the US Army had come a long way since the days of the Spanish - American War half a generation before. That war had been fought with only minor differences from the tactics, strategy and technology of the Civil War, where the Great War was much more modern in scope and approach. Certainly trenches, tanks and aeroplanes and machine guns had turned the Great War into a more defensive engagement, with troops taking cover in trenches and using the other innovations to defend rather than employing tactics more suited to man to man combat. Rapidly changing technology rapidly changed war. In fact war was the catalyst for much of the technological advancement.

The US military had completed its mission. There had been enough casualties that the US would be taken seriously at the peace talks - despite their late arrival to the fray. They had arrived at an opportune time as the Russian Revolution had ended the war in the east and freed huge numbers of German troops to fight on the western front. The Germans had pushed hard in the spring of 1918 knowing they needed a knockout blow. They failed and the weight of US involvement helped push them back towards Germany, the end becoming more and more inevitable. As the war wound down, they retreated bit by bit, unable to keep their supplies and their morale up while those opposed to the continued fighting grew louder and louder in Germany.

About half of US deaths were from the influenza, a fact lost in the fog of war - and still many thousands of US troops had died in combat, about as many as had succumbed to the flu. A respectable 110,000 deaths in this European war, coupled with the US throwing off Spanish influence in the western hemisphere two decades before, had bought the US its full flower of inclusion among the great powers. The traditional powers had losses many times greater, but they had been grateful for the US decision to tip the balance of the war and force Germany into an unwilling, but necessary peace.

There was no "Remember the Maine" moment nor anything like the Roughriders charge up San Juan Hill to be etched into American military lore, but the Great War engagement had cemented the US into the first run of nations, perhaps still as a junior member, but one that was watched with a wary eye.

Hathaway decided to walk through Paris on his way to his meeting. He had come to like these walks through the streets where even the old buildings and leafy trees were interesting and occasionally gave way to a storied monument or other ancient pile. Once he figured out the lay of the main streets he tried to take alternative routes through the maze of Paris, sometimes finding little markets or a series of shops that he poked into or more often, just getting lost in the unpredictability of the road network. He could never be sure that a street that appeared to take him where he wanted to go, would actually get him there. More than once he was forced to retrace his steps and try again.

Walking along the Seine on the Left Bank he had a magnificent view of Notre Dame across the river. Guessing a bit he turned away from the river expecting to intersect with the Boulevard St. Germaine. He reached that major thoroughfare, looked around and turned to his right, where he found the Cafe Flore about a block on.

The cafe was quiet at this early hour. Hathaway approached the bar and ordered a cafe au lait and a bain du chocolate before finding a seat at one of the tables along the back wall. It was completely mirrored to give the cafe the illusion of size. Heavy on the milk was the only way he could handle French coffee, and he always had it with something to eat, as the coffee was always too strong. The bun wasn't even as succulent as the ones he had become accustomed to from Eisenrick, and it was three times the price he'd been paying near his hotel north of the Arc De Triomphe, but it was necessary and would do nicely as the alternative was the army mess.

"Ah, there you are Captain," said a youngish, blonde woman, as she strode to the table undoing her overcoat. He rose.

"So nice to see you again, Miss Robert."

"Please Captain, I am Rosalie outside of the office."

"But I understood you wanted to speak of department concerns, leaving us physically out of the office but metaphorically in the midst of it."

"Such precision is unnecessary Captain."

"Then you must call me Herbert for now, Herb by the end of our meeting and Herbie when I call you again for coffee."

She smiled, unsure how to take Hathaway's approach. "I asked you here to speak of my concerns regarding the intelligence that you and other platoon commanders have provided is not getting through to army brass. There seems to be a roadblock in the chain of command - but I don't know where it is."

"Why do you think there is a problem? What evidence do you have?"

"I am present in the interviews and type up all the notes, they are approved by the officer who conducts the interview and then they are sent up to Army Command, where they are reviewed and assembled into facts and evidence from which our future military policy will emerge. So far, what seems to be emerging as policy is a far cry from what we are feeding up the chain of command."

"Are you qualified to make that assessment? Perhaps you should start with an example?"

She made a face, looking at once incredulous while narrowing her eyes and opening her mouth to speak, before deciding to say something else.

"The influenza deaths for example. From our tallies about one half of all US army personnel that died in the Great War, died from influenza rather than battle or consequences of battle. Nowhere in the ensuing policy are there measures to stop this."

"Perhaps brass feels the influenza is only a one-time occurrence. A bit of bad luck as it were."

"Well they do seem to be selling our total death numbers as a ticket to the diplomatic big league. However there is much, much more. Technology for example. Some commanders are almost of the belief that the technological changes will be removed from future army tactics as they proved less than totally effective. They have no sense that they will continue to be refined and improved."

Hathaway looked at her a bit more closely. She was young, but apparently quite sharp and in fact unable to hear the evidence and not draw conclusions. Her determinations were not shocking. What concerned her was the inability of army brass to see the future clearly.

"In addition, and perhaps more disturbingly, statistics show there were a number of companies, platoons and other small units which sustained almost no casualties. While other units were decimated and in some cases completely wiped out."

"Is that strange? How does it compare to other US military actions?"

"A good question. It doesn't, if you take away from the study any units that never faced hostile action. I have looked. So the conclusion is that there is evidence that some commanders determined to keep their platoons out of harm's way or perhaps more than that, they were positioned in a way to reduce their casualties. Almost like there were certain favoured battle groups and others simply tossed to the wolves to die in numbers sufficient to build US credibility."

Hathaway paused. Had all his efforts to protect his men left a trail?

"Well that is certainly a significant conclusion. And frankly one I would be very certain of before making public. There are many commanders and brass that would very aggressively fight any accusations of that nature. I never received any specific orders that were contrary to our mission. My platoon was engaged in clean up operations and occasional supply. We only faced two actions at the front and both were late in the war when tactics led to substantially fewer casualties. We did not spend significant time at the front."

"Certainly I am looking for your perspective. Perhaps I'm on the wrong track here, but I am not specifically referencing your command."

"What else could I reference, that is my experience. You mean you called me to a clandestine meeting about your concerns without looking at my background in the report? I'm a bit surprised."

"Quite, Captain Herbert, perhaps it isn't my place to be concerned, however, I thought if I passed on my feelings that a seasoned officer might take up the cause, and give it a bit of credibility. I called you because I remember you from meetings with Colonel Hart. I was the receptionist at Baupame HQ. Your Corporal might remember me better. I took the minutes of meetings. And, there are other things that alone do not appear to be much, but added all together are unsettling."

"Please tell me more and let me know how you think I can be of assistance." Hathaway didn't think of himself as a 'seasoned officer' however he had to concede that he had more battle experience than many US officers who arrived at the front far too late to really understand the course of battle. He had never felt entirely comfortable with the expectation of battle and wondered if that was his lack of experience, or fear of death.

She took a sip of her tea. "It seems that many of the regiments under direct command of Pershing were cut up badly. In fact it appears that those regiments were reformed several times in the field. So much so that army records had trouble keeping up with the changes. Regiments that fought alongside, or under the command of British officers seem to have found much fewer fatalities. Your platoon for example fought its engagements with British troops and seem to have had a high degree of survivability. It is well known that Pershing did not want our troops fighting with the British or the French, that's why we fought to regain much of the Marne Salient by ourselves in the summer of 1918."

"Yes, I am very proud of my platoon, that we were able to avoid many losses. Poor Jimmy Albright was killed delivering ammunition and rations to the front. Larry Schilling was killed by snipers when he was running to deliver a message - that message, carried on by another soldier, probably saved hundreds of lives. Of course several of my men were wounded, some grievously, in our actions and sent to England to recover. Some contracted the influenza. A few never returned to us and were sent home. We did not emerge from this unscathed."

"I'm not suggesting you did. What I don't know is how some units were able to keep their casualties down while others were almost wiped out. Was it merely the luck of the draw? Unfortunately, the interviews with ground commanders like yourself have provided no clue as to how you survived. Not even a pattern of actions or locations have emerged, only that you fought largely with British and in some cases French troops."

"I'm afraid I have provided all I know to the debrief. I would be happy to provide more if there was anything or anyone had additional questions of me. It would be nice to think we discovered some effective way of staying alive but in the fog of battle we were assigned a role and we fulfilled it to the best of our ability as others were counting on us. Was there a preponderance of deaths among other units in actions we took part in?"

"Yes, but that alone is not material. As you said units had different objectives and as such were either in harm's way or were not during the fighting of any particular engagement. That's just it Captain, there appears no way to explain it other than perhaps the experience of the British and French troops you fought with provided some measure of survivability that American troops alone did not have."

"Can I get you more tea, Rosalie?"

"Please. Captain, it is not my job to do anything more than the clerical work compiling the information from the debriefings. However, I cannot help but want our experience here to pay dividends to American troops in the future. I had two brothers fighting, one of whom is not coming home."

"I'm sorry to hear that. How is it that you yourself are here with the military?"

"My father is the Deputy Quartermaster at the department of defence. He is serving in France and could not leave me at home. My mother died when I was quite young. After a few months of haunting the art galleries I asked for something to do. He found me this job with Colonel Hart thinking the experience would be good for me."

"So you are bored by the art collections? I find them fascinating. Especially the painting. Sculpture is remarkable but just doesn't capture my imagination."

"I found them fascinating as well, but once you've seen the Old Masters 20 times, close up and studied them at length, you either become an artist yourself, or you remember the pleasure and move on to something else. I remember the new realists like Delacourt and Delaroche, I liked their style. I have moved on."

"I am not so studied in the arts. However, I was fascinated by the impressionistic works of Monet and Renoir that I saw in galleries. They at first appeared sloppy and without necessary detail, but they sit in your mind giving you the view of a memory, with the swirl of the essential and the flash of colours central to the experience. Perhaps you could find the time to give me a quick tour and lesson?"

She paused. And took another sip of tea, trying to have the moment the question was asked pushed into the background.

"Yes, Captain Herbert, I might be able to do that, if only to save you the time I spent in the galleries and museums. I am no expert on these Impressionists. I failed to see the paintings as you have - as memories of moments in time."

Before he could respond she said, "However, I am more concerned about what we can do for those who leave here wounded, missing limbs or eyes, or horribly disfigured by fire. The dead have given their sacrifice. I want to make sure that it is a worthy sacrifice by understanding how to limit casualties in the future. The damaged are only now beginning to live their particular sacrifices. In hospitals, and I visit them often, they are unexceptional among the other wounded. Once they return home they will be ignored, rejected from normal society as their wounds are too hideous to look at. Even among their families there will be change and disbelief and revulsion. I want to know how some of you avoided that so we can try to avoid it in the future."

"So you think all this will happen again?"

"It is inevitable Herbert. Men disagree. Men fight. Wars are won and lost, but the idea of war has never been disavowed."

"And yet, this has been called 'the war to end all wars' because of the carnage and destruction. The carnage simply beggars belief, especially when you are in the midst of it."

"If you believe that there is a level of death past which men will not go when confronted with their existence or that of their families and homes, you do not understood the human psyche. People are capable of anything if the right conditions surround them."

"That is a remarkably horrible way to see the world."

Hathaway was tempted. The lovely young woman before him spoke with such passion. Her intentions appeared pure. And yet, something held him back. He was not contrite about his approach to the battles, but neither was he willing to speak of it as even the slightest suggestion of a shift from the orders of the battle plan provided a chink in his armour of duty, a flaw that could be exploited. He was never entirely comfortable with the foreknowledge. And there were others players in the effort at self-preservation, their motives in his mind, pure, who would inevitably be drawn into anything he suggested. The code of the soldier remained.

He gazed thoughtfully into the ceiling, trying to appear as if he was considering his entire wartime experience, then he hesitated theatrically for only a second before returning his gaze to her.

"I'm afraid Rosalie, that there is nothing more I can think of, that might have led to the lack of casualties you describe. I always thought we were just a bit lucky. We were present south of Arras for a large offensive in which we were ambushed at the end. It might have been a trap. My unit was assigned a sector that was not immediately targeted. The main thrust of the ambush was a few hundred yards to our north. When it occurred we were able to hit the dirt before we were targeted. There were some significant injuries from shrapnel and machine gun fire. After a time in the south to regroup and avoid the influenza outbreak in our sector, we moved back into the line. A few weeks later we were north of Arras in a quiet part of the front when we were assigned to storm a small town. It was I who issued the warning of the ambush, largely because I had seen the warning signs in our previous ambush and recognized them. In fact, I received this DSM for my recognition of that. Two of my men, who ran to tell the forward fighters, received higher commendations as well. One posthumously."

"I would think, mathematically, that luck would have evened out. In other words you would be lucky in one or two actions but eventually you would not sustain the luck and it would run out," she said.

"Are you a mathematician, a philosopher or a clerk? Rolling seven, three times in a row isn't unusual."

"No Captain it isn't. I'm just someone who has a lot of information pass me by and who has tried to make sense of it."

"And speak to Larry Schilling about the odds, of course he isn't here to reply, but he might disagree with you as would a number of men in my charge who were wounded," he was a bit annoyed, but he softened. "Actually, that has made me remember that Corporal Rollins, with whom you spoke, was badly wounded in the leg in our first engagement and the British officer that was with us was able to take charge of his battlefield needs get the wound dressed. He survived without losing the leg. So maybe there is something to your thought that the British experience helped our survivability."

"Is that in your report Captain?"

"I don't remember. It should be as it was fairly dramatic at the time. Though it was our first taste of battle and perhaps became a bit more forgettable in that he survived and we faced additional combat."

"I will check your official account. I may call you back to add this new information into it."

"Perhaps you should share your calculations of the odds of casualty with the analysts who compile the information into policy?"

"I have tried that Captain, but I've been ignored. The Army is not inclined to take seriously the claims of a young woman. That's why I wanted to talk to you. In our previous discussions you seemed to be of the same mind as me. Perhaps you can carry this discussion and have some influence on policy, or at least ensure that all aspects of our data collection are included in the analysis."

"To be fair, in our case anyway, the mathematics are hardly daunting. We faced only three actions, two of which were at the front and in both we were in supporting roles. It's not entirely unusual to roll three sevens in a row. I would guess that many of the American troops did not face a high number of actions thereby keeping their odds of being decimated within a simple yes or no of casualties, like us."

"Perhaps you are right Herbert."

"By all means continue your pursuit of this cause. Speak to your father of your concerns. Maybe he will carry the torch for you. Perhaps you will find more compelling evidence."

"I have been reluctant to draw my father into this. He is very much the straight nosed army bureaucrat. Logistics and supplies are like that, not very fluid. We need a certain amount of something and it needs to be in a specific place at a specific time. There is not a lot of uncertainty."

"If you have some specific information you would like me to pass on, I will. With something concrete I can pursue this with my commanders to help get the points you made across to them. And that can only be a good thing for future Americans who fight. I certainly will let you know anything that springs to mind. As you might expect much of what has occurred here is being constantly turned and examined in my mind. These are extraordinary circumstances and unusual actions for people to be involved in. Give me statistics and details and I will try to make your point. Please call me if you want me to add to my report. Now, how about dinner tonight? I am staying north of the Arc. Where can I pick you up?"

Chapter Eleven

The troop ship sailed triumphantly into New York harbour, sounding its horns, with the deck full of happy soon-to-be ex-soldiers. Fire boats launched a celebratory spray into the air. An unflappable Lady Liberty watched the joyful proceedings.

The ship docked and disgorged its passengers to a general liberty. A formal leave taking would begin the next day and the ship would remain in New York as a floating hotel for three days while all the men made arrangements to travel from New York to their home towns across the country. Eisenrick invited the platoon to his family bakery early the next day before they all began to get shipped out the following morning.

"I won't pass that up, Frankie," said Jocko Rollins. "I'm guessing your mom makes better stuff than you. I'd like a little bit of heaven before I head home to Missouri."

Momma Eisenrick faced quite a sight at precisely 0-800. She had just completed the rush of morning orders and was standing behind the counter with her head down, thinking of her next task, when a noise caused her to look up from her ledgers as she was reorganizing her mind for the morning.

The boys worked it perfectly. The entire platoon entered the bakery by the front customer entrance, filling the small sit down area where croissants, bread and pastries were sold to walk-in customers each morning. There was a huge hubbub of noise and confusion as they all piled in, much to Mrs. Eisenrick's amusement and consternation. She knew a troop ship had landed the previous evening, in fact it was a regular occurrence.

She put her index fingers to the sides of her mouth and whistled loudly, instantly quieting the hubbub. "What can I get you boys this morning?"

Clancy chimed up, speaking his lines, "We're looking for Frankie. He promised us a bun, like he used to make us in France."

"Oh, you know him? I'm afraid my Frankie hasn't arrived home yet," she said with a sad shake of her head.

Then the door to the ovens behind the counter burst open.

"Momma, momma, I see you've met my friends," said Frankie, who had quickly snuck in the back way through the delivery doors and donned an apron. "I promised them an Eisenrick apple pastry for bringing me home safely." He smiled a huge smile.

His mother began to shake. Her eyes welled up with tears which rolled down her face as her feet were rooted to the floor. The room was silent. Her legs felt like over cooked spaghetti.

"Oh Frankie, you're home, you're safe and you're whole. And you promised pastries to these boys for brining you home. That's all?" She threw her arms around him and hugged him tight, but only for a moment to make sure he was real. She caught herself, wiped the tears from her eyes and cheeks and mastered herself to take a stern look at her son.

"That's all? She grabbed trays of pastries and put them up on the counter. Please, eat. Everyone of you, eat with my thanks for bringing my boy home safely."

A huge cheer went up and Mrs. Eisenrick hugged Frankie again, all the harder.

"Fire up the ovens we are going to need another round of morning pastries," she yelled into the back part of the shop, always the pragmatist. The pastries disappeared in moments so more croissants found their way from the ovens and were offered and then bread was cut, slathered thick with butter. The late morning orders would be a bit behind that day.

"What's all the commotion?" asked a greying man, coming through the oven entrance to the sales area. He was wearing a heavy coat, fresh back from deliveries.

He spied Frankie still being clung to by his mother.

"Father, I am home."

The elder Eisenrick took a step back, blinked a few times and then flung his arms around his son's head. "Safe, as I always knew you would be." He recovered himself quickly. "When can you start delivering for me?"

Everyone laughed.

The Eisenrick's afternoon customers received their orders a bit late that day, but not one was upset once they were informed of Frankie's return. He was well known to their customers.

The next day as they left the ship, the Eisenrick's had made sure that every member of Frankie's platoon took with them a fresh loaf of bread and a bag of pastries for their journey.

One by one the platoon members took their leave, most bidding farewell and reminding each other of their promise to their Captain to meet again in 10 years.

Jocko was one of the last to go. It had fallen to Eisenrick and Martin Wilson to lead the goodbyes as they were New York City boys and would remain.

"Frankie, where do you think we'll meet? Where's the Cap going to get us together?"

"Don't know his plans Jocko, but knowing the Cap he has something in mind already. Could be Philly as that's pretty central. I think that's near to where his family lives. Could be California if a bunch of us end up out there. Take care of yourself Jocko. Stay in touch. Look me up if you're back in the City."

The men shook hands and Jocko turned for the platform.

As he walked away slowly Wilson turned to Eisenrick, "You know, I think it really is over now Frankie."

"Yeah Marty, I know what you mean. Everyone has gone except you and me and we're supposed to be here. Our platoon didn't really see a lot of action, more inaction from the hurry up and wait army command. Except for those offensive pushes near Arras we didn't we much action. I guess that's good. We almost all came through without a scratch."

"Oh, there were scratches, though not much that remains for most of us, except Jimmy and Larry. And don't forget that shelling we took in the village just after the battles. I think that was the last time I was actually shot at."

"Stay in touch Marty. Get back to your property deals. I've got a bakery to run. My dad said he wants to expand our operation and open a second retail location near the Battery. His brother wants to run it and his sister is talking about a third bakery in Brooklyn if the second one is a success. Hopefully the start of good times."

Frankie Eisenrick fell back into the bakery business. His uncle took a stab at running the downtown location but it was quickly apparent that he couldn't handle the early morning hours the bakery business required. The store was thriving but the logistics of running two locations was threatening to kill the second outlet.

Frankie began to run the second shop. He spent his mornings baking and supervising new employees and his afternoons drumming up business alongside his uncle in the hotels and restaurants in the twenty blocks at the tip of Manhattan.

"Yeah, I've heard of Eisenrick's. It's in the theatre district up around 50th Street, right?"

"Yes, that's our original location. We now have an operation down here on the corner of Fulton and William Streets, retail on the bottom, our commercial bakery in the back and a whole lot of customers living all around us. Fresh, is our trademark. It's fresher baked here than baked uptown and delivered downtown."

"You are right. And it's good to know you take your product seriously and are now down here. Eisenrick's has a good reputation," he thought a minute. "Look, we are doing a special New Year's Eve dinner at three locations within two miles of your bakery. If you can supply us with our needs for the night, and the product is good, we can talk about our future needs."

Frankie took the order and details. He knew from experience that getting in the door of these hotels and restaurants was all he needed. Product quality was necessary but Eisenrick's had that in spades. It was punctuality and customer service that was perhaps more important. Pastries with minor imperfections were much less of an issue than no pastries. As long as they were fresh. And Frankie paid close attention to both.

Getting the restaurants was even more important than the hotels as most catered to the evening crowd which allowed his ovens to be busy most of the day, rather than having a huge rush in the morning, and nothing later. Business was good, so good in fact that he was settling into a pattern, baking for the morning rush at hotels and a few morning breakfast places, getting those deliveries to the customers by 7 am and then doing a lunch and dinner run to ensure the freshest product possible. He had several customers who paid extra if they got the first delivery when the bread and pastries were still warm from the oven.

Frankie enjoyed the business and the constant changing of orders, delivery times and needs of his customers. He worked seven days a week, with reduced hours on Saturdays and only a half day in the morning on Sundays. People in hotels still ate their breakfast, no matter what day of the week it was.

He took great pleasure in hearing some of his customers tell him that there was another Eisenrick's bakery up on 50th street, but it wasn't as good as his. He didn't have the heart to mention the left handed compliments to his parents, but he did keep them apprised of his delivery arrangements which helped the quality of his product.

After a year, and a third Eisenrick's opening in Brooklyn, Frankie had a long talk with his father.

"Dad, I'm getting more and more orders from big retailers and these new grocery stores. They want to stock bread as their customers want to buy it there for convenience. Problem is I cannot guarantee quality and that's the backbone of our business."

The two jawed about their problem for some time. Then Frank hit upon a solution. They decided to bake bread and rolls in their stores at the end of each day and deliver them to the grocery stores in the evening, so they would be available for sale. This bread would have a bit more salt as a preservative to keep the bread fresher and edible for longer. The most important point was to call it something else because it really was a different product from the very fresh bread they had built their reputation on.

"What should we call it? How about Frankenrich Bread? It sounds German, it has 'rich' in the name to sound expensive and the whole thing is your idea," said the elder Eisenrick who was still not sold on the plan.

Within five years the demand for bread in grocery stores was 50 times that of the local bakeries which still thrived on the hotel and restaurant business.

Frank had opened a commercial bakery with no retail component and made sure the bread was delivered late in the evening or early in the morning. Frankenrich Bread was on practically every table in New York. Eisenrick Bakery still held an envied spot on the tables of hotels and restaurants in lower Manhattan and in Brooklyn.

After a time, Frank married, with Martin Wilson as his best man. In fact, it was through Wilson that Frank dabbled in the property markets in New York, buying and selling properties in mid-town Manhattan that were being gobbled up as the city grew. The Roaring 20s roared loudest in New York. Frankie financed a number of ventures and grew to take Wilson's advice as a virtual guarantee to riches.

"Frankie, I'm making a killing in stocks. You buy in the morning and sell a week later in the evening and you've made 20-30 per cent."

"It can't keep going up forever, Marty."

"Yeah, I know. I'm not all in. I put in a substantial stake and get out a week or a month later. It's gold. I use the money to finance some property acquisitions. The property seems safer to me than the stocks, but you have to make money while the sun shines."

"And when the sun sets?"

"Don't get caught too far from home without a light by which to see."

"Gee, so profound. Not sure your exit plan is the best. However, I do like the idea of taking a lot of small risks - as long as I only get burned on the last one, I've made a lot of money whenever it finally ends."

"It's a new world out there Frankie. It may not end, at least not for a long time."

"Make no mistake Marty, it will end. Just don't be caught without a place to park yourself when the music stops."

When the crash came, both Frankie and Marty took a hit. Predictably Frankie held a significant share of an electricity venture that was going up on October 28th and went down hard on October 29th, 1929. Marty was in a bit deeper, holding three companies that fell off the market on the fateful day, but it was only a small part of his substantial holdings. Both men waited it out and bought back in a few years later, making all of their losses back and more and both becoming very rich men.

Chapter Twelve   1928

Frankie held the envelope and waved around the letter it once held.

"It's already been 10 years. Cap said he would get us together but I don't know if I can get away."

His wife made a face. She knew he had been looking forward to the reunion. She also knew his dedication to his business. She looked at the letter.

"You have to Frank. It's being held on a weekend in Jersey. You will only be gone a couple of nights. You can travel down with Marty. The bakery will survive. It did last year when you went down sick for almost a week."

Frank's expression lightened, "Cap is having it at a hotel outside of Philadelphia, and he's paying for everything. He must be doing pretty well to manage that."

"Everything?"

"That's what this says. He really wants us all to come and realizes the time is the biggest commitment, he says, so he doesn't want excuses. It's for us vets only though he acknowledges that future reunions might have to include spouses and even children. It's two weeks before Thanksgiving."

Frank and Martin went together in Martin's Pierce Arrow. The car was stately, reliable and large enough to take both men, their overnight bags and some croissants and pastries for the reunion.

The hotel was on the east side of the Delaware River in rapidly gentrifying New Jersey, only a short distance from central Philadelphia.

They entered the hotel and immediately encountered Hugh Coleman, looking just the same as he did 10 years before, tall and strong, and Charlie Hauser, who was a bit more worn down, even though he still towered over everyone.

"You guys seen Ruth?"

Frankie was momentarily confused. "Ruth, Ruth, who is Ruth? Somebody brought their wife?"

Hauser looked down at him strangely.

"Oh, you mean The Babe. Of course, but I see him all the time, I'm a Yankee fan and George stops by the uptown shop sometimes. He loves our sandwich buns. Marty sees a bit less of him as he's a Giants fan."

"Oh wow. He's unbelievable - 60 home runs. I never thought that was even possible."

"It's not only possible but other guys are starting to hit them too. It's a new way to play the game. Exciting too when you can put up two or three runs with one swing of the bat."

"I prefer the Giants, mostly because they are a bit easier to get to see up at the Polo Grounds," said Marty. "Terry, Groh, Freddie Lindstrom and Hack Wilson are all pretty good players. We're always in the first division and usually have a shot at the pennant."

"New York must be crazy. Prohibition; but liquor everywhere. The markets making millionaires left and right. Big buildings and cars everywhere. It's gotta be a different world from what we live in."

"Well, tell me about your world. You aren't that far from New York. Charlie you still in the milk chocolate business?"

"Yeah, and we've expanded. This whole effort by the government to buy up our production has meant there have been some good profits. In fact I'm heading out to California to buy some land out there. My dad says they have a longer planting season. He doesn't think this over-supply support will last and he wants to turn the profits he's getting into land. They aren't making any more of it, especially in Pennsylvania. I heard Bernie Smith is out there. I've arranged to meet him."

"What about the farm here?"

"Hopefully it will support our expansion in California for a while. My older brothers operate it now, mostly, but my dad is wily. He's been around long enough to take advantage of things while they are there to be advantaged."

"Sounds exciting - California. A lot of people are heading out that way, and Bernie's already out there, you say. Where is he? What's he doing? What about you Hughie? You don't look any different from the last time I saw you at Grand Central Station."

"Geez, slow down Frankie, we got the whole weekend."

"Bernie is in San Francisco - well, near San Francisco, in a wine making valley just north of it. He's making wine or at least growing the grapes. Now Hughie, fill him in."

"I feel different. Got into General Electric like I thought I would but it's expanded all over the place. I've been at several different plants mostly in the north east but I was out in Cleveland for a couple of years. I've moved into facilities management. I don't run the business, I make sure the buildings where we do our work, from manufacturing plants to office buildings, are operating properly and efficiently."

"Wow, that's a huge responsibility."

"To be honest, once things are running well, they continue to run well. It's mostly paperwork about deterioration, upgrading technology and the like. The only problems come when the big guys decide to move plants or retool them or build new ones. Come to think of it, that's most of the work and it's never ending as GE is growing so fast."

"What do you guys do for laughs?" asked Marty.

"I don't laugh, I'm Amish," said Charlie with a dour look and a very straight face.

"Really?" said Frankie, caught by surprise.

Charlie held his face for another second then burst out laughing. "Got ya. Used to be Amish. Out in the countryside there isn't much to do except go into town and maybe watch something at the movie house. Most of my neighbours are Amish and pretty much keep to themselves. We do have get-togethers usually organized by the local church. Of course with our outsider status we have a bit of trouble with this. Not that we aren't welcomed but we are treated very much as lost sheep."

"My brother Bill and I have been volunteering over at Gettysburg. The government is building a large museum and memorial to the Civil War battle that was fought there. We have been helping out with setting that up - pulling a lot of stones, moving some cannons into place. It's quite a big deal. I had no idea how spread out the battle was. In fact it's like there were a number of large engagements and another larger number of smaller ones, that turned the battle in small increments. We go over there for a couple of weekends in the spring and fall, just after planting and harvesting."

"How about you guys, what have you been doing?"

Marty spoke up first, detailing his career in property development, stock market purchases and general prosperity in the huge run up of the 20s.

"Got married a few years back. The former Lynn Calderon, the daughter of a friend of my father. Her father is a bank executive. We currently have two children, Max who's almost three and Abigail who is one. They keep my wife busy and I try to keep them busy when I have the chance."

Charlie spoke of his growing family. He married a girl he'd met at Penn State whose family owned significant farm property north of Harrisburg. They had three children, still all very young.

Hugh Coleman explained that he was interested in football. He coached a team in Troy, New York and sent many of his graduates on to college teams.

"Mark my words, the professional game will take off in the next 10 years or so," he said. "The college game is fun to watch, and it's nice to be in the crowd, but the professional game will be very popular. People want to see the college stars continue to compete. Media makes them famous and the media wants them to continue to sell papers or radio spots."

"Anyone going to play golf today? I understand Cap has us a few tee times at the Merchantville Country Club a few blocks from here. It's one of the oldest clubs in the country. There was a two time US Open Champion who was the professional there."

"Yeah, I think I'll play a round. Who else is in?"

Eight men gathered at the first tee, two of whom had never played the game before. A few declined. Hathaway divided up the group putting one newcomer into each group and placing the better players in the first group, so the second would not be waiting to play.

LaRue, Endicott, Allen and Clancy made up one group. Clancy's size and strength made up for his lack of form. Even though his score was high, he thoroughly enjoyed himself whacking balls huge distances. He decided he was going to take up the game when he returned to Pittsburgh and tried to get Duff interested.

Duff played with Hathaway and Wilson and Shawcross. He did not enjoy his play particularly though he did hit a shot that he thought would be good to retire on - smashing a ball high and far over a pond and having it drop softly on the green and slowly rolling right past the hole before stopping only two feet past it.

"After hitting that you've got to come out with me when we get back to Pittsburgh. We'll try a few of the local courses and if we like it, maybe we'll try to play Oakmont which I understand is a bit tougher than the others."

"I guess I could try it again Clance, but I didn't really like it. Swinging wildly at a little white ball only to have to chase it once I managed to hit it. It's like you get penalized for being successful," said Duff.

"Just work on making contact first, and then work up to a big swing. It feels real good when you hit it right. Remember your shot over that pond?"

"Kinda nice being out here in the middle of nowhere, eh Marty?" asked Hathaway. "You city boys like the slower pace out here and a little elbow room? Manhattan is a bit too go-go for me."

"Aw Cap, you know, I love New York. I love the speed of life, the pace of making deals, finding new deals and how easy it is to meet your friends and socialize. I don't think of it as hectic. I think of the opportunities to do something almost any time you want. For me, this is a nice change of pace but it's all a little slow. The air is nice and fresh though."

"I travel there a couple of times each year usually for a big industry pow-wow. I find it fun and exciting for a couple of days but then I just need some quiet time to recharge. I don't know how you and Frankie do it - never ending, day after day."

"I guess we've just got our routines and we use the city the way it works best for us. I know Frankie gets around a lot more than I do. He talks to his customers who are in Jersey and Brooklyn and the Bronx. Me I stick to Manhattan and rarely leave the island. In fact I don't often go north of 59th Street. There's a restaurant there that one of my friends likes who lives on the Upper East Side. Course I go into the Park once in a while for a bit of quiet time. If you get deep enough in there it almost seems like another world."

"Where you living Cap?"

"Baltimore," he said, pausing before reluctantly adding, "I moved there not long after I returned from Europe. I landed a job in the chemical business. We develop new chemicals and industrial processes in a range of manufacturing businesses. Everything that's made needs some kind of chemical in the process even if it's just a cleaning solvent to make the finished product sellable. The market seems endless right now."

"Any family?"

"My parents are still doing fine and my younger sister is completing school. She'll be looking for a husband soon, I expect."

Marty waited expectantly for Hathaway to fill him in on his own family but he said nothing. He was no longer wearing the wedding ring he had sported in Europe. Marty decided not to press the matter. He waited for an opportunity to ask Shawcross if everything was alright with Hathaway.

"Yeah, he's a bit guarded on that stuff. I see him a fair bit. He's in Philly a lot and sometimes he stays at my place overnight. We play golf sometimes. He has some contact still with the Navy down at the Yard in Philly - I think he is working with them on their chemical needs," said Shawcross, in an after dinner conversation.

"He split with his wife. Apparently she tricked him into marriage just before he enlisted. His father was livid with his apparent disregard for the young lady and his determination to escape to Europe, so he disowned him. Cap had said the pregnancy was not his doing. He came back from Europe and found the child he was supposed to be responsible for had been stillborn, so he chose to end the marriage, which had been forced upon him by his father."

Marty's eyes widened. "Wow, that is a powerful lot of responsibility."

"Cap told me this without any detail or fanfare. Just wanted to explain his lack of a wife and lack of family ties. He sees his mother but only quietly, usually for a lunch in Philly. She's afraid to cross her husband and sides with Cap. He still corresponds with his younger sister, but has only seen her a couple of times in the last 10 years, at her boarding school in Washington."

"I remember him speaking about being married when we were in France, but he never elaborated. Now I know why."

"What have you been up to Dick?"

"Living across the river in Philly. That's where I was from. Well, west of Philly on a farm out there. I had a bunch of brothers and what with farm machinery making it easier to work the land, I took the opportunity to get some mechanical background when I returned from France and got into the farm machinery business - it was something I knew. Business is pretty good, as everyone wants to make their lives easier, and increase their productivity. Charlie was right, the government is buying up surpluses, so farmers are going hog wild buying new equipment as demand is essentially unlimited. They are making it now. It can't last. I just hope that innovation in farm machinery will keep that market strong for the foreseeable future."

"What about the western farmers?"

"Yeah, there has been a major push to get our people out there. It's a different kind of farming and in some places it's actually ranching, completely different. There is a market for machinery though. I'm happy to stay close to home. I like the new spacious sections of the city that have been built. It's not as crowded as the city itself, and there is space and distance. Most of the properties in my area of the city are a couple of acres, only made possible by the motorcar. You can't build railways to service the areas as people are too spread out. Some have small farms attached for local produce. Most of my neighbours have office jobs in the city but preside over a couple of acres of orchard or chicken coups or some such little business on the side. The country is changing Marty."

"I haven't seen Jocko. He's from St. Louis right?"

"Yeah, he wrote to let the Cap know he couldn't get here. Sent him a long letter and asked that it be passed around. Invited anyone passing through St. Louis to stay with him for a night or two. I'm not sure who has it, but it'll find its way to you eventually."

"What about Bernie Smith and Pete Delany, and Tom Billings?"

"Same as Jocko. Bernie is in California. I think that's what inspired Charlie to go out there. Delaney is in Detroit in the auto business and nobody knows where Billings is. He seems to drift around from

170

one place and one job to another. I think his last address was in Buffalo. He's just not the settling down kind I guess. I've heard there are a few veterans from France who haven't been able or willing to put down roots. It's not uncommon. He was always a bit solitary even in France. Nice guy but not much of a joiner."

Chapter Thirteen

The men gathered on Saturday evening for a final meal to conclude their first reunion.

Duff Richardson heaved himself to the table, still nimble but a larger version of the man who had served in France. He sat beside Frank Eisenrick and enquired after his family.

The Eisenrich family had grown with a son and another baby on the way. Frank explained he had plans for top flight education in the best prep-schools in the city while keeping the kids grounded with their family's hands-on business beginnings and expectations of work in the bakery. Preferential treatment was not going to mould his progeny's view of the world. He knew that hard work, a little luck and a lot of careful planning had gone into his family's success.

He told Duff about his growing family and his hopes that he could pass the bakery business on some day, as he was poised to take it over from his parents.

"The old man loves it. He doesn't have to deal with the problems of retail though, he just arranges the deliveries, connects with customers and generally is the face of the operation. I'm having to do some of that with the expansions we've undertaken. The actual baking and packing is the hard work and my mom still handles the retail part of the operation uptown."

Frank's oldest son, William, was born the year before in 1927 and his wife was expecting another in the spring of 1929. New York was a huge growth area, as was much of the country.

"Well Frank, I hear you. Pittsburgh is quite the place. I worked for a long while in the steel plants, working my way up from the floor to the pour and into quality control. From there I got involved in the financial operations as poor quality steel was costing the company money. Then I ended up setting up insurance programs for large contracts and eventually ended up working for the insurance company."

"It's been a strange ride and its only just begun. I still know a bunch of guys from the plant, and that is tough work. Unionism is growing, despite the labour battles they've had there in the past."

"I cannot understand Mr. Carnegie. He had so much opportunity to set things right in his own operations. But he gave away much of his fortune building things for the general public while ignoring his own employees. I know he's dead and sold long ago, but he set the tone, and now the corporate boys follow. How difficult would it have been to build schools, pave roads and pay the workers a bit more, instead of building libraries all over the country. Heck, it was those workers in Pittsburgh who made him rich."

"Unionism is a curse," said Frankie. "Nobody who has put their sweat and heart into building a company wants to cede any autonomy in its operation. I think the enlightened management does what you suggest to stave off the labour movement. However, I have seen some benevolence turned against owners and employees who have received better pay and working conditions, then turn and demand more still."

"What is the solution?"

"I wish I knew Duff. In my business I am still very much a family concern. Unionism hasn't really hit us yet, though there have been some hints. My bakers want more money and better conditions. Frankly, baking is hot and needs to be done early. Automation is not really there yet, but it's coming. So for now all I have left is improved wages. I have given increases to my best workers, and dangled them to others. I hit upon giving a raise to those who learn the trade after a year on the job. It helps retain employees and gives some value to the skills they have learned. Thing is, many of my employees are very low skill - drivers, packagers. They can be easily replaced."

"But Frank, don't those people need to earn enough to buy your product?"

"You mean like Henry Ford upping the wages so his employees could buy his cars? I suppose, although that is one of the perks of working for me. I allow the employees to take a loaf of bread home each day. It saves them from buying it and it ensures they will attend to the highest standards when they make it. I just don't tell them which batch they get to take their loaf from. A lot of my workers are part time, usually the second job in the family or sometimes an older kid. The problem for me is they rotate through pretty quick. I try to take on the best ones with full time jobs and better pay."

"You always were a smart one Frankie."

"I learned a lot of that stuff from my father. If you watch long enough some of the strange things he does have very practical beginnings. How about you Duff; any family to speak of?"

"No, not yet. I'm about to be married. Next spring to be sure."

"Does she know yet?" laughed Frankie.

"Oh yeah. We've been courting for a while now. I think she's always been on-side, at least as long as I've been in the office at the plant. She was a bit aloof before that. Her father is in contract negotiations with the large buyers of steel. He even met Carnegie once when he was really young. My family knows her family so I've known her, Charlotte, for some years, even as kids. Her dad moved up in the company at the same time my father did. Come to think of it, they always left the door open to us, but didn't warm up to me until I'd moved off the plant floor."

"That's the way of the world Duff, old man. The families of young ladies want to ensure they are positioned at least as well as they have been accustomed. There is a large difference between a man who works hard with no prospects for improvement and a man with connections, hard working or not. Success and comfort are the keystones for betrothal. You are perhaps lucky that Charlotte appeared to like you even before she was allowed to by her family. It makes for a better union."

Duff's straight line expression, moved into a small smile.

"Yes, perhaps you are right. We are to be married in April. Her father has had several discussions with me of a very odd nature. Your insight has somewhat cleared up his message."

"What did he say?"

"Oh, pretty much what you've just outlined. 'Duff my wife and I have been fond of you since you were a child, and the care of our daughter is a must' and that sort of stuff. It's all starting to make a bit of sense."

"What do your folks say?"

"Nothing much. I think this may have been a plan for a while."

"And you are good with that?"

"I guess. Charlotte is very nice and attentive when I call at their home."

"You have had private conversations?"

"Of course, this isn't 1880 or something. We are just folks moving on up in the world, we're not the Vanderbilt's. We have spent several afternoons together and attended a couple of events with each of our families. I am content that I could not do any better on my own. The whole thing is a bit of a whirlwind to me. I'm satisfied that my mother has a good handle on it."

"Well, best wishes Duff. I think it will all work out fine. Family blessings are a good start. The management of expectations seems to be handled and you actually like the young lady's character and carriage."

"Now, what about your future prospects?"

"I like the insurance business, especially since so much of what I am doing relates to the work I did before in the plant. I know my stuff and that is comforting to take to work each day. I remember when I was new at the plant and lived with the daily anxiety of no experience. Where does this go? I don't know, perhaps into the extension of uses of steel, the construction uses which are growing 10 fold, and the uses in specialty products which are just catching on. I've been advised to purchase some company stock in the steel enterprise and am advised that it will be a smart investment."

"You should talk to Marty Wilson. He's involved in all of that stuff. He advises me from time to time and I've done well. Though I am a bit wary of the exuberance of the markets so I have positioned my-self to reap the gains and minimize the losses which I believe are inevitable."

"I don't have a lot to lose at this point. I need something steady and not speculative. I know my gains will be lower but I am not interested in taking great risks."

With the main part of the dinner over the men began to move around the small room, nursing drinks and making small talk with their friends and renewing bonds.

"Hey Clance, come and sit down. You're in Pittsburgh too, right?" Marty Wilson patted the chair beside him.

The big burly former cook smiled widely and ambled over to take a seat.

178

"Shoot, I forgot my drink." He moved slowly to get up but Marty yelled down the table to have Clancy's drink retrieved and passed up to where they were sitting. Clancy settled back into the chair.

"Well Clance, what are you up too? Please don't tell me you are in the restaurant business?" He laughed, but suppressed it to a smile when Clancy gave him a look.

"I thought about that," he said, thinking back a few years. "A nice greasy spoon, regular customers, guys who appreciated the basics of a good, quick and cheap meal. But I realized there wasn't much money in it, though I did a stint as a cook in a place frequented by the steelworkers. Then I overheard one of them mention that the plant was looking for some big guys to position things for the crane operators. Seemed like easy work so I got in. Duff spoke for me. Now I'm operating the crane. It's not real tough and it pays better than most of the jobs in the plant as it takes a bit of skill and practice."

"That's good - a steady job is a good thing. Any plans for a family?"

"Yeah, I guess. My steady girl, Becky, sorry Rebecca, she wants to get married and I can't really see any reason not to. Although maybe this golf thing might take up a bit o' my time," he laughed. "Naw, she's fine and is great with her two nieces."

"So when is that going to happen?"

"Sometime soon. She's pushing and I'm just not saying. I guess it's about time. Everyone else here seems to have started."

Allan LaRue and Freddie Allen were sitting across from Clancy and Marty and were listening in.

"Hey Clance, just let her do the cooking," chimed in LaRue.

"Shut up LaRue," said a very annoyed Clancy. "You didn't lose any weight over there. In fact you're a bit scrawnier now than you were then. Maybe I should pass on a few recipes for your missus to use. Of course they feed anywhere from 25 to 200 at a time. You could go into the banquet business."

LaRue smiled, "Now Clancy, it's just a bit of good natured ribbing. I haven't had you around for a while and I feel like I have to catch up."

"Enough. I put up with that in France and frankly, cooking for you lot was no easy task. I was up earlier than any of you, working hard on the next meal while you clowns were chowing down on the one at hand. If it weren't for the helpers that Cap assigned to me I might have gone AWOL."

"You might have gone AWOL to the Germans. The war would have been shorter that way," said Freddie Allen.

Clancy started to say something but Wilson cut him off.

"And Freddie here knows," said Marty. "He liked the army so much he re-enlisted. How does Clancy's cooking compare to the rest of the army grub you've got? What are you doing now Fred?"

"Sorry Clancy we are just having some fun. Truth be told, your efforts were among the better ones I've sampled in my time in the army. The cook we had at Fort Dix was fantastic. The guy made meals for several thousand men at a time. He was more like a field marshal in the kitchen as he had a team of people working for him but he always managed to get things together perfectly. Then there was the guy in Texas. I served there only briefly as the army was being reorganized a few years back. He was obviously a greenhorn. Some things were okay, but he had all kinds of trouble getting things done at the same time. Often we'd eat each item of the meal separately as they came finished. I think they promoted him into logistics. That's Uncle Sam for you."

They all laughed.

"Truth is Clancy, I thought you did a great job for us. Meals were always on time. Yeah, they were simple but that was their charm and having that rotation of main courses simply meant that you got better each time through. By the end, and we were only there a short while, your beef stew and spaghetti were top notch. In fact I still compare your versions to any others I've had and you're the tops," said Marty. "And I eat at some nice places in New York."

Clancy nodded his thanks.

"Now don't get a swelled head. I think it was Eisenrick's bread that hurt your reputation. But he was a professional. That's not your fault. And frankly your version of pretty much everything else probably topped his."

"And what has the army got you doing?" asked Hathaway.

"Now I'm in Georgia commanding a tank corp. They call me Major Allen but commanding is a little strong. The boys are young and willing but teaching them to drive tank is a challenge sometimes. They love squashing stuff, so much so that everything on the range is flat. We put out things for them to practice squashing, so they have a sense of how heavy the tank is and what it can and cannot master. We train tankers in driving, mechanics and tactics. Brass

181

thinks future battles will be fought between tanks with only a little infantry to clean up and support the tankers."

"So all my extra time in Paris advising the army on future tactics has resulted in young men crushing whatever is in their way in armored vehicles?"

"Yeah, I'd say so. Of course there is the Air Force too. Sometimes we engage in mock battles with them. Mostly us trying to figure out a quick way to signal enemy troop movements from the planes to the tanks. Mixed results at best."

Chapter Fifteen

The invitations had gone out, RSVPs returned and almost everyone said they would be able to attend the gathering - the 20th anniversary of the end of the Great War.

The original reunion, a 10th anniversary affair, had come off, but only after much wrangling and rescheduling. It seemed the former platoon members had busy lives, were more spread out across the country and simply couldn't manage to get together. Eventually Hathaway arranged a two day affair of meals and time together in New York City in the fall of 1938. It had been a difficult decade for almost everyone. The Depression ripped through America leaving its mark on every family, especially those with people at the beginning of their working lives, or nearing the end.

Technological innovations kept the economy in perpetual motion as old industries were destroyed while new ones rose out of nothing but a new idea.

While the Hathaway family home had remained in the family, it was not Herbert who owned it. His mother had remained in the house after his father died in the early 1930s. His sister lived near-by and was poised to take over the family estate as she had married and put together a large family.

The original plan of having the reunion at his sprawling family home had not worked out for the first reunion as the rift with his father remained unrepaired. And by the time of the second reunion it was obvious that he had to abandon the idea of ever having control of the home, though he did visit from time to time as he passed through the Jersey side of the Delaware.

He had held out hope but his father was intransigent. The two men remained at loggerheads. Herbert insisted he had nothing to do with the pregnancy of his father's friend's daughter and should not be bound if there was no child. The elder Hathaway clung to the social convention of his time, refusing to believe his son at the expense of his long time social network. The elder Hathaway's death and nearly two decades of forgetfulness of the original events allowed Herbert to be rehabilitated at a distance to his family.

He had pleaded with his father, insisting he was not responsible for her condition and wondering why his father sided with the young lady rather than his own son.

"I did not impregnate that girl," he had pleaded with his father. And yet, the former Annie Black had identified Hathaway as the cause of her predicament. No amount of denial was going to convince his father that he had no responsibility. The Blacks were a respected area family, Annie and Herbert were childhood friends and the senior Hathaway could not conceive that Annie Black would lie.

She had.

Hathaway was forced by his father to marry Annie Black. He had enlisted in the US Army expecting to be shipped to France before the child was born. He was. The child was stillborn. Hathaway again pleaded his case with his father, believing the matter ended. His father disagreed and threatened to disinherit him should he leave her.

He did.

Without hesitation the younger Hathaway left his wife, filed for divorce and never had contact with his father again. Hathaway's mother harboured a sliver of belief that he was telling the truth. In fact as time passed, it ceased to matter to her. Herbert's sister knew in her heart he was being honest. She believed that her father did not want to cause a rift with the Blacks and had insisted upon doing the right thing to avoid becoming social pariahs. Both mother and sister managed to steal a few moments with Herbert from time to time but kept their time together short and secret from the elder Hathaway.

Some years later Annie Hathaway - Black had moved away with a second husband to Columbus, Ohio. There was grudging animosity between the two families as Herbert's decision rippled through their lives. They never said anything directly but they blamed him for the estrangement of their daughter.

Without his family's backing Hathaway secured a job selling industrial chemicals to large manufacturing companies. He had done well, moved up in the company and was poised to gain a position in the front office. He had established a relationship with a lady and they had moved to Chicago as he was currently based there as the western agent for the company.

As he was moving into a vice president's job he travelled frequently to New York where he dealt with the top executives of companies that he sold chemicals to.

Knowing when he would be in New York, he chose a hotel, issued the invitations and spent two days with his mates, or at least the 10 of them that could come, reminiscing about their experiences in Europe.

"Remember that time Duff risked his life for a keg of beer?"

"It wasn't just a keg, it was three kegs, and he didn't really risk his life, he just risked our wrath." They all laughed.

"Well, he did get shot at."

"Only right at the end, by then he was back in the truck and moving back toward our lines," said Andy Endicott, with a big grin on his face. "If he'd come back empty handed he might have been shot by us."

"I never totally bought the story that he got lost and drove out into no-man's land with a truck full of beer kegs. Crap, the Germans might have thought he was carrying big bombs," said Hathaway.

"I always said it was a good thing it was Easter. That's why he was there, bringing the beer for us, and that's why they didn't kill him; a little Christian charity. I'm guessing they just took a few shots at the kegs to see if they'd explode."

"I think he was single-handedly trying to end the war. A gesture of good will. A bit of suds for the Krauts and voila the hostilities are at an end. They were about ready to quit anyway. They were just looking for an excuse," said Duff.

"I'd never seen anyone manhandle a whole keg of beer the way he did. Picked three of them up like they were empty. It's amazing what fear and duress can do for you," chimed in Dick Shawcross.

"He says he was fearful of us, if he lost the beer. I'm guessing he was in fear of getting shot, by them or us," Eisenrick laughed. "Too bad he couldn't make it here. We could get the whole story once and for all."

"How many of us made it?"

Hathaway mused a moment. "Well, there are all of us, what 10 guys? And then you Frankie, and Marty are joining us when you can, mostly for evening meals. Charlie Hauser said he'd make Day Two only. So it seems we have a quorum but we are definitely missing a few.

"I wanted to talk to Hughie Coleman about that night we wandered around Paris, before we were sent back north of Arras, but I don't see him."

"He's another that's coming in for tomorrow only. He lives up in Albany."

"I thought he was in Cleveland?"

"He got transferred back."

"God that was a funny night, you know. He and I, and I think Hauser and Jocko wanted to see some of the sights before we shipped out. So off we went one night after dinner. We checked out the Arc de Triomphe and naturally we wandered down the Champs-Elysees. Eventually we found our way to Notre Dame and then across the river to the Pantheon. And then we got lost."

"It was getting late, and we spoke no French, and nobody seemed to sense that we were in any distress. We started to wander back towards the river but got caught up in the streetscape and moved more or less north towards the Eiffel Tower. Once we got close to that, we got lost again. You think you'd be able to see the tower to give you direction but the nearby buildings block it out and then you move two or three blocks in the wrong direction before figuring it out. We were gassed, that's a lot of walking - hours."

"Of course now it's really late, and the street people have come out. They are begging and accosting us in a language we don't understand, so naturally we try to brush them off, which results in a few localized fist-fights. We manage to escape the gendarmes and the locals long enough to get back across the river and spying the Arc, make it back to our hotel sometime long after curfew."

"Not sure if anyone actually missed us, but I can say it's good we had nothing much to do the next day as we could hardly stay awake."

"Oh, I knew you gentlemen had been out and about. But the idea of being in Paris was to blow off a bit of steam. I actually encouraged others to take in a few sights. Remember we all went to that dance hall as a group. It was only occasionally difficult keeping you guys in line. A much different story for some of the other units. As long as you were back before dawn and you weren't upsetting the locals I was happy to look the other way."

"You were a good CO, Cap. Gave us enough leeway to be human and keep us in line enough to be a fighting unit."

"I tried my best boys. I was pretty confident that when things got tough you guys would pull together and do what was necessary. Lucky for us we were never really in the real bad stuff, the thick of the fighting. Oh, we got shot at often enough but the real nasty stuff seemed to pass us by."

"Yeah, we were near it a couple of times, but never really in the central part of the action, even at those two battles. Just lucky I guess. You never know what sector the Germans would target or what their battle plans were."

"We had our three pieces of action," said Hathaway. "That was enough for me. Remember, I stayed with the army for a couple more years working out the best approach to building our modern army. I was in Paris for a time, London and then back here in Washington."

"So what was the plan for the US army?"

"Not sure they actually decided when I was there. It seemed obvious to me to work on armoured units - remember how scary those tanks were when we saw them, and how they took the pressure off the ground infantry. That's the way Freddie said they were going. Oh, I heard he got promoted to Colonel. I also liked the idea of an improved air force - only problem is the rapid improvements in aircraft design make it almost impossible to gear up in advance as all your planes would be obsolete if a conflict broke out. Some of the brass were afraid of technology and the ones that understood it, understood the obsolescence caused by rapid improvements."

"Let's hope there isn't another conflict. Though it appears the Germans are mighty ticked off about the peace treaty. Once the Allies had the upper hand they just stuck it to the Germans knowing they had little stomach for continued hostilities and maybe no actual capacity to make it happen. It isn't commonly known but their population was practically in open revolt."

"You reading about this Hitler chap? He's putting the country back together again but the undercurrents of things I'm hearing are not good. They are coming out of the depression and people are back working, but he's all about scaring people into line with his plans - they have supremacist leanings and are forcing out all the non-Germans, and I hear rumors that they are intimidating people who are not ethnic Germans into selling businesses and leaving the country."

"They just took over the German areas near their borders and everyone there seems okay with that. Peace at all costs, it seems. Nobody wants another Great War."

"I'm just as happy if we stay back here," said Coleman. "Why should we get ourselves all tangled up in their problems again?"

"Anybody here in the markets?"

"Hey Marty, that's dangerous stuff. Remember what happened in '29. Goes down as fast as it goes up. You don't want to get caught with your pants down."

"You are right there Allan, but if you are smart there is real money to be made on new technology and growth industries. The depression can only last so long. I only play with the money I've made already. There is real growth in real things. And I figure to keep cashing in and turning the profits into real estate."

"Good luck to you. My advice is don't be greedy. That's when you will lose big. Steady gains are good. This market is volatile."

"Things are different now, Allan. The crazy stuff is gone. The Crash blew it all up. It's all about the new technology, like radio and movies and the growth in our economy thanks to immigration - people leaving Europe for a better life. It creates demand and opportunity. No telling when it will stop."

Fortissimo Ostinato

Frank got a visit from Freddie Allen who had been directed to the wholesale bakery after a visit to the original shop in midtown.

Freddie had remained in the military moving up the ranks and was now Brigadier General Allen, commander of a division of Patton's Third Army Group.

"Frankie I'm shipping out to England. We are mustering for an eventual offensive against the Nazis. The army has been good to me. What the last time we met, for our 20th reunion a couple of years ago, I was Colonel Allen in charge of a tank corp. I'm telling you, if you are in the right place at the right time, you can advance rapidly. Patton is passionate and absolutely convinced he is the smartest guy in the army. He probably is, but he is a bit less circumspect than a few of the other high ranking guys. He's convinced he's right and he moves very boldly - excellent when you are right. Deadly when you are wrong. He hasn't been wrong yet. It's just that most of the brass figure he will be sooner or later."

"You know these guys. What's going to happen? What are the chances of getting sunk while you are getting across?"

"Yeah, I know some of them. No surprise to me that Eisenhower is the Supreme Commander. He is a very calculating general and very aware of loyalties and keeping his commanders happy. He has the least ego of any of the top brass. It appears we will take a very calculated approach to an eventual invasion. First off, there will be battles and skirmishes in North Africa and along the Mediterranean coast. Frankly I expect that is where the eventual invasion will come, but that depends on naval supremacy and quality landing areas. If it was up to me, and it's not, I would likely land in Vichy France and get organized there. As a Brigadier General I am just responsible for my men in the field."

"What about the crossing? Those U-boats are scary."

"It's always a possibility but we are very aware of the threat and take great pains to minimize the potential losses. We move in large convoys which might make good targets but they can only get some of us and the rest get through. We also have significant air cover from both sides meaning there is only a narrow space we have to traverse where we are not covered."

"Good luck. It appears to be a completely different thing than our time in France."

"Yeah, no trenches and the tanks are bigger, faster and more deadly."

The United States was pulled into World War Two almost willingly, though it took the Japanese attack on Pearl Harbor in Hawaii to do it. Before that the Americans had been not-so-subtly backing the Allies but refusing to be fully engaged. Post war analysis suggests that the unwillingness to commit to the war and hold their power in reserve is largely what led to the final truth of America as a world power.

The Russians poured their entire nation into what they saw as an existential struggle. Central Europe used its final reserves of power stored since colonial days in fighting for their positions in the post war world. The Germans spent their stores of honor, militarism and self-determination in a last gasp battle for hegemony in Europe.

After the Nazis had claimed Europe the ensuing reclamation of several national prides presaged battles in North Africa, Italy, Stalingrad that were hugely significant. However, from an American perspective, the battle for France and specifically the landings in Normandy, were the epic struggle they endured, co-ordinated and accomplished in the European theatre. While it is true that once a landing was accomplished, the steady drive of the Allies into Germany was never really in doubt, and there were no more hugely decisive battles to show.

It was the same in the Pacific, where the large Battle of Midway and Battle of the Coral Sea, essentially put the Japanese on the defensive, where they were no longer determined to win, but rather to lose as slowly and painfully to their opponents, as possible.

The steady drumbeat of island hopping victories by the Americans echoed the steely determination of their push through Europe. Not without setbacks, but entirely without drama, at least until Hiroshima.

Their late entry into the war, their relative lack of bruises from the conflict and their move to an industrial economy sowed the seeds of the Pax Americana. And while nothing lasts forever, combined with economic vitality, that hegemony endured for decades.

Chapter Sixteen

Martin Wilson started in the property game in New York but quickly moving into property development and redevelopment as Manhattan quickly grew. Small, old and dingy tenements and small factories were slowly cleared out and large office towers, apartment blocks and grand buildings began to transform the New York cityscape.

Was it ever thus as New York seemed to have transformed itself multiple times in the previous 100 years.

Of course the tenements did not go away, they simply moved to the Lower East Side and to the west along the Hudson. Through the 20s and 30s these were still factory areas, shipyards and warehouses as New York was a very busy port. Manhattan was surrounded by wharves, docks and quays from the Battery all the way up to the lower reaches of Central Park. And the New Jersey side of the river and Brooklyn were similarly arrayed with one shipping dock after another. Some were for passenger ships but most were for cargo.

Wilson bought some of the old buildings and redeveloped the property making way for marvels of engineering. The Empire State Building, the Chrysler Building, the Woolworth Building were all built in this manner creating an uptown hub of commerce and industry just south of Central Park to the east of the theatre district. The tip of Manhattan was still the financial centre with Wall Street and the New York Stock Exchange dominating blocks of banks, brokerages and financial businesses. Hotels and restaurants catered to this business, while a different type of hospitality industry, one that was more family oriented, took root uptown.

Martin Wilson did not go anywhere in New York without apprising himself of potential redevelopment opportunities. On several occasions he had seen blocks of property that he didn't even know were for sale scooped up for major building projects. He took the necessary steps, joining clubs, getting involved with major city-wide philanthropic efforts and meeting the right people, to get himself into a position to get first shot at these land purchases. He had not wanted to engage in speculation, preferring to buy and sell, engage as the developer, or try to put deals together pulling from the bits of information he gleaned at various functions. He would find out that this bank was running out of space, that hotel wanted a new addition, this land developer wanted property to build a skyscraper. The city itself looked to build cultural institutions or redevelop older buildings for the purpose. New York addresses were highly prized by various organizations. The gravity of the city grew and drew in more and more activity as it became the center of banking, publishing, broadcasting, and finance. Martin Wilson was busy and wealthy.

"Frankie, nice to see you. How have you been?"

Frank Eisenrick was always happy to see his old friend. After all they spent some time together and often saw each other on the same event circuit. It was Martin who had turned Frank on to the business possibilities of social encounters. Frank had been able to purchase property for his bread factory through information from Wilson, who knew of an old warehouse on the West Side that was for sale, but was not in a part of town that lent itself to large building projects.

It was on Little West 12th Street near Washington Street. Eisenrick was spending most of his time running the large factory while his relatives took care of the two specialty bakeries. Given the difficulties in keeping the product fresh he was limited to where he could deliver in a few hours. And he had just about tied up all the business he could in that radius. He was considering an expansion into New Jersey or onto the island. He mentioned it to Martin.

Martin looked at him strangely and said he would look into it but warned him that he had few contacts outside Manhattan.

"Frankie I have a line on some prime space on Central Park South. A few old buildings I can buy up and build a large apartment building or maybe hotel. The office guys don't want it, Central Park is too much of a distraction but the hoteliers love it."

"What happened to the Rockefeller property near there?"

"I played that all wrong. And you know, I'm not sure how I should have played it. I may not have gotten it no matter what approach I took. Rockefeller bought the land from Columbia University and wanted to lease the land, long term, but that's not a way to develop property. I was on them with offers, you know, negotiating; then a bunch of other guys got the same idea and things were going nowhere. I let it go and now I hear Rockefeller realizes the value of developing the land and is going to do it himself. He's got a few square blocks in there. Apparently he is building a little bit of everything. It's going to be huge."

"I'm beginning to see Manhattan, not as the central section of a great city, but as a collection of neighbourhoods," said Wilson. "Some are hot, in that everyone wants to be there. Some are not, as in everyone wants to get out. Some attract various economic strata like artists or blue collar guys, but most seem to grow along ethnic lines - Little Italy, Chinatown, Greektown and the like. I'm trying to figure out how to approach development along these lines. If you are right in your timing and approach it's a quick and easy sale. If you are wrong you had better get it right or you will be holding on a long time."

"It seems as if all the factories are moving off the island, the port facilities too, all seem to be going to Jersey," said Frankie.

"It's all about the money. The land on Manhattan is limited and that pushes up the price. In your case you could probably make a big dollar selling your factory property - but then you would be faced with having to find a location that did not hinder your delivery times. That's almost impossible off the island - unless you were to bring it across by boat to waiting delivery trucks. Hey, think about it, your footprint would be reduced to only the needs of the delivery system and your ovens could be built on much cheaper land in Jersey."

"That's a big change Marty. Is this the right time for such a venture? You said timing was everything."

"It is. Leave it with me, I'll bring it back to you in a few years when the right property comes available."

"You had a chance to talk to any of the boys recently?"

"Of course. I heard Jocko is in a bad way. He had a heart attack just a few weeks ago and is not recovering very quickly."

"I hope he gets there. How old would he be. He was older than us, right?"

"I think he'd be around 50 now, he enlisted in his late 20s, he was looking for a job and a bit of adventure, I remember him telling me in a trench somewhere."

"Yeah, Marty, that would have been France," said Frankie with a grin. "I'm guessing that there will be a few of us who don't make a 40th reunion. We're getting on. Well you maybe, I'm only 47. What are you, 49?" His smile widened.

"I'll be 49 later this year," said Wilson matter-of-factly. "Still feel 30 though. Okay, maybe not 30, more like 33 . . . and a half."

"What was Jocko doing?"

"He was selling cars for a bit, still in St. Louis, or near St. Louis in some smaller town. Seems like everyone there was needing a car to drive from the town to jobs in the city. This whole sub-urban thing is really taking off. He was doing pretty well, he said. There is some of that sub-urban stuff going on here, but I hear about it mostly from beyond Brooklyn and out in Jersey too."

Chapter Seventeen

"Remember that time in Paris?"

"It was only two days and a bit."

"I think I remember every second of it, even when I was sleeping," laughed Endicott.

Duff laughed, "Have you ever been back?"

"Are you kidding. Uncle Sam paid my way the first time, not sure he wants to do it again, nor do I want him too, not if I have to fight for it."

"It was me sowing my wild oats, those days in Paris. I certainly saw things there I haven't seen since, and don't want to. But my eyes were opened up to a crazier world than I knew existed."

"That bar near the Eiffel Tower, remember that?"

"It was pretty crazy, especially to a young man from Mechanicsville, Pennsylvania. I sometimes wonder what those people were doing. There couldn't have been much of a future in that unsavory stuff."

"I guess that's just it Duff, they likely came from areas devastated by the war, maybe had relatives killed, children maybe, and they really didn't have much to live for, survival I guess. Have your whole world ripped out from under you, everyone you know, everyone you count on or that counts on you, and you might well end up like them."

"Andy, I sure hope not. Watching people collapsed in the street, no place to go, too wasted to get there or find some kind of shelter was not good. Almost made you happy to get back to the lines, where you knew you were going to get three squares, a dry place to sleep and a reasonable likelihood of waking up the next day."

"You remember sleeping dry?"

"Dry without liquor and dry from the knees up, most of the time even in the holes."

"All I remember was the water in those trenches. It never seemed to go away and was so awful that I can't ever remember it being dry."

"You musta done a lot of front line sentry duty. I only remember it being wet after a hard summer rain. And that wasn't so bad. There was one time right near the end when it rained for a couple of days and was getting cold. That wasn't much fun, but we got pulled back as they must have known the war was soon going to be over."

Andy, changed the subject, "Was in Pittsburgh a couple of years ago and went around the town after working a deal for steel for my business. Duff, some of the steel works reminded me of France, Flanders, the smoking ruins and heavy machinery, tired men, not a pleasant thing around."

Duff grimaced. "Those works keep a lot of people employed, put food on the table and generally help build the country. Steel is the backbone of industry and of Pittsburgh."

"I was downtown and such as well. It's a thriving place where the rivers meet. Certainly you are right, Pittsburgh is thriving. How is the steel plant?"

"Funny you should ask," said Duff. "I still know a bunch of guys down there and I'm around it often, given that I underwrite a lot of the production. Insurance is a little cleaner and more civilized than the steel plant. Frankly it was the unions that got me out. They'd have you know that they are all about the workers, but the truth is they are all about themselves, and by that I mean the union bosses. We had a problem with a couple of guys on the floor who were concerned about the dangers of the molten steel pour. A couple of guys had been hurt. They suggested a couple of things that would help keep the workers from getting injured but the union backed the mill saying it was too expensive and that the experienced workers should have no problem. All they did was tell us never to pour without an experienced man there. Railings, a little splash protection would have done it for us - a few bucks in steel or wood and a couple of hours to install it. Hell their own industrial mechanic could have done the job in his spare time - but they refused."

"So how is insurance?"

"It's okay. I miss the drama of the floor. You know there is nothing like the big hoppers sliding down the upper rails towards the moulds, with the wispy, red glow at the top and the light reflecting on the mill ceiling. You know you are dealing with the essence of hell, the magic and fury of the base elements, fire and air. The fear at the beginning of a pour is real - keeps you very aware. Once the pour has started though the magic of the molten metal is beautiful and the thrill is that of an alchemist successfully turning base elements into something special."

"Stamping paperwork and keeping an eye on contracts - as nice as that is, clean, civilized, doesn't quite cut it. Having said that, molten metal is a young man's game. I saw some accidents in my time, usually because of nonchalance or repetition breeding a lack of awareness. Figured I'd get out while I was still whole. Some of the wounds were quite gruesome, burns, lost limbs."

"Making is more fun than shuffling papers, but the sales and accompanying paperwork is where the money comes from. The insurance biz is actually pretty good. And I still get to watch a pour once in a while. What business brought you to Pittsburgh?"

"I'm in the car business. I own a couple of manufacturing plants, one in Youngstown, another in Canton and a third in Cleveland, well just outside Cleveland, that make parts for cars. It's pretty mundane stuff, take the orders from the manufacturers, build the parts to spec, get another contract for something else."

"What kind of parts do you make?"

"In Youngstown its body mouldings. In Canton it's radiators and heat exchangers. Near Cleveland its engines. We build everything to specs provided by the big manufacturers and a few smaller ones, so we are sort of an extension of their operation but they get us to do it and buy our entire production."

"Sounds pretty lucrative."

"Yeah, it's pretty good that way. Very little chance of going bust. Just a matter of keeping the price low for the manufacturers and making sure the whole thing runs smoothly. Of course there is the juggling of contracts and the retooling of plants but we can usually get the contractors to take on part of these costs if that's what they want."

"Where are you living?"

"Canton, now. I started in Cleveland and moved to Canton just recently as it is midway between my other two factories. I started the Cleveland operation when I bought up a long term contract from Ford for engines. The others came to me in deals and mergers. There are a lot of manufacturers out there but the business is eating those who have trouble and those who are doing well, as they merge with some of the bigger companies."

Endicott enquired about the insurance of steel products and said he would make an effort to visit Pittsburgh specifically to see Duff Richardson as he wanted to enquire about insurance for his contracts and manufacturing processes. He had seen a competitor ruined when his factory burned and he failed to deliver on his contracted business.

Chapter Eighteen

"I actually considered postponing our 30th anniversary reunion this year," said Captain Hathaway, "but I think the plan to make it small was a good one. Only a few guys could make it. Maybe the next one should be in some more exotic locale."

"You mean Pittsburgh isn't exotic enough for you?" Allan LaRue laughed. "It's pretty good for us guys in the midwest. And really good for Duff and Clancy."

"So far we've stuck pretty close to the east coast. Isn't Freddie Allen down in Georgia or someplace? Maybe we should head south next time?"

"Yeah, Capt he's the commander of Fort Benning, Georgia. He could probably set us up. They training tank troops there. He said he was going to try to make it, but nothing yet. There is some sort of connection with Fort Benning up here somewhere. This is the smallest showing. Only eight guys and a few wives."

"Nobody is dead yet, and that's a bit of a surprise. Although nobody has heard much from Bernie Smith who is out in California or Tommy Billings. A lot of guys are finishing up their careers. I'm told by everyone who couldn't make it this time that they will definitely be here the next time - the 40th."

The usual sorting out of what everyone knew of the others took up most of the first night's dinner conversation. Jocko Rollins was there from St. Louis for the first time and mentioned he'd seen Tom Billings when he passed through town a few years before.

"He's a bit of a drifter, but not in a bad way. He just gets bored I think. Keeps a job for a few years, gets a bad break, like the shop closes down or something, and he moves on - looking for new horizons. He's restless I guess. I'm sure some of us feel that way too but with obligations and responsibilities we let it go. He has none and so he answers the call."

General Fred Allen swept into the dining room mid-meal, just arrived from Georgia. He was replete in a full dress uniform, covered in medals and the colours of various citations, with gold braid and crisp folds in everything he wore. He sported a big grin knowing how puffed up he looked compared to the civilians who surrounded him.

Most of the veterans were awestruck and unable to speak. A few almost rose from their places to salute, and had anyone done that virtually the entire company would have followed.

Only Hathaway seemed unmoved. Deep in his heart of hearts he knew that despite Allen's rank, he would forever be Captain to him and his superior officer. It was unspoken but every man in the room knew it to, even if they didn't think it consciously.

210

"Tell us Freddie, what was France like a second time?" asked Hathaway.

"You know Cap, I've decided to go again sometime when it's not ravaged by war. Both times I've been there it's been a bit of a mess. France appears to be an interesting place now that I've seen some of it intact. I'd like to go when I could actually linger over some of the historic places and monuments. Most of the places I've been are a bit beat up. Nothing like seeing how the people live, but having a roadside view into their third and fourth floor apartments was not the way I envisioned it."

A voice chimed out for Allen to run through the whole of his experience in the Second World War.

"You know, the whole thing, in less than 20 minutes. Then we'll have the quiz."

The war had ended three years before and the country was well on its way to getting back to normal. Integration of the troops back into the economy had gone fairly well as several years of privation had swelled demand for consumer goods, leading to prosperity and the belief of prosperity to come.

"I landed with the troops on D-Day. Second wave. By the time I got there, on Utah Beach, most of our guys were up off the beach and engaging ground forces. I'm thinking, "if it was this easy why did we wait so long'? Then I heard about Omaha. If we'd a known how bad it was there we would have done something about it. Gotten there quick. Thing was, at the time, I thought brass wanted to ensure we were solid on at least one beach before we worried about the other. But who knows, communications were pretty bad. Remember, this is the army we are talking about. More paratroops I

211

guess, would have helped, but they were being held in reserve. Only problem is the first groups in were so scattered that dropping them was almost more trouble than it was worth. Instead of a lightly equipped fighting force behind enemy lines we had a scattered, scared group of soldiers running around in twos and threes just trying to survive."

"Once we got Utah it went pretty well. We certainly didn't expect the Germans to fold up and go home, but they had little support of the people and that went a huge way for us. Liberation is good."

"Where else did you go?" asked Pete Delany.

"I was with a unit in Patton's tank group. We formed up a couple of weeks after D-Day. Before that we just did what we could in the bocage, a crappy, dense underbrush that is murder to fight in and through. It forms the borders of many farm fields and really slows down tanks and infantry. Once we were going, I was charged with getting the fuel. An almost impossible task. Patton was so pissed with me when I was unable to get him the supplies he needed. Lack of fuel is what halted the advance near the German border. I think Ike had the gas he just wanted to keep Patton from running around on his own. We'd essentially broken through but were stalled for lack of gas. We could have ended the war much differently if Patton had fuel. Ike was always the cautious one."

"In the end the delay allowed the rest of the Allied force to catch up. But Patton was pissed. He thought he could end the war in the west with a week's more fuel. He might have been right. The German's were on the run and were half of a mind to surrender. It would have put a stop to the whole Battle of the Bulge thing. They would never have gotten that arranged if we were still on the move."

"We had some fuel and I was able to secure us a trickle but we had to have huge quantities of fuel and the secure supply lines to support it or we were in danger of becoming stranded or worse. So we sat on our reserves and waited. Patton would have taken the risk I think, just pushed on ahead and taken the chance that fuel supplies would follow. He might have succeeded. Imagine that. We'd have been to Berlin first and maybe even beyond. A lot of Germans surrendered to us rather than surrendering to the Russians. The whole balance of the peace could have been different if Patton rolled the dice."

"Then we were getting ready to go to Japan, outlining our invasion plans when the war ended there," said Freddie Allen. "The army has been good to me. They call me General Allen at Fort Benning and who knows what they'll call me when I retire in another 10 years or so."

Allen turned to Hathaway and gave him a stiff salute.

"Cap, I want to thank you for the way you handled us, so long ago. The lessons I learned in leadership and in patience and organization started back then and have served this General well."

The men all rose and gave their Captain and General Fred Allen a round of applause. They settled back into their dinner and conversation.

"Freddie, I mean Generalissimo," laughed Clancy McDonald. "Was it as brutal the second time as it was for us?"

Allen dipped his head and looked at the floor thinking. "You know Clance, I have wrestled with that. In some ways it was far worse. Though, in our day, the first time, it was more immediate, closer, more in front of you. Colder. Dirtier. Bloodier."

"The second time through it was at arm's length. The fighting was further away and the carnage was there but cleaner, more distant. Often the Air Force would bomb columns of Germans ahead of our arrival. If we were right on their tail it was awful because of the sheer scale. If we arrived days later it had sometimes been stripped by the retreating army or scavengers and was a bit less horrible."

"Certainly the destruction of the German cities was dramatic. In the first go round, the villages had been pounded so much there was almost nothing left. You didn't know anything had been there. The second time the cities were much bigger and the destruction less complete and much was still standing enough to recognize what had been. The worst thing was the concentration camps - the death camps where the Nazis killed multitudes of Jews and others. What really horrified me was the systematic way the Germans went about it and the fact that they simply treated the Jews like cattle; women, children, old people, everyone. It is unbelievable how they just eliminated people like we would clear out a hornet's nest, or kill an ant infestation. They killed everyone with a systematic ferocity that is all but impossible to grasp as possible from people who are supposed to be civilized and enlightened. I don't know how they managed it. Any civilians that we used to help clean up the camps were horrified by what their countrymen did. They were complicit without knowing, I guess. A hard concept to grasp. They supported the idea of dehumanizing of Jews but would likely never have done it on their own. They certainly stood aside as others committed these acts in their names. I still don't really understand why the Jews didn't fight back - how were they cowed into submission until their time came? I guess they too could not fathom what was about to happen to them, at the hands of their own countrymen."

There was a silence at the table as no one could think of anything to say. Eventually Clancy broke the spell.

"To bad about Patton," said Clancy, like everyone else, unable to conjure anything of substance to add to Allen's observations.

"Yeah. It's almost like he was destined for death," said Allen with a shake of his head. "He just fought everything and did everything right at the edge. A car accident is a damn stupid way for a guy like him to die, but it cements his legend and I think he would be okay with that."

"You like the tank corps Freddie? asked Pete Delany.

"Well I stuck with it. I saw the fear those big mothers inspired the first time through. God they were magnificent when they rolled over or through a trench, back in Arras. Scary as shit. Especially when they worked. They are much more reliable now. That's why I got involved in the corps after the Armistice and given that the army was moving that way I advanced pretty quickly. Being with Patton certainly enhanced my standing, even though by then I was a logistics officer, sort of past the nitty-gritty tank battle stuff. Right now, the corps is good, but sometimes it feels like I'm the head of a driving school for delinquents," he laughed.

"Some of those green kids can't help themselves, they gotta run over something to see how flat they can make it." The circle of veterans started to laugh. Allen continued, "And then there are the ones who want to blast the targets. They think it's a good thing to get it from as far away as possible. Of course in the simulations their shots go wild and their tanks are hit while they move into enemy range while recalibrating. If Patton taught us one thing it was to get the first good shot off, not just the first shot."

"Hey Pete, is this your first reunion? What have you been so busy doing?" asked Duff Richardson.

"It is Duff. Been a busy man, my daughters are still in school. I bought a place on Lake Erie to hang out in the summers. What about you Duff?"

Oh, you know the same old stuff. In the steel product insurance business, couple of kids, living the life and looking for better now that the fun is finished in Europe. Things are changing though as steel production is now more commercial than government related. We're adjusting though."

Chapter Nineteen

Peter Delany made his way from the army into the automobile business. In the 1920s Detroit was booming and it didn't slow down. The automobile was king. His father was a mechanic with a few auto repair shops in the Cleveland area and Peter got into the parts business.

Right after the war he would run parts from the local distributors to his father's garages and then a few others and then a few others. It didn't take long before he was running a small fleet of trucks delivering parts all across northern Ohio. He came to the attention of the big boys in Detroit. They bankrolled him and soon he was running parts between the manufacturers and their subsidiary factories in Michigan, Ohio, Indiana and Illinois.

He married late, in his 30s which was unusual for the times and had a small family. His two daughters married in the late 1950s and had children of their own. Pete had made a bunch of money in the trucking business with solid long term contracts from both Ford and General Motors. He bought a property at Put-In-Bay on Lake Erie which he used as a summer home. Eventually he set up his sons-in-law to run the business and they expanded from auto parts into consumer goods and food. Pete settled into a semi-retirement. He held stock in the company and acted as an advisor.

Long before he retired he would spend much of his free time at his Lake Erie cottage.

"Dad, I want to get married," his daughter Glenda told him one afternoon sitting on the dock on the Bay.

"Well, that's fine. You are what, 22, that sounds about right. I'm guessing it's to that young man you brought around at Christmas. Why now? The boy, what's his name? George? Did he finally get a job?"

"Dad, it's not that he is waiting to get a job, lots of companies were after him. He is waiting until he graduates. He's an engineer now and took a job in Detroit at Ford."

"You should have said something. I know lots of people at Ford. I could have set him up."

"Would you have done that if he was just someone I knew? I know you could have Dad, and you might put in a word for him still, but he's taken a job with the design department. You know, thinking up the kind of cars people might want to buy in the future."

"Does your mother know about this. Seems the young man should be paying me a visit."

"Yes, she does and yes he will. But I insisted that I let you know the basic situation prior to that so you wouldn't be caught surprised."

"Surprised? You always surprise me. Probably because I never had any brothers or sisters. Not quite sure what to expect from you and your sister. Anyway I never had to worry about what people might want in the future. Just move these engines from Cleveland to the plant in Toledo or even up into Canada. Mind you some of those cars they put out have been mighty ugly. Nobody bought them. Didn't matter, I still made money."

"Well you need to think about the wedding. It is traditional that the bride's family pay for it. And it's first in the family. It's planned for mid-November in Detroit, enough before Thanksgiving that it won't interrupt the holiday."

"Who are his people? What's his name?"

"Nothing to worry about Dad, mom's checked that out. In fact she's already had lunch with his mother - last month when she went shopping in Detroit."

"Sounds like this has been cooking for a while," he made a face with a little grimace.

"It has, though mostly so it would all fit together for everyone rather than have a thousand cooks throwing in their suggestions. George is from a fine automotive family in Canada, the Windsor area. He was taking some of his engineering courses in Detroit with the brother of a friend of mine from school. We met at Sally's house, when he was there visiting her brother. His name is George LaRue. He's like all the French in Detroit, very American, or in his case Canadian and American. In fact his father is an American and he has an uncle living in Detroit too. His dad took a job with GM in Canada and has been there for years. He was born there so he has dual citizenship."

"LaRue. I know a LaRue, served with him in France. Haven't seen him since we left New York after the troop ship brought us back. A little short, but not aware of it, or at least it didn't bother him. He was only a little French. He was from northern Vermont and had a touch of Quebec in him. No accent though, 'cept for a faint New Englander one."

"Probably not the same family but I guess you never know, could be a relation somehow. Anyway, we have lots of work to do for the wedding."

"I'm sure your mother will help you with that, she loves that kind of thing. Just tell me where and when, and I guess how much, and I'll be there, in a nice suit, with a lighter wallet and only the hint of shell-shock. Just tell me the food will be good," he laughed.

The wedding was two years in planning. On the big day the guests gathered. The church was full and everyone was in their finest.

"With this vow I give thee this ring," said George, sticking to the script and looking only mildly uncomfortable in his starched tuxedo. He reached into his pocket and pulled out a small gold band. It was a perfect circle save for a 'v' shaped notch. At the outside of the 'V' the ring sported a mid-sized diamond, sparkling in the bright lights.

"This is a family heirloom," said George, when he had Glenda try it on for sizing. "My mother gave it to me and it had been her mother's wedding band."

George held the ring up to give to Glenda saying, "Despite the trials and tribulations of life, may the circle remain unbroken, as it has in this ring."

George placed it on Glenda's finger. She smiled at him. He looked back, solemnly at first and then matched her grin.

After the service guests dutifully looked at Molly's ring as the group was waiting to form a receiving line, to greet all the guests. Glenda showed off her wedding band, odd though it was.

"It was George's grandmother's but she was killed in the Great War, oh, George, my father fought in the Great War, didn't you Dad?"

"Yes, I did. That reminds me. I have a present for you. He took out a small jewelry box and handed it to Glenda. "I want you to have this heirloom of sorts from me to remind you of your heritage and the sacrifices that have been made for you and that you will have to make as you build a family of your own."

Glenda opened the box and saw the ring that Pete had found in the mud of France all those years ago. She very much liked the design with the square box setting holding a lovely mid-sized diamond. The setting sat turned to its corners on the ring forming a diamond shape. She slipped it on her finger alongside her new wedding ring, but the look was quite chunky with the 'V' from her heirloom wedding band pointing to the square setting.

"Maybe if you wear it on another finger," said George.

"Or perhaps I could wear it offset, like this . . . " she twisted the ring so the two diamonds were not at the same point. "No, that doesn't work. It's kind of uncomfortable. But I really want to wear it - especially if it's important to you Dad."

She took the ring off, turned it around and put it back on. A little twist and she gasped - they fit together perfectly. "Wow, look at that."

An older gentleman, gasped. He nudged a woman standing beside him to look. She swooned with a cry and fell, the older man catching her.

"Mother, mother, are you alright," said George as he moved quickly to reach under his mother and ease her to the floor with the older man still standing over them.

She came to and drank some water before being helped into a chair. It was warm in the building and the excitement had gotten to several guests. The young people turned their attention back to the curious ring co-incidence.

Soon George's mother came with the older man, George's great Uncle and joined them the circle.

"Of course you know my mother," said George. " And this is my Great Uncle Pierre, my grandmother's brother from France. He emigrated to Vermont after the war," explained Pierre. "Uncle what is it?" he asked the obviously agitated man.

"Please young lady," said Uncle Pierre. "Let us see the two rings."

Glenda held out her hand. The two rings fit together perfectly, with the diamond shape of the setting fitting into the 'V' shape of the ring Glenda's father had given her leaving the two almost identical diamonds perfectly aligned. The two rings together formed a larger diamond shaped square but didn't look exactly right.

"Where did you acquire that ring Mr. Delaney?" the older man asked.

"Well, to be honest it is a war time heirloom. I found it in the mud in France during the war as we were being shelled. It has a special significance for me because of that. It is very much connected in my mind to the trials of our unit the Diamond Company, and all my friends I served with, because of the diamond shape to the setting and the diamond in the middle."

"If you don't mind me asking where in France were you at the time?"

"It was north of Arras in the autumn of 1918. It was the last engagement we fought as the Armistice was declared only a few weeks later."

The older man wobbled on his feet, clutching at a nearby chair he sat down. George's mother remained unmoved.

"I've seen that ring before. Do you not remember it Molly? Perhaps not, you were young," said Pierre. "Both these rings come from my sister's wedding band set," said the old man weakly. "I gave the one that Glenda received from George today to his mother Molly, my niece, when she was young. It was my sister's, George's mother's, and had been the ring she was expecting from her husband in a wedding ceremony the day she was killed by a German shell, prior to a formal church wedding with her husband. I was best man, and it was Molly's only memory of her mother after she was killed. We had to leave the area quickly to avoid the German advance."

"They fit together perfectly," said George. "Perhaps there were multiple sets made. How do we know it was my grandmother's?"

"Her husband had it made specially," said Pierre. "They had been married in a civil ceremony prior to the church wedding which she insisted upon. She wore it always. It is inscribed. There was a third ring that went on the other side of the main band. My sister and that ring were lost when she was killed on the day of the church wedding in St. Giscard, a small farming town north of Arras."

Pierre continued, "She wanted to complete the church service which had been arranged long before the town was threatened by the German advance. As we arrived for the service German shells began exploding around us. One hit my sister's carriage directly killing her and both my parents instantly. In fact there was nothing really left. My sister's husband Charles Augure begged me to escape with his parents and his daughter Molly, George's mother. I did, and never saw Charles again. He had an additional ring which completed the set - which is what the church wedding was doing. It is a mirror of the one I gave to Molly and fits the setting on the other side. It too has a diamond, making three diamonds to complete their family."

"There is one way to tell I suppose." He asked for the pair of rings and looked closely on the inside of the bands. On one ring was inscribed 'amours' and the other 'toujours'.

"I think it was a common inscription but it says 'Love Always' when the bands are put together."

The group stood agape. They were trying to comprehend the tying together of events. More than one of them asked Pierre to explain the circumstances again.

"George's grandmother, my sister always wore the central diamond ring as she and her husband had been hastily married in a civil service. They had always planned a formal church wedding and tried to get it completed as the Germans were advancing through the area in 1914. My sister was killed when a shell hit her carriage as she was going to the church."

"I had the second ring, the one with the stone at the apex of the 'V' as I was to be the groom's attendant, and the rings were made as part of a set. I gave it to my niece after her mother was killed as a heirloom of her mother. She was only 7-8 years old at the time. I gave it to her when we emigrated. She was sad that we were leaving France and worried her mother would never find us if she was looking. Given the destruction of the carriage and the battle that ensued we never had the chance to bury or formally grieve her mother."

"I remember the wedding day. As family, we were going to the church in a group of three horse drawn carriages. There was a fourth carriage with friends who had been invited. I was in front with my niece. Charles the groom's family followed, the carriage of friends was next and my sister and parents were riding in the last carriage. The German's had been advancing. So much so, that we had stripped nearly everything from the town to leave quickly after the ceremony. The ceremony had been scheduled at the church and we had been assured we had a couple of days left at worse, so we decided to keep the date. The Germans broke through and started to shell the village as we approached the church. We started to move off, the wedding guests fled from the church. Most were never seen alive again including the groom. Some thought he had used the occasion to flee the wedding but I knew better. They had been together married for almost a decade and had a child together, your mother, George. He would never have gone, he had plenty of opportunity to do that in the years before."

The story spread through the wedding guests and everyone had to see the perfectly matched rings for themselves. The guests filtered through the newly formed receiving line to get the story and see the rings. Several of Peter Delaney's friends were also at the wedding, including his long time friend Andy Endicott.

"Oh my god," said Endicott, when he saw the rings on Glenda's finger. He reached into his pocket.

"I always carry this ring for luck, especially when I attend weddings. Couldn't think of anything else to do with it, and it meant more to me than I could sell it for. So I've kept it."

He slowly opened his hand. "I found this ring in the crypt of the church in the town we investigated, when we were shelled. Is that where you found the ring in the mud?" he asked Delaney.

In his palm he held a simple gold band, notched with 'V' and decorated with a mid-sized diamond at the bottom of the 'V'. There was a gasp from several of the guests.

"I have brought this ring with me to any wedding I've attended over the years. I'm not sure why."

He gave it to Glenda who slipped it on her finger. It snuggled up to the other two rings and completed the triple diamond setting by mirroring the other 'V'. Now there were two 'V' cut rings, one on either side of the center cut square forming a larger triple setting.

"Good lord," said Endicott when he saw the effect. "The ring was in a box on top of a monument in the crypt of the church. I often wondered if it was a wedding ring but it seemed too simple and I could never explain the notch."

"I thought Charles was killed in the bombing. It never occurred to me they would have hidden in the crypt," said Pierre. "When the shelling started we all ran. Molly was in the carriage with me. The church was hit and destroyed by several shells as we moved further away from it. George's mother was born before the marriage. It was for her that they wanted to complete the ceremony before leaving town. Do you remember that day, Molly? he looked at her.

"We've not spoken about it in years. When she was seven or eight when I gave her the part of the ring set that I held as the best man. It was meant to be bestowed during the ceremony to complete the union. The groom had the matching ring as my sister already wore the central section as an engagement / wedding ring, which she had worn for several years as the wedding ceremony had been delayed several times for various reasons. After the war I adopted my niece, and gave her the ring as the only memento of her mother that I possessed. She has given it to George and George has given it to Glenda."

Pete Delany spoke. He sounded far away, starting as if in a dream, trying to remember any details he could add to the story he told.

"I found the ring in France, as I was being shelled in the later stages of the Great War, in the ruins of a village north of Arras," said Pete, speaking slowly. "I fell on the ground from the shock wave of a nearby explosion and when I stood up the clump of earth I held had this in it. Good Lord, what a co-incidence."

"Do you know the name of the village?"

"No, I don't but my platoon commander might. We had been assigned to clear it of booby traps and shells. At the time it was behind the lines and the war was nearly over. We thought the shelling that day was target practice from a distant ridge."

"I remember how scared I was when the shelling started," said George's mother Molly. "I was riding in the carriage, with a magnificent horse pulling us along. My uncle told the carriage driver to run away, not that he needed any instructions."

"Oh, my," said Pete with a loud exhale, as he remembered more details. He was having trouble keeping his composure. "It was late 1918, and there wasn't much left of the village but the last thing we checked was the ruins of a church. My CO and another guy cleared a door in the floor of the church and found a crypt and a number of bodies. About the only thing they said was that everyone was very well dressed and nobody looked like they expected to be there for very long. A fallen piece of masonry had held the door shut - nobody could escape."

There was an audible gasp.

Uncle Pierre couldn't speak. "And that was reported to the authorities?"

"Yes, I remember the Cap saying he would pass on the info. It would have been in the fall of 1918. There was nothing else there save a few low walls of stone, the remains of some foundations. The place had been fought over four or five times in battles in that area. I'm not even sure what it was called. Only that there was a crossroads, maybe 20 buildings and a small church."

"We never heard anything about that, but then we had moved away and emigrated. We weren't land owners so we had no claim to anything that might have been left."

"Well, your story fits. The ring I had included two dates inscribed on the inside of the band - two dates about eight years apart."

Chapter Twenty

It was the 40th anniversary reunion. Pete Delany told the story to the hushed group of veterans.

He had to go over the names of people and their relationships very carefully as the story of such a co-incidence seemed almost impossibly difficult to comprehend.

Andy Endicott was there to corroborate the details. "I remember the fine clothes and shiny shoes," he paused and took a sharp breath of air. "I need a drink."

He continued, "As we left the crypt I grabbed a small box that had been left on top of one of the grave monuments near where the people were gathered. I didn't even look at it until later, long after the shelling that day. It contained a ring."

There was stunned silence.

"Well, I'm not sure what to say. There are just so many co-incidences in that story it doesn't seem real," said Hathaway.

"That's what I thought too, Cap," said Endicott. "But if you think of it the only real co-incidences are Delaney finding the ring in the middle of nowhere, and the fact that his daughter married the grandson of the person who lost the ring he found. Large co-incidences to be sure but the rest of it isn't that far-fetched as the other parts of the ring follow the first two co-incidences. The fact that Molly married a man named LaRue is not material to the story, even though we know a LaRue, because the two LaRue's are unrelated."

The men contemplated the strange events when Hathaway broke the silence.

"Tom what ever happened to you after the war? We could never catch up to you to invite you to the reunions."

Tom pushed back his chair and stretched out his legs. He was still wiry even under a shock of grey hair. The lines of his face gave away his age, but his arms were toned and he appeared as strong and agile as ever. He looked up at the ceiling.

"I guess I just moved on a lot," he said. "Got bored with whatever I was doing. Came back from France and got a job in a factory in Buffalo. I grew up there so it was natural to go back and get a start. I still knew people there and I managed a factory job. That got boring so I took off for Chicago. Stayed there for a few years, mostly working in a paper warehouse but also was a printer, and became the guy who fixed all the machinery. Eventually they just hired me out to other factories to fix their machines so I figured I could do that myself. They didn't like that and black-balled me. I left for Detroit and got a job keeping machines going in some of the GM production plants. That seemed to be all work and no play so after a while I moved on again. Eventually I just got sick of fighting for my independence. Everyone wants to control you, sort of like the army, but all subtle-like, not so much in your face as the army. After a while I had enough dough so I went west. Ended up in Denver a while and then moved to California - built a little place in the woods and lived quietly. Park Rangers eventually forced me out, and I drifted some more.

"Never did marry. Had me a woman for a time in Chicago but she left, she wanted something more permanent and I could never bring myself to give up my freedom. The ability to just up and say 'screw it' and leave is very seductive. I didn't want to go along to get along and then have a couple of kids tying me down. I am a man of my word and it wasn't a commitment I couldn't make wholeheartedly."

"That explains why we couldn't contact you."

"Yeah, my father was already dead when I came home from Europe, my mother went to live with her sister in Atlanta not too long after I got back, so I was a bit adrift."

"You know, they bleat about how we are all free in this country. We aren't and never really were. Too many government regulations, to many permissions, government people telling you where you can live, how you can live and demanding taxes and fees and other BS. It was great living in the woods in California but as soon as campers and tourists and vacationers started moving in, the government figured I was more of a hindrance and they regulated me out of my home. They liked me there to keep an eye on fires and wild animals but as soon as I got in the way of profits, I was gone."

"What is Freedom anyway?"

"The ability to make your own decisions, to reverse course and to go where you want, I guess. Freedom doesn't imply the ability to do whatever you want, you are always beholden to a social contract. You don't have the freedom to kill someone, right?"

"Not unless the government ships you to France with a gun."

"I always figured I was free to do with my life and to chase whatever happiness I chose as long as I didn't unreasonably butt up on anyone else's freedom to do the same thing. You know, 'the pursuit of happiness' thing. Now there are so damn many of us it seems someone's freedoms are always in the way of mine - and for some reason the government places their freedoms ahead of mine."

"What is it that you want to do?"

"I just want to be left alone. Don't make me fill in forms, reducing me to a number, a number that must register for this, pay that fee, follow that regulation. Just leave me alone."

"So where are you living now, Tom?"

"Well, right here. When I heard that you were having a reunion, I figured that would be good, and I'd never been to Florida. I heard it was warm," he said with a smirk, and an exaggerated wipe of his brow.

"So you are staying here for a while?"

"I'll check it out. Appears there are plenty of cheap places to live. I took a place up the road for the season. That'll give me time to look around. Might even do a bit of fishing."

"What are you hoping to find?"

"I don't know. I've never been one to settle," laughed. "What I'd like is freedom to be. Fix a few machines here, do a little fishing there. I really don't like it when it all closes in. Renting a little place will keep me here for a while, and whatever I find will either keep me here longer or give me a reason to move on."

"Have you had a chance to speak to some of the other guys? There's Frankie talking with Freddie Allen. Remember Frank would bake for us? Well now he's baking for most of New York City. And Freddie, he's made some money in the retail business, he owns a small chain of hardware stores in the Atlanta area. He retired from the army a few years back - full Lieutenant General. Both those guys have done pretty well for themselves."

"Yes, I said hello to Freddie. He and I were together the in the trench after the fighting near Lille, when the Kraut tank rolled through. Crap, I've never been so scared in my life, before or since. Never seen anything like that, big metal thing rolled up to the edge of the trench and then slowly tipped in. Both of us scrambled out of the way. Just managed to avoid being crushed. Funny thing was we were actually safe because we were so close to it. If we'd had something to blow it up with, we would have. Freddie managed to jam a few rocks into its treads and that stopped it from moving for a bit, that and the incline up the other side of the trench."

"In the end we just moved down along the trench before scrambling up and out after the trench turned a few corners and we were out of the line of sight of the tank. It was a most unpleasant scramble back to our lines."

"What do you mean, after that we didn't have lines anymore. That was half the trouble with those offensives. By the time you sorted out where you were and where everyone else was, as some sectors pushed forward and others were pushed back, it was hard to gain any actual ground that was defensible. That's why we moved back. It was obvious from the lack of fear of the guys in the tanks, that we were among the few who had gained ground into German territory, eventually we would run into lots of them and not our own guys. Time to go."

"Was that where we saw the card party?"

"Yes, it was. Another reason to move out."

"The card party? I'm not sure I've heard about this."

"As we moved along the trench from the tank - the major part of the story, we turned a corner and saw a covered room, probably an ammo dump and store room as there were parts of a destroyed machine gun nest nearby. In front of the doorway there was a small table, looked like a nice antique, probably something picked up from a bombed out town. There were six guys sitting around the table, most on chairs, some on ledges cut into the side of the trench and a couple others on sandbags."

Freddie continued, "When I rounded the corner I stopped, and pulled back, thinking they would take us prisoner or kill us. But there was no sound. Funny how all the extraneous sounds of battle are filtered out in such a situation - and all you can hear are the sounds that are right there, absolutely integral to the situation at hand. There was nothing. At first I thought they were being cautious because they knew we were there and were planning an attack. I thought quickly and started to scramble up the side of the trench. Tom grabbed me and pointed to the other side - they wouldn't expect us coming from the German side, so we reversed and scrambled out of the trench, staying as low as possible. Still no sounds."

Tom picked it up. "We inched along the top until we were near the turn in the trench. I looked over and there they all were just as I'd seen them originally, though this time I could see why - they were all dead. It appeared that a shell had hit their machine gun emplacement dead on, the resulting explosion and shrapnel had neatly killed everyone playing cards. Not one of them appeared to have moved after the explosion. Two of them had neat little holes in their heads where they'd been hit. Two others had wounds in their torsos, you could see the blood soaking through their clothes when you looked a bit closer."

"We scrambled down into the trench, mostly looking for some food. We found some in the storage room and stuffed it in our pockets and got out of Dodge. I did pick up a souvenir on the way," he reached into his breast pocket. "This was lying face up on the table so I grabbed it."

He gingerly took out a thin plastic pocket and extracted the contents pulling a playing card, the King of Spades, out and holding it up. It had a hole the size of a dime cut right through, taking out the King's head, as if someone had done it deliberately.

"Well, I'll be damned," said Freddie. "I knew you grabbed at something on the table, I figured it was money."

"I carried this around with me for years in my wallet. That's why it's so worn. After I noticed the damage, I took it out and put it in the plastic sheet. It's a constant reminder of," he paused, "of death, the suddenness of death and of my experience in the Great War."

"Those guys never knew what hit them, it must have been one of the first shells as they were still playing cards and had not moved, not even to hunker down for the barrage."

Pete Delany wandered over to their table.

"Tom? Nice to see you, I was wondering if you might make it some year."

"Well I'm living in the area now, at least for a few months. Anyone else living around Sarasota?"

"Yes, I heard that someone was living in Palm Harbour now. Can't remember who."

"Oh, better wait on that. Cap is going to do his usual welcome."

Hathaway, had risen and moved up to the front of the room, where he stood behind a small lectern and tapped a microphone to get everyone's attention.

"Hello, hello, is this working?" He saw a few nods. "Okay, hello members of Diamond Platoon and welcome to our Fortieth Anniversary Reunion of the end of the Great War. After Pete's story our platoon nickname has taken on a different significance."

There were some murmurs though the room.

"I am particularly pleased this year, as all members of our platoon are here, except one, including three who have never attended before and several who have not been able to make the previous events. This year, my granddaughter is trying to speak to everyone to compile a short book of memories. She will ask you some questions. Please be open to her questions as this is an opportunity for everyone to say things that need saying and to speak to each other and to the future. I will put the book of memories together and mail a copy to everyone once it has been completed.

"I know there are things that you may not want to say but please consider this opportunity for what it is, a chance to say what happened to you, how it may have changed your life and anything else you may find interesting about your experiences.

"This year we have a treat or two in store. Frank Eisenrick is going to conduct a bake off tomorrow morning and bake break and croissants the same way he did for us in France. In addition Allen LaRue will take us through his trip back to the battlefields of Flanders with a slide show just prior to dinner tomorrow night, right here in this room. He took a trip back last year.

"Our first reunion was a small affair. Ten years from our service we had moved into our lives and the reunion was for only vets. For our 20th reunion our numbers grew a bit, with the occasional child coming as well. We had 41 people for our 20th but that slipped a bit to 31 people for our 30th reunion in Pittsburgh. Today, I am proud to say that with children and grandchildren and the complete attendance of the surviving members of our platoon, save one, we are at 75 attendees. Please take a reunion program on the way out tonight. We have a meeting for platoon members only, scheduled after dinner tonight in the hotel bar. Tomorrow is your own, to explore Sarasota, fish or play golf or shop. Tomorrow evening has the slide show and dinner event and cocktail party and dance following it. Read the program for more detail - including seating arrangements for dinner."

Chapter Twenty One   1968

"Shit, if it isn't Bernie Smith."

With the sharp, late afternoon light coming through the windows, Bernie was only half visible in the glare, but entirely unmistakable. The light cast a long sharp shadow on his entrance and highlighted his cautious nature.

A few heads turned. A slightly stooped figure entered the room, stopped momentarily as if to sniff the air and moved slowly away from the door, along the wall. He didn't want to be seen before he could scope out the situation.

"Look at him," said Freddie Allen, "that's Bernie a mile away. He used to do that style of checking out the room even when he entered the mess."

The guys in his group laughed. "That's so true," said Charlie Hauser, who squeezed his comment out through intakes of laughter.

"Only thing is, he was the smart one. Remember, he was doing it in the mess tent," Allen retorted. "There are times I wish I had had a bit of patience on what they fed us."

Still smiling, Charlie beckoned Bernie Smith over. He started to make his way through the crowd of men and their wives reacquainting themselves with old friends. It was the fifth 10-year reunion of the platoon. Being the 50th anniversary of the end of the war Hathaway had made a special effort to get every surviving member of the platoon to the event, held this time at a small hotel in Sarasota, Florida.

Canvassing some of the more well-to-do members of the group, Hathaway had even managed to provide a little incentive to those who had a bit of financial difficulty getting there. A number of the men had retired to the Gulf Coast, and the few remaining who hadn't, were able to make it to Florida with little difficulty, save one or two whose financial situation was a bit precarious.

"Hey Bernie, so good to see you. Did Marie make the trip with you?"

"Oh, yeah. My son drove us to San Francisco and we came by train through Denver, Dallas and the south all the way to Tampa. Rented a car there and came here."

"How is California treating you?"

"It's the land of milk and honey. Only problem is the milk is spilled and spoiled and stinks to high heaven and the honey is sticky and difficult to clean up. I think it might be that way for every farmer," his growl turned into a smile. "Actually things are looking up, planted grapes, lots of grapes and they've been sold to a winery for years. So I know it's going to be a decent year. Added to the spread a bit again last year. A couple more acres. Wineries are growing like weeds out there."

"How long you been out there now?"

"Wow, a while, let me think, I went out there just before the depression, so what, a bit more than 40 years. This is only the second reunion I've been to. It's hard to get away from the farm, but now my boys have taken on a lot of the day to day stuff."

"You picked the right time to go out there."

"My Dad was right, the farm business in the east was good, but fixed. You couldn't get more land, and farming practices meant that you needed more to make it work. He sent me out there with some cash and I bought an acreage in the Sonoma Valley, basically scrub land at the time. Got it real cheap with enough water to make it go. Then I kept buying land right through the depression and I still buy it. Dad came out there once to see what we'd done just before he died. I think he was impressed with things, though he'd spend most of his time asking why we did what we did and providing suggestions. Some of them were pretty good too. And of course some of them were too eastern to work really well. Things are a bit different out there. Unless you're in the Central Valley, crop production is like ranching plants. The water situation is a bit precarious, there's always water but it seems that we are almost perpetually playing defence against draught."

"We've got a pretty good sized operation out there, some cattle, some almonds, some cash crop and I've been moving into the grapes now for about 20-25 years. It's been getting bigger and bigger. I've had no trouble selling my crop each year and for a while now a couple of wineries have offered to pre-purchase the grapes at a premium. Crap they were outbidding each other. I went with the biggest company, figured they'd be more inclined to remain in business and pay me. I even get paid extra if the crop comes in larger than expected. Only downside is they have a couple of their guys come by the farm regularly to see how we are making out. They ask a lot of questions - figure I have to give them answers as they are paying. But I don't like it."

"What wineries are pre-buying?"

"A couple of brothers have put together a large operation but they are processors almost entirely. They contract with farmers and then make and bottle the wine. They promised us a case once it was finished. I held out for two. That sealed the deal."

"How about your boys?"

"They have been on the farm, Joe and Eddie, that is, for as long as they've been alive. They work well together, Joe is the detail guy and Eddie can't pass a job without getting it done. My other boy, Winston, the middle one, he's not really interested in the farm. Oh, he worked there as a kid, that's part of growing up on the farm, but now he's a lawyer with a bank in San Francisco."

"How about you, Charlie? How's your farm and family."

"Well, it's all pretty good. I just stayed on the family farm until mom and dad passed. My brothers run it. I moved out to California as well and got into vegetables in the Valley. My inheritance set me up and I just kept growing veggies and buying land. My wife got some cash from her family farm when her parents passed. We put that into our operation as well.

My brothers made good money selling all their milk to Hersey's and run a small herd of beef cattle. They got into breeding them a few years back, trying to get more milk production and now we are trying to get a higher quality of beef. Problem is, it's not at all clear what a higher quality of beef actually is. My sons tell me that quality of beef cattle is in the quantity of meat they produce. Some of the processors are trying to get a certain kind of meat, and that requires us to handle the cattle a certain way, how we feed 'em, how we move them around and stuff. The boys are on this more than me. I just worry about building repairs and stuff."

"Got to admit we kinda went past merely being Reformers when my mom died. It got harder and harder to justify not having a bit of technology - so we electrified the Pennsylvania farm and used some modern appliances, mostly in the house though and in the barns. Nothing crazy. Been doing things the old way so long it just seems like the way to do it."

"California is a bit different. Good thing I did that stint at Penn State, the operation out there could not run if it wasn't partly automated. It's too large and the water resources have to be precisely organized. Like Bernie said, even if there is no draught it seems like there is going to be one so we are constantly planning for it."

"Well, that's a big change, going electric. Kinda like this Bob Dylan fellow my boys talk about. He went electric and all his fans kinda went crazy."

"Who? Dylan, the only Dillon I ever heard of was Matt Dillion on Gunsmoke. Now he ain't never going electric."

"He's a singer. Used to sing folk songs now he's gone and started playing electric guitar - loud as hell. Can't sing a lick. Sounds like a soaking wet, scart cat in a thunderstorm. The grandkids all love him."

"Well some of the Pennsylvania neighbours thought the electricity thing was bad, but they are using it now a bit and I think they'll string wires to their places in the next year or so. Once they see how easy it is to preserve food and to operate the bottling and some of the farm machinery with a bit of power, they shake their heads and the next thing you know they get wired up. The old ways aren't going away though. It's only a small nod to the future. Some of the families worry we have hit the slippery slope of modernization."

"Nothing much happens on the farm of note though, no real excitement. I'm guessing that's why we stay in farming. It's all pretty predictable. We certainly don't crave excitement. We'll I guess I did a bit when I signed up for the Army, but that made me decided the old ways were pretty good. Excitement only gets you killed like old Jimmy, or maimed like a few of the others who we saw."

"I'm not sure if I crave excitement Charlie," said Freddie Allen. "Or even if Smithy is the same as you. He travelled across the country and started from scratch. That's pretty exciting even if his life wasn't in danger most of the time."

"Got me a nice bit of land south of town and built it up bit by bit. Had Dad's backing too, so we weren't destitute - though it was a bit touch and go there until just before the Second War."

"I was in California for a time, but just moved back east when I retired. Made some money out there in real estate, south of Frisco but mostly in the Los Angeles area. Couple of my daughters are still there, but my Jennie wanted to come back to live in New England where her friends are and where we lived for a time when she was around 16. The army was good to me, especially after the second war. Went to California with the army but the money opportunities couldn't be missed. I ended up retiring in Atlanta and got so bored I started a hardware store. Now I have a half a dozen. My boys runs 'em now. I'm thinking of retiring again. Might scout out a few properties down here. I hear the Atlantic side is a bit more developed."

"Oh here comes Marie. Dear, you need to meet my friends Charlie Hauser and Bernie Smith." The men introduced their wives and there was a bit of awkward silence while everyone tried to find a topic to bring up.

"Charlie never says much about the war but he insists on coming to this reunion every time," said Jennette Hauser. "Maybe you gentlemen could tell us a bit of what went on over there?"

The men looked at each other uncomfortably for a moment or two.

"As Americans, not much went on over there. We got there late and didn't fight too much but our presence seemed to take the fight out of the Krauts."

"I remember a lot of moving around, a bit of R and R in the south by the sea, a couple of battles in Flanders and us getting shelled that time east of Arras, just before the Armistice."

"Yeah, that sounds about right. We were backline troops in the northern offensive in the late summer and early fall of '18. I know there were a lot of nervous guys but we really never had to be the main attacking thrust on the front lines. We were the support guys. The English guys had some harrowing tales to tell. We'd complain of our conditions and they'd just laugh like hyenas without really saying to much. From what I gathered it was pretty gruesome, with a lot of blood, a lot of craziness and not much in the way of comfort. They talked about the number of animals, horses I guess, that were killed in the explosions. Time makes us forget how many things were still moved by horse in those days. Some of the survival tales that were the worst were just making it through each week in the trenches. They didn't talk much about the battles."

"We got a bit of a taste of it when we went on those two attacks. We were shelled that one day but it really wasn't an attack, at least not like the constant bombardment the Limey's talked about."

"Yeah that was more target practice rather than a full on offensive."

"It scared me half to death."

"Come on Freddie, as I recall you were standing up on one of the foundations trying to see the artillery emplacements. They shot, what, maybe 50 rounds at us. I'm not even sure they knew we were there, They were just practicing their ranging on the remains of that village."

"Come on," said Marie. "There has to be some stories you can tell us. We've all heard about the rings and Peter Delaney's daughter.

There must be more, even if they are a bit less farfetched. Isn't that why we're here."

That's why WE are here. You are here for a different reason," he laughed.

"Well there were that few days in Paris and there was the R and R in the south of France," started Charlie. "We set up our camp. I remember that."

"Yeah, that's where we found out that Eisenrick was such a good cook."

"Not a cook, a baker. His family owned a bakery in New York City. There he is over there, talking with LaRue and Endicott."

"Boy, he made the best bread and croissants. Like a little piece of heaven."

"He used to call them Manhattan's finest - a slice of the Upper West Side."

"That's a New Yorker for you. I thought Manhattan's finest were the NYPD," he laughed. "Wonder how his business is going?"

"Oh, it's your first reunion in a while. Frank is the master bread maker of New York. He made a fortune by getting into the supermarket supply business early on. His company has most of the sliced bread business in the Tri-State area and western Pennsylvania."

"That is the Tri-State area," said Hauser. "Once you get to Allentown you might as well be in New York."

"I always thought it included southern Connecticut."

"Oh, maybe it does. It's probably a local thing. Is there a Quad-State area?"

"No, but I've heard of the Quad-Cities. Not sure where they are though, somewhere in the midwest, maybe."

"Maybe it just depends on your location. The way things are growing it could be a number of places."

"Maybe . . .anyway Eisenrick could bake bread, and apparently still can."

"So what else happened in the south of France?" asked one of the women.

"Well, we set up tents and we hung out a while. It was just down time from being at the front for a few months. You were able to wake up and know that there was no possibility of being shelled, nor would we be on the move anywhere until our time was up. We all had a few jobs to do each day, cleaning stuff and repairing equipment, mostly little things and much of it wasn't even important or watched. Just something to keep us busy."

"It would have been nice to travel around a bit."

"Our camp was lovely. We were away from the main part of town in a park area. We scratched out a baseball field and played a game every day or two. By the time we had to leave we had it down to a couple of even teams. Cap had a few balls which he guarded zealously. There ain't no place to buy a baseball in all of France. Had to get them from Army brass. I remember he used to trade with other units and made a big production of getting sporting equipment for the boys from HQ. We used to hand stitch the balls if the stitching was frayed. I remember the CO coming around giving him a few and told him that's all he'd get. No wonder he was so protective of those balls. He must 'a winced every time they got hit."

"Not every time, maybe when you hit one Charlie. I didn't know the Amish were such good ballplayers."

"The Amish not good ballplayers? Ever heard of Honus Wagner?"

"He was Amish?"

"Close enough, he came from an Amish family. He might have been the best ever."

"Some of our guys had never really played until France. I remember Jocko was pretty bad but he learned real quick and could hit pretty well after a week. Cap was real good, but he wouldn't play after the first two games, preferred to umpire - especially after it became apparent that we badly needed an umpire. He could protect the balls that way too. Only dispensed them when we really needed one. He used to take a toothbrush to them after we played to whiten them up a bit."

"Oh come on," laughed Smith.

"So the holiday time is all you boys can remember?"

"Well there was the time we were shelled when we went to clear out a village that had fallen behind the front lines. We had to check to see if there were any minefields or booby traps. Cap split us up to cover the ground a little quicker. Good thing to, as the Germans decided to take that time to shell the village from their high ground about two miles away."

"A bomb could be shot from that far away?" asked one of the women.

"Oh yeah, probably much further. In the battle you couldn't see the artillery. In fact you could barely hear them they were so far away. All you could hear was the muffled thump of it firing, very faintly, off in the distance. The shells themselves would scream as they cut through the air, so you had some warning to get down. Unless one landed very near you would usually manage without injury, though some guys got hit by pieces of them or bits of the stuff they blew up. That could be deadly. We were lucky in that village, nobody was hurt. I guess there wasn't much left for the explosions to fling around and cause injuries."

"Of course everyone here has heard Pete Delany's story about the ring he found." They all nodded and shared a few shakes of the head and "Small world."

"Hey Cap, why did you pick Sarasota for our reunion?" asked Duff Richardson.

"It's close enough to Tampa to make it fairly easy to get to. It's far enough from Tampa to reduce the cost significantly. Plus I really like the hotel location on the key and the lovely beach. I asked everyone what they preferred, didn't you get the letter?"

"No I didn't actually, but that's probably because I moved recently. I only found out about it from Clancy - who called when he found out. I'm living in Palm Harbor just north of St. Petersburg. I retired there about three years ago. Once the insurance business was done - Violet and I took the plunge, sold the big house in Pittsburgh and bought a nice bungalow a mile or so from the Gulf."

"Well Duff, if I had known, there was nothing stopping me from moving our little reunion north of Tampa. I wonder how many more of us will end up down here?"

"Us? Are you in Florida too?"

"Indeed I am Duff, I moved down to West Palm Beach on the Atlantic side about five years ago. It's a lovely spot and full of old Northeasterners who have retired there. Not sure why but there are a number of French there as well, outta Quebec. Makes things a bit more lively."

"So you gave up the family home?"

"I never had it. My sister owned it for years and recently sold it to her son. I'm glad it's still in the family. They are contemplating a significant renovation. I'm not sure I could leave that place entirely - it's been in the family for about 200 years; the property anyway. The house is more than a century old, though it's been added to many times. It's quite the ramshackle affair."

"I remember, you had mentioned it as a possible location for our first reunion in '28."

"I would have done that but it seemed to me to be a bit remote and a little small for the whole group of us. By '38 with wives and kids we were swamped. That hotel near Philly in '28 was nice though. That's 40 years ago - it only seems like a touch over 10 years."

"It's funny but I've met a few people who also served and they have their unit reunions from time to time. We share beers and stories at the Legion Halls. I see those guys more often. You get to know their back stories, but it's never quite the same as this."

"I know what you mean. I remained back in France at the end of it all for a while and even thought about remaining in the army for a while. They kept me for another two years while they worked out all the logistics over there and started the process of building the army over here. Those guys I worked with get together from time to time, but it's not the same. Those were desk jobs mostly and it's just not the same. Being shot at has a way of sharpening your memories."

Duff laughed. "Yes it does. Found that out in France and it proved useful during a robbery I was caught up in back in the late 50s in Philly. Everybody was panicking and I was cool, hyper-aware. I could see the robber was nervous and might shoot everyone so I took the chance to try and calm him, and told him to grab what he came for an hightail it out of there before the police surrounded the place. I didn't want him panicking and shooting the place up. It worked."

"Anyway Cap, I'd heard some of what you were involved in after the war but never knew the whole story. That's a bloody long time to keep you on. The rest of us were gone and done for a long time by then. Well, except for Freddie."

"Not a big deal Duff, like I said, for a bit I thought about making the army a career," said Hathaway. "In fact my time at US HQ sharpened my mind a bit on the subject."

"Were they shooting at you?"

Hathaway smiled and shook his head. "Not sure there is much more to the story, Duff. Once the war was over, they asked me to stay on a while as the US Army was really a ramshackle affair, from personnel and training to arms and armaments. Don't forget the last thing the Army had done before the Great War was the charge up San Juan Hill. God, that seems so long ago. The Navy was far ahead of us. I toured French and British installations and had long meetings with their people regarding the war, the tactics and the technology. We even looked at some of the German bases, trench emplacements etc. It became obvious to me that technology would outrun the tactics of the Great War - that in fact, the War was a one-of-a-kind affair and that tactics are entirely dependent upon the prevailing technology. I recommended that our efforts at building the military be directed entirely into the air force and technological improvements to everything. I was among the minority. My work done, I came back to the States and started in the chemical business."

"So the army brass didn't see it your way? What did they want?"

"In the end I think they did. But Duff, there are competing interests. At that time the Army barely had an air force so there was no one to speak for it, except Rickenbaker. He knew. There was an infantry and a cavalry and the Marines and Navy were very powerful. Those interests were deeply entrenched and won the day. Even the old cavalry people put up a bit of a fight saying the mechanized army was unreliable. Deep down they realized they had to go mechanized but it was contrary to everything they knew. The most senior guys didn't want to overhaul everything just before they retired and couldn't get up the energy to change. However, enough of them saw the inevitable and worked to set the wheels in motion in that direction. The Navy also pushed the Marines to be a bigger portion of the military and I thought at the time that the versatility was likely a good idea. Not that I was prescient of course. I never even thought about the Pacific or the Japs or any of that."

"So what you're saying is that we weren't particularly prepared for the Second World War but we at least were thinking about the First One in a way that lead us to make some sound decisions?"

"Yeah, that about sums it up.

Chapter Twenty Two - 1978

"A couple of the guys can't be here anymore. Freddie Allen passed last year, Andy Endicott the year before that and Duff and Clancy died within a few months of each other back in '74."

"I guess it's inevitable, eventually, you know."

"We are all old men. Every one of us is over 80."

Hathaway took a deep breath. I've been holding out on you guys. I've been wondering for years if I should tell, or take it to my grave. I guess I want to know if I did the right thing, it weighs on you."

"What are you taking about Cap?"

Hathaway looked down, studying his feet. It took him a while to start. An old man, he wanted to collect his thoughts before speaking.

"Well, there was a plan. Before we got to the front some of the unit commanders had seen how some of our units were being sacrificed. We weren't real sure of the motivation of brass, an attempt to buy us battle experience, credibility among the allies or a stronger place at the peace talks . . . they were all possibilities but I didn't want my guys, or me, to die for those reasons. In retrospect it's all geo-politics I guess, but at the time it just seemed like a poor reason to sacrifice yourself and your mates.

"So what we did, a string of unit CO's, was tell each other, several of the non-commissioned officers and small unit commanders, what we knew about troop movements - the unit commanders for certain US units - and tried to figure out how best to complete our assignments while dodging the bullets, so to speak and stay alive. We never shirked our duty but we certainly managed to remain in the best position to survive craziness, without it being obvious to brass. I know from conversations after the war that brass just thought the theatre of operations made the logistics difficult - little did they know that we had a hand in that."

"Did your actions hampered other units or put them in difficult positions?" asked Jocko Rollins.

"I suppose they might have, but not on purpose, more in the heat of battle. We never really knew what the Krauts were going to do. That was the reason for our co-ordination. We didn't want to leave each other hung out to dry, so if one unit was going to do something we let all the units in on our plan. Some of these things were pretty benign - moving out on an offensive a few minutes later than expected. If you gave the Krauts a few extra minutes after the bombardment they were able to fight back more effectively or if

258

they were dead from the shelling, they'd still be dead. If they fought back better, then we wouldn't be caught in the open when they figured it out. More people survive - really just a better battle tactic. Brass may have fainted at the thought but they weren't the ones dying."

"What other things did you do?"

"All kinds of things to delay our participation in effect buying us a little time to react to battle actions - especially where it appeared to be suicidal. You guys never knew, although I think a couple of the brighter ones had an inkling something was up - we just dodged trouble a bit too much to be random. I for one, did not believe that the brass had the right to sacrifice my life for some minor and fleeting advantage on the field or in negotiations. The tide of war was with us, and a death or two in my unit was not going to change that one iota."

"We would hold back ammo deliveries so the units on the front line had to hold back, especially as the Armistice neared. We stretched out bad weather to stop us from fighting, we would purposely get the trucks stuck in the mud to slow our operations. Well, I did it, by insisting deliveries were made, by sending trucks on roads I knew would be difficult to pass. It wasn't all delay and avoid, it was more like completing ordered tasks to our advantage in timing or logistics. In one instance we exposed ourselves to draw fire so we could locate their artillery and allow our guys to try to take it out. A few times brass changed their battle plans based on our intelligence. They never said it directly but when deliveries are stepped up and troop movements indicate a coming offensive and then they are pulled back without explanation, well, you know they changed their minds."

"Did anyone else in our unit know about this? How high up the chain did it go?"

"I don't actually know," said Hathaway. "Nobody else in our unit knew, I kept it to myself. I only had one contact with another unit. In my post war discussions there were some indications that it went up pretty high, though of course no one would admit it out loud. Just hints. You never knew if they were involved or merely digging for information on suspicions that something was afoot.

"I only had dealings with a Major in a nearby regiment, I don't know who he dealt with. All I know is that it wasn't just us two, he had a contact and his contact had a contact. At least that's what he told me. We weren't around long enough for me to get my own contact further down the line - I was the end of it. The biggest problem I had was trying to appear competent to brass while purposely making small changes to some of their decisions.

"You might note that most of the American casualties in the Great War came from actions in other sectors and from the influenza. Whether that was because those sectors had better Kraut defences, or they were targeted more, I cannot say. All I know is we managed to push the Krauts back with a minimum of casualties in the last six months of the war, the time when the American involvement was beyond a token force."

"I am proud of the fact that my platoon came through the war with only a two deaths, and one was a driving accident in the war zone but not during battle. It was more like a traffic accident for someone who drives a lot - almost inevitable; if you drive that much even on city streets eventually you will have an accident. Only the severity of it was unknown and unknowable."

"I sometimes struggle with the idea that I do not know all the consequences that came out of our actions. However I sleep well at night knowing that what we did was human and right, protecting our mates and making sure their service was worth the sacrifice of the lives we lost. Some guys never recovered from the war - shell shock, gas attacks, lost limbs and disfigurement. A couple of my guys were burnt pretty bad, but on their arms and legs, not of their faces, that's the worst."

"I'm not sure how to react Cap," said Rollins. Bernie Smith nodded and Hugh Coleman did too. The rest appeared confused.

Eisenrick spoke slowly, "We didn't shirk our duty? But we did things that did not follow the battle plan? I'm uncomfortable with this Cap. Are you sure we didn't go soft long enough that others took more of the pain - by essentially fighting in our place?"

"Frank, I never took us out of anything that was expected of us. I simply tried to give us a better chance of survival in the tasks we were asked to accomplish."

"Remember the village that was booby trapped? We were expected to attack the north-west corner of that village, essentially make a blind charge over the open field between that hillock we hid behind and the first buildings 150 yards away. I made the decision to move the unit further east through the wooded area as the frontal charge to dug in positions would have been suicidal - as those units who tried it found out. Even if we had succeeded we would have been in the midst of the town when it exploded and likely would not be having this conversation right now. By moving to the lightly defended north east we saw the evidence of the boo-by trap and were able to warn the others making the frontal charge from the west."

"But we were expected to support that charge by drawing fire off to the north?"

"Think for a moment Jocko. How much fire did the other unit that moved into that breach draw. None. They swarmed the town be-cause they were being drawn into the booby trap. We saw it and saved hundreds of guys."

The men sat around the table in an awkward circle. A few stood in behind those who were seated.

"So you want our blessing regarding your actions?"

"Well, as long as we didn't endanger other guys with our actions, you have mine," said Martin Wilson. "We survived and I think most of us have had long and interesting lives."

"But Cap, assure me we didn't make others take the heat for us and maybe that's all that needs be said right now," said Delaney.

"As far as I can tell, we did not. Remember we were only in two planned actions. Frankly it was only in the booby trapped village that I really had to steer us away from the suicide mission, or what looked like it. In the other action, the offensive that ended at the tent city, I steered our unit to the south, away from the direct line of fire of the machine guns hidden in the tents. And that idea came from the Brit officer. His experience saved our lives, or at least some of them. Remember we had some injuries there - a couple of guys were shot and wounded, remember Hughie's leg wound. Thankfully no one was killed. Remember our guys did some of the dirty work in taking out the gun emplacements from behind. I think that's why I was more cautious the second time."

"And brass after the war wondered if our light casualties came from our interactions with the Brit troops. Apparently those in strictly American units did not fare so well."

"I guess it makes sense, Cap. Don't torture yourself. You were a damn fine CO and officer. If you helped us survived by being smart we should be grateful," said Billings.

"I have wondered if it was the right thing to do, Tom. I keep coming back to the conclusion that I can never really know what might have happened otherwise. In any event, you guys have nothing to be ashamed about. Me, I don't think I do either, but because I cannot know the outcome of things that did not happen, the alternative history, it keeps coming up in my mind."

Chapter Twenty Three

The brown Buick moved along the old country road, slowing at each drive. Houses had been built to fill in the once rural area, but this road didn't have curbs or sewers as it was an old farm road, now a gentrified old country road, surrounded by higher density suburbs. The properties were still large as owners were reluctant to sell off and subdivide the old farmsteads. Financial incentives had pried much of the large acreages from the long time owners but those sales had occurred years before with the famers keeping a few acres to themselves and often ran small market garden operations. Some of the driveways were very long, and many of the homes had a little shed down by the roadway where they sold fruits and vegetables in season.

The Buick slowed as it approached each driveway and paused. After a few it turned slowly into one, a ramshackle farm house that had some modern touches obvious to even the most casual viewer.

"I think this is the one, come with me."

They made their way up to the door, the older woman, moving very deliberately, picking her way across the uneven ground. She held a cane in one hand and her other arm was cradled by the younger woman, perhaps in her late 50s or early 60s.

They mounted the steps to the porch and moved towards the door. It swung open.

"Hello, I heard your car turn in." He was tallish, looked about 50 years old, with short dark hair, a hint of grey, and an easy manner. "How can I help you?"

"Well, I hope you can," said the older woman. "My name is Rosalie Roberts. This is my daughter Frances, she helps me get around. Are you the homeowner, Rodney Montgomery?"

"Yes, I am, but I don't know who you are."

"I am a writer and I'm looking for the family that originally owned this house - the Hathaway family. Town records show you purchased the home only a few years ago. Do you know where I might find any members of the Hathaway family?"

"Sure yeah, I'm one I guess," he said poking himself in the chest. "Which members are you looking for?"

"Oh, well anyone who can help me with a bit of background. I'm writing a book on battles that the US Expeditionary Force fought in France during World War One. This was the family home of Captain, later Major Herbert Hathaway, a platoon commander of a unit that has an interesting history with actions at several battles."

"Oh, yes, that would be me, um, us, I mean my mother . . . " he shook his head and smiled. "Sorry you caught me by surprise. My mother was a Hathaway, she sold the home to me, so I suppose I am a Hathaway too. Herbert was her brother but did not come here after the war. I know very little about him."

"Well perhaps I can fill in some of the blanks. And maybe you can help me with whatever you know."

Montgomery paused a second, looked around, and decided to invite the women in.

Settled around a coffee table, proper introductions were made and Rodney put on a pot of coffee. The living room was large, to match the house, with much brocaded furniture and a huge and deep fireplace. It was no showpiece. The giant stone fireplace dominated the room and harkened back to the days when the fire would have heated much of the house - despite the installation of radiant heat and the abandonment of the coal cellar.

"Well, Ms. Roberts, what would you like to know? I only really know what my mother told me, though I did meet my uncle once in New York when I was young. He was a nice man, and my mother really looked up to him. In fact I believe he was instrumental in my parents financial dealings. He was a businessman, though he never had any children that I'm aware of."

"Please call me Rosalie. Your uncle did, after I insisted on it. He was a very nice man."

"You knew him?"

"Yes, for a while in France. I was working for the US Army in logistics and did a large survey of US Army actions in the Great War as part of a research project the army commissioned right after the Great War. Now I am trying to visit with as many of the commanders of units that I can in order to piece together US actions in the War. The Defence Department in Washington still insists that the actions in the Great War are classified, top secret and will not grant access to records. Even though I wrote most of them. So I have to speak to the sources. Fortunately I know of many people to talk to and gain names from them for subsequent interviews."

"How can you track all the US actions - it would be impossible, there must be thousands."

"Actually no. There are really very few as the US involvement in the Great War was only very short. And frankly I'm not interested in the early token involvements but only in the later stages of the war, from the spring of 1918 to the end in the autumn of that year - about six months of battles."

"I spoke to your Uncle after the war as part of my US Army research into successes and failures of the war. The US Army was a very young entity at that time. No real experience and warfare was changing rapidly from civil war type tactics that dominated the thinking of the time and the naval engagements and sieges that occurred in the Spanish - American War."

"We had a war with Spain?"

She smiled. "Yes, short and very sweet for us, before World War One."

He blinked a number of times and shook his head.

"My Uncle Herb died a few years ago. He had organized his unit reunions every 10 years since the war ended. I guess they will go on, but one of the other men will have to take on the task. They've met in Florida for the last several reunions as many of them live there now."

"I was wondering if you knew any of the stories of the battle actions you uncle took part in?"

"As I said, I only met him once or twice. Battle actions were not on the agenda. I think it was ice cream and Coney Island."

"What stories did your mother relate to you? Is she still alive?"

"Yes, she lives in Florida now. You might want to speak to her. I know very little. She spoke of a battle where a German supply depot was turned into a booby trap. I think my uncle was wounded there, but not too badly as there was no mention of him taken away from the front. I do know he was immensely proud of the survival rate of his unit. My mother used to say that he made it a priority to keep his men safe. She spoke of a baker that her brother talked about, now a major manufacturer of bread in New York. In fact I remember going to a bakery in New York when we saw him and he gave me some pastries. She also talked about his action in spotting a booby trapped village, wired with explosives, and how Uncle Herb recognized it and warned everyone saving many lives."

"Does your mother have any mementos of that time?"

"I don't know. She never mentioned any," Rodney said. "I have something that I like, but I'm afraid it doesn't have any battle significance. You might be able to identify a few people though. It's a photo of the unit taken in the spring of 1918. Let me get it for you. I had it framed after I found it when we cleaned out the attic when my mother moved to Florida."

Rodney returned a few minutes later with a framed photo. Sepia toned and inscribed 'Biarritz, 1918" in the bottom corner. It showed two ragtag lines of men, almost as if two teams had joined together for the photo after a game. There was a youngish man in the centre, holding a bat, and two others partly crouched down who looked like officers.

"This is interesting," said Rosalie. "I haven't seen anything quite like it. Perhaps this is what is so top secret at the Pentagon," she laughed. "I believe that man," she pointed at the photo, "is Major Ewing of the Screaming Eagles. The man beside him was his adjutant. I can't remember his name."

"And I have a couple of balls that were likely used. They have names on them. Do you want to see them?"

"Yes, absolutely and anything else you might have from that time."

Rodney returned with two old baseballs, dirty and marked with faded ink. He handed them to Rosalie but her eyes remained fixed on the old baseball bat he also brought.

"Is that one of the bats from the photo?"

"I don't know. It was just with Uncle Herb's things that had been left in the attic from years before. He didn't appear to want them as he could have easily gotten them for many years."

"May I see that bat, please." She looked at Frances. Rosalie made a show of looking at the bat near its business end, at the label and for any other markings or identifications. She saw the faint impression of a 'Property - US Army' stamped in the handle.

Then she inspected the knob scratching at the base of it before placing the bat head on her foot and propping the handle between her knees. She pushed on the knob but nothing happened.

"It's too stiff I think dear, can you try it?"

Frances took the bat and put it between her knees and hunched over it with her right palm pushing down on the knob.

"I think it's moving a bit, yes. Left, left," she could feel the clicks, "Down, right, down, left, down, right and pop." The knob popped up.

The room was silent.

"What is that?" Rodney was almost too shocked to speak.

"Something I had heard about long ago, I think," said Rosalie. Frances tipped the bat back and extracted a roll of paper. "Careful now dear. I need to read that."

The late afternoon sun shone in through the large front bay window. Catching furniture and decorations near the window the light was casting giant shadows across the room and throwing them up across the people talking and onto the large fire place at the end of the room.

She carefully unrolled the paper, brittle with age and it's tightly rolled nature, she gently held it top and bottom to reveal its contents.

To whom it may concern:

This baseball bat was given me by Colonel Douglas Hart at US HQ near Arras in the spring of 1918 at the behest of Major Ewing of the Screaming Eagles squadron. The Major used this method to include me in the plan to wage war in a way that would protect our soldiers without endangering the success of the mission. I understand that Colonel Hart went to West Point with Pershing and knew that he would not hesitate to spend the lives of US soldiers to achieve a wide range of goals. The colonel was determined to do something about it.

I did not tell any of my men of this initiative during the war but I did provide some information about it, perhaps looking for some absolution, at our reunion in 1978.

I have always tried to do my duty and modified battle plans within the scope of our stated objectives only inasmuch as I could preserve lives and limbs. For my part I believe I succeeded. I do not know of anyone else involved in this effort - though it was suggested that it was widespread and extended into the British ranks.

It was unsigned. She finished reading. Rodney waited for her to speak.

"I spoke to Major Ewing and he said he had only told Captain Hathaway, that they were the only two in on the plan but that he had alluded to Hathaway that there were many more involved. The mention of Colonel Hart is not news to me. Unfortunately I believe he died some years ago."

"So you had some knowledge of this?"

"Yes, as I said I was involved in battle analysis in the immediate aftermath of the war. I was aware of a secret project to test the wits of platoon commanders and how they would react to peer pressure to modify their battle plans. It was really an ill conceived experiment as it quickly became obvious that there were too many variables to be able to draw any significant conclusions. Still, I could not believe the huge disparities between the battle casualties of some of the units. American units were either decimated or came out almost unscathed, there was no in between."

"I have pursued this inquiry for many years - in fact well past my retirement. That's why I cannot easily get access to army records but I do have some insider help."

"So was my uncle shirking his responsibilities?"

"Some in the army think so, others merely wonder. That was part of the study - to determine motivations and actions when the unit commanders were put in this position. The enlightened among us, them, want to know what happened so they can learn the lessons of battle. They want everything. Did we win the battles in question? Where were the units who modified their plans stationed? What was their casualty rate. Were people in the know injured or killed at a higher or lower rate than those who knew nothing?"

"I don't know anything else."

"Rhetorical questions now I guess. Thank you so much for your time and efforts to help me corroborate what I knew and suspected. In the end, several of your Uncle's platoon can probably thank him for their survival - but of course we could never know which ones, it's all just speculation in the numbers game."

Oh, and before we leave perhaps you'd like to see something Frances has.

The younger woman reached around her neck and pulled up a chain that had been beneath her blouse. She quickly slipped the chain over her head and reeled in a medal that it harnessed.

"This is your uncle's Distinguished Service Order which he won for his actions in seeing the booby trapped village and warning the other units," said Frances.

"How did you get it?"

"He gave it to my mother to safeguard for his daughter until she was old enough to receive it. She gave it to me."

Chapter Twenty Four

Rodney and his mother attended the 1988 reunion - more of a final farewell as the men who attended were all in their 90s.

Bernie Smith came in from California, Allan LaRue was there, Charlie Hauser and Dick Shawcross both came as did Frank Eisenrick.

Hugh Coleman had died of a heart attack in 1985 at the age of 89. Pete Delaney died at his Put In Bay cottage in 1986. Martin Wilson had died in an auto accident in 1986, sliding off the Henry Hudson Parkway on some black ice. Jocko Rollins was dead of old age though no-one knew the circumstances or date - they had only received the invitation to the reunion back with a "DECEASED" stamp on it - maybe from a nursing home or something. Tom Billings sent a note saying he was in hospital and could not attend - but wished everyone well.

The group met at the Waldorf- Astoria hotel in New York City. It was now 70 years after the end of hostilities in the Great War.

"My friends, I'm sure we have all taken some time to ponder the actions of our much loved Captain, Herb Hathaway, after his revelations at our last reunion," said Frank Eisenrick after asking for everyone's attention at the dinner table.

"Personally I believe our Cap did what he thought was right and we will never know all the details that went into his decisions. I do struggle with the thought that we did not do what was expected of us in France, and that maybe others took our places among the dead. However, I also know that individually we did the best we could with what we were presented with in our actions. Some of us are here or had long lives and much to be proud of because of the actions of Captain Hathaway. Is he a hero? I'm not sure we will ever really know, as the consequences of his actions cannot be completely understood. I do know that my son, your daughter, my granddaughter and your families in whole or in part think he's a hero as they exist because of Captain Hathaway's actions and for that I am profoundly grateful."

There were a number of nods around the table.

"Human life is precious," said Charlie Hauser. "I thank my maker every time my family grows and I look at my wife and wonder why it is that we have been so blessed."

"Life may be precious but human deeds, especially profound deeds and accomplishments are worth more than extended life. It is really an issue between quality of a life lived and quantity," said Dick Shawcross. "Our Cap had both in some ways. He made the decision to help us all have lives we could look back on, at the cost of doubting his decision for the rest of his life, and he himself lived for 85 years. I only hope he did not struggle too much with his choice in his lifetime."

"It consumed him enough that he felt he had to share the burden with us," said LaRue. "I'm guessing he wondered long and hard if it was the right choice. And if it was the right choice to let us in on the secret."

Rodney Montgomery met with the remaining attendees after their private dinner. He told them about the visit from Rosalie Roberts and the baseball bat. He read the note to them.

"I remember that bat he carried around, said it was like a safety crutch in case we got into unexpected close combat. I preferred a sharp knife for that possibility," said Hauser. "In fact I still do. Sometimes you get some unruly wild things out on the farm."

Final Chapter

Rodney Montgomery checked into the hotel, an older dowager hotel on the Upper West Side of Manhattan, New York, the greatest city in the world. Some might disagree, reserving that distinction for London or Beijing or even Rome, but New York had married the old and new worlds and sat astride the strongest country in the history of the world. It may not always be so, but in the autumn of 1993, the 75th anniversary of the end of the Great War, New York was it.

The Upper West Side teemed with activity. Stores being stocked, shoppers, theatre goers in the evening, even the parents of students, travellers and those on hand for a special conference at the nearby Museum of Natural History.

Rodney was there on behalf of his great uncle who had died some years before. He was there to preside over the final chapter in the Great War for that last two veterans alive.

Both were in their mid-nineties, and both were still remarkably able despite their ages.

New Yorker Frank Eisenrick, soldier, baker, businessman and father had lived in New York his whole life. He had attended most of the reunions, his wife Donna joining him when she could.

Rodney had arranged a private room in a nearby restaurant for the final meeting. He met Mr. Eisenrick and his wife in the hotel lobby and walked with them the two blocks to the restaurant, chatting amiably, mostly about their day in New York.

"I could have met you at Gianties, instead of you fetching me from the hotel," Rodney said.

"Oh, no, we were walking right by it anyway. We stopped by our operation on 52nd Street. It's just a couple of blocks. We're used to it," said Mrs. Eisenrick.

"There we are, Gianties; this place had been here for a long time," said Frank.

"Well, you picked it so it must be good."

"They have the best rolls and pastries in town."

Rodney caught himself and then chuckled. "You must know almost all the restaurants in the whole of New York?"

"Indeed I do. However, we rarely eat out, so I try to patronize certain places when we do. Eddie Fiarona is the owner, well, used to be the owner, but he's retired now. We have been friends for a long time. He helped me build the business and I used to take him to Yankee games. His sons run the restaurant, or maybe his grandsons now. Actually it's restaurants, plural, there are two of them."

He pulled on the door. "This is the original, and there is another called Really Gianties, on account of his patrons not believing the two restaurants were run by the same owner. It's down in the 20s on the Lower East Side."

They moved into the restaurant where Frank was greeted by the elder Fiarona himself. A wiry man in his mid 80s he still stopped by the restaurant often and made a special trip when he heard his old friend Eisenrick was coming for dinner.

The small party took their seats with Eddie Fiarona sliding in himself after inquiring if they were still waiting for more of their party.

"Join us for a bit Eddie," said Frank. "Or if you prefer come back after dinner and have desert with us."

"The two chatted for a few minutes until Tom Billings came in, escorted by the restaurant manager. Tom was even more spry than Frank. He hopped up a little rise and settled in behind the table. Eddie took his leave promising to return after their meal.

"Tom Billings; we have only seen each other a few times in 70 years and yet I think I know you better than anyone in the world."

"Frank, every time I eat fresh bread, or get a little pastry confection, I think of you and Biarritz in 1918. Even the smell of such things takes me back."

"Why are the memories so powerful?" asked Rodney. "My uncle told my mother the same thing."

"Well, son, we were only there for a few months, but those days were like living a lifetime each day. Not that it was particularly memorable or profound, but so many things stick with you, when you are out of your element, especially when you cannot see the future laid out. We made a pact to only speak of the good things, the Soldier's Code, and that's why they bubble up, as that's what we have forced ourselves to remember."

"And now there are no good things left. My best friend Marty Wilson died a while back though his wife Lynn still calls. It is the bad things which affected each of us, though we decided to never talk of them."

"Can you speak of them now? Perhaps that would make you feel better, unburdening yourselves."

"Well, chief among them I think is why we each survived when so many did not. And after your uncle's confession we understand some of that, although in my case I had to reconcile the guilt with the knowledge that I had no understanding of what occurred and can have no hand in any guilt. I wish your uncle had held his tongue, but I understand the burden he carried and frankly don't blame him for speaking," said Frank.

"Yes, I see that," said Tom Billings. "But I don't hold any concern for any of that. It was his choice, made freely. Certainly that was a damn sight better than choosing which of us should die."

Tom went on, "Like when he sent me and Larry to warn the forward units of the ambush. Snap decision, just like Larry hesitating at that hill when I was certain to run behind it. What's worse is I never told anyone that I saw him get shot. Right in the head, boom, it exploded. He was dead in mid-stride. It was after that shot that I dived behind the hill. I rolled and knew he was dead, so I recovered my breath and picked up and ran to deliver the message. Finish the job, don't think about what happened."

"You saw it?" asked Frank.

"I did, and it was horrible. He was a few strides in front of me. I was just following him. As the hillock approached he moved to the left to round it on the village side, then hesitated. He was shot almost immediately after hesitating in making that choice. I leaped out of the way of his falling body, to the right, and tripped and fell behind the first rise of the hill."

"Why didn't you tell anyone?"

"Because that was the code, don't burden everyone with your horrors. What about you Frankie, did you see anything you held back?"

"Frank, took a sip of wine and pushed himself back in his chair, extending his legs. Donna moved in closer to hear.

"Well, I guess it's long enough ago now . . . "

"Please tell. The story and understanding of those events will lose your voices and experience if you say nothing," said Rodney.

"I'm a sentimental guy, you know," he said, glancing at Donna and dabbing a wet spot in the corner of his eye. "It's like all the bits and pieces, swirl around and I try to bring them together, try to see what they all mean. And then I see that they all revolve around something. They all revolve around love. Of people, of things, of ideas. But it's hard to get them to stick together. Almost like they have the gravity to move in orbit around what we love, but they won't quite touch it. Like the opposite poles of a magnet. They won't quite get close enough to join it and are content to simply revolve around. As long as they are close, that's right where they want to be, independent, not subsumed into the mass of love, but distinct on their own. I'm rambling. It's a hard concept to under-stand and harder to explain."

"All the things I've seen . . . And like you Tom, I expect there are far more things you could speak about if you chose to."

Tom nodded slowly.

"Hauser, Delany and I dropped into a trench, in one of the battles near Arras. The Germans had been driven back by our shelling. We dropped into the trench and moved along it, worried about finding a machine gun nest or something. Nobody ever told us what we might find or really what to do. Training in those days consisted of mostly cleaning your gun and trying to stay dry. In any combat it was survival of the most ruthless, I guess."

"We rounded a corner and there was a German on the ground. He was alive, but I don't know how. He was literally cut in half by something during the shelling. Fortunately it was muddy and it was hard to tell where the soldier was and where the dirt began, save for the blood. He motioned us to do something. Hauser thought he wanted water so he grabbed his canteen and screwed off the lid and tipped some into his mouth. He lay awkwardly and after a bit of gingerly looking about it was apparent he was leaning back on an unexploded shell."

"As we were trying to decide what to do, we heard voices coming from around the corner of the trench system. German voices. Once the shelling stopped the Germans who had abandoned the front line trenches would come back to defend their forward trenches from the offensive charge that usually followed. Our near dead German mustered up as loud as he could and said something in German. We scrambled the other way around the corner we had come in from when four German soldiers came into view. They spoke briefly and then one of them pulled out a hand gun and shot the dying soldier. With them clustered around his body, Delany, shot at the shell and it exploded killing all four men. I told Cap about it without some of the details and that's why Delaney got the DSM. A medal for service to be sure. Distinguished, I don't know."

"Afterwards I tried to figure out what the dying German said. As best I can figure he wanted us to mail a letter in his pocket. I don't know if that ever happened as it was many days later that I was able to figure out what he said."

The room was silent for a few moments, the veterans still in the trenches in Flanders. Donna broke the spell.

"Frank, why didn't you say?"

"It was our pact to keep quiet and I didn't want to burden you. Also we felt that if we spoke it might put younger generations off of battle, and sometimes those battles are necessary. Pacifism always results in a worse outcome than standing up and saying no."

"Oh, I don't know," said Tom. "After the war I simply couldn't fight anymore. I moved from town to town and job to job whenever things got tense. I just left. And I knew I left some good places and some good people. But I couldn't bear to fight about anything. I couldn't even fight for myself, I just up and left."

"I eventually retired in Florida. Liked that trailer park where I rented just before our 50th reunion. I liked the area, warm weather, living was easy and cheap. I could put myself out there as a handy man, and I had plenty of work if I wanted it. Eventually met a nice lady, Doris Corrall. She had moved there from Boston with her husband when he retired. He died not long later but Doris had made friends and she decided to stay in Florida. I did a number of jobs for her and we became friends. I resisted the urge to leave Florida a couple of times, forcing myself to wait a few more weeks before pulling up stakes. Those few weeks always let the tensions die down and I got to wondering what might have happened to me if I had taken the same approach in Buffalo, Cleveland, Chicago, Denver and St. Louis. My life would certainly have been different. And then it probably would have been different if Larry had swerved right instead of left when he came to that hill."

"So it isn't all about love, I don't think - God I hate that expression but can't help using it - I can't stand describing thinking negatively as not thinking at all, 'don't think' arrghh. Anyway, It's mostly about fear, whatever you are afraid of is what drives you, either to conquer it or to avoid it."

"The fight or flight response," said Rodney.

Tom nodded. "I didn't want to lose my life, and I certainly didn't want to lose it unexpectedly, suddenly without warning like Larry did. I guess my moving around gave me the feeling of control, even when it appeared I was losing my life, or at least the life I had built in each of those places. No regrets though. I've seen and done a lot."

"So did the war affect your thinking or were you always that way?" asked Rodney.

"You know, for me I think I always leaned that way, away from a fight, away from anything unpleasant. The war just enhanced those feelings."

Frank chimed in, "There might be something to that. I was always happy to have a plan and follow it. The war seemed to be that exactly. I followed orders and was always willing to do something different if the obvious reward was there. I wished I'd known German. I would have posted that letter. It probably had nothing important to say, but it was important to that guy. It was the last thing he wanted done, his last command in life. All he wanted was his final thoughts to be transmitted, probably to his family."

"We used to receive those letters, my mother tells me. Her father who was upset with my uncle refused to open them. But his mother did. They never had much to say, an amusing anecdote, a bit of an observation perhaps. The army was worried about detailed info being transmitted so they were general in nature. And still I know those notes were treated like gold by my grandmother. My mother said she would read them and it was his voice, his mannerisms filling the room. Powerful stuff."

"You gentlemen were in France for only a short time."

"Yes, but so much happened."

"But it seems as though there was much time between engagements."

"There was, except reliving the harrowing hours of an engagement usually took weeks because every single moment needed to be reviewed in three or even four dimensions."

"I agree," said Tom. "I can practically tell you the shade of mud we were existing on top of or the nature of the clouds and wind for each day we were there. For me it's much more than the battles. It's the everyday life that I remember. The actual fighting, not so much. But the preparation, the movements and the outcomes I remember in incredible detail. If I could draw, it would be so detailed it would be like a three D photograph."

"A hologram!"

"Yes, I suppose. Like a hologram. Do they have those now?"

Rodney nodded. "Is there more?"

"Oh, yes son, there is much more. I have tried to jot these things down in some detail but I always get lost in the tangents of detail," said Tom. "I'm afraid I'm not much of a writer."

"There was the time that Hughie Coleman was hit in the leg. It was at that tent battle," said Frank.

"The tent's battled?"

"No, that's just how we remembered the action. We moved deeply into German territory and came upon a tent city, a camp I guess. It looked abandoned but it wasn't. When we got close they opened fire from the first row of tents which were all machine gun nests dug in under the tents."

"Hughie ended up with a mixed American - British unit after the initial onslaught. The British officer was very experienced. He struck the charge that knocked out the machine gun nests but Hughie was hit badly in the leg. He fought on and receive a medal for it. I think the Britisher got the Victoria Cross. Funny thing is the way Hughie told it, they were just trying to avoid getting shot and ended up knocking down the whole ambush."

"Hundreds died in the assault but thanks to the Britisher and Hughie, a lot more did not."

"Hugh spent about four weeks in the hospital after that one. He nearly bled to death from a leg wound which didn't appear to be that bad when he showed us the scar. He said they told him he might have bled to death if it weren't for a tourniquet and a few 16ths of an inch."

"You know, by the time we were there almost everything was an offensive. We did the majority of the shooting. We were shelled and sometimes they came over the top, but only a bit here and there. Almost like they were probing for a weak spot that they never found. I'm not really sure what it would have been like in the trenches during a full blown German offensive."

"Our unit was lucky. One of the guys in another platoon near us, took a flamethrower clear on his left side. The Kraut had survived the barrage and holed up in an officers lean-to, meaning it had walls and a roof. As he approached to look inside the Kraut blasted him. Took it full on. The rest of us learned to take several shots at these structures before taking a look inside."

"The poor guy was melted on the entire left side. I remember talking to one of his mates who was there. He said watching his buddy's face after the blast was like seeing an egg, sliding down a frying pan. His skin melted down his face taking his left eye with it. The skin began to firm up quickly but the damage had been done. The poor guy was horribly disfigured. Though if you saw him in right side profile you'd never know."

"I asked after him some years later when I ran into someone at an American Legion function who knew guys in that unit. They didn't know much about him. He seemed to have disappeared."

"Oh, my god. How horrible. Now I know why you didn't want to speak of such things."

"Yes, dear. And those were just a few of the things. People forget there were animals there, mostly horses but also birds and dogs. They suffered horrible injuries but were usually put down, we couldn't do that to the men, though I heard some stories."

"Me too. I was sitting with a few English fellows during one of our resupply weeks and one of the guys, a sergeant I believe, started speaking about one such incident. He claimed he'd heard the story third hand from someone in a different unit, but the detail he provided was too much, he must have seen it firsthand."

"You mean, they killed one of their own?" asked one of the women.

"Strictly speaking yes, but according to the story the guy was horribly injured and would not have survived. His stomach had been ripped open by shrapnel and his intestines had spilt out. In those cases he would be transported and hospitalized in great pain only to die a day or two later. He said the man had also suffered huge wounds to his face and shoulder. They shot him at such an angle that he never saw it coming."

"Good lord, how could they do that?"

"How could they not? His suffering was beyond human capacity. Often times these cases simply passed out and then they died hours later never coming back to consciousness."

"Don't forget the trauma of doing this caused many to shoot themselves. Sometimes fatally. Suicide. In our group we never spoke of this, except to acknowledge that sometimes it must be done. I'm certain that every man in our unit did not want to be the one called upon to perform such a task. And thanks be to God, nobody ever did. At least nobody that I know of."

"Tom, did your war experiences have any effect on the way you lived your life?" asked Rodney.

"Well, young man, I have asked myself that question almost every night since I left Chicago. At that point, my pulling up stakes was becoming a pattern. I wondered. I think my natural make up is contrarian, and while I am not likely to fight I am also not likely to put up with things I don't like. So I move on. I think my war experiences, especially Larry's death, and the manner of it, probably reinforced what was already there in my personality. It seemed Larry made a fatal choice and did it carelessly and by simply following instructions. Me, I'm more complicated than that."

"What about Captain Hathaway's admission?"

"That one is easy for me. I support him entirely. Told him that too, right after he 'fessed up. In fact, his admission is almost like the mercy shots we just talked about. I'm sure that being provided the opportunity to protect his men was something he almost wished had never occurred because no matter the choice he made he would have to live with guilt and second guessing himself for the rest of his life."

"What does anyone want in life? Most want a quiet life without significant want. The rest want some combination of virtue, glory and immortality. In the end when they find these things are beyond their grasp, most of them settle for some measure of virtue, living a good life, contributing to their families, their communities and their friends. War service has a way of helping men to fill that gap. I know that my actions in the war were done with the best intentions and with the welfare of my friends and countrymen at heart. I must admit, only once did I feel that my experiences in Europe were insubstantial. I was at an American Legion once and overheard a group of men speaking about the battle of Iwo Jima with two marines who were involved with the discovery of extermination camps in Poland at the end of the second war. I was glad they didn't include me in their conversation as I felt much like the ladies here today feel when they hear details of the fighting."

Light in the restaurant had faded. The large buildings in Manhattan make it difficult to actually see the sun set, rather it is signalled by softer light and shadows in the streets. Natives grow accustomed to the change in the quality of light, almost the indescribable ethereal light of a solar eclipse. As the conversation wound on, the light changed until there was no more. Candles in the restaurant flickered. Eddie Fiarona sat down with them.

Rodney and Donna and Eddie wanted to keep the two veterans talking, but they were done.

"You know, anything more is just more of the same. Blood, death, fear, and suffering, from trench foot to wounds to bad food. It's all suffering of a kind. I suppose life is like that really. Just a constant effort to avoid suffering. How many people actually get what they really want in the way they imagine it. I've never seen it. Even successful people will tell you it isn't quite as they thought it would be. And even successful people struggle with doubt, battle misfortune and find themselves bitterly disappointed, sometimes by the very success they sought."

"I've been blessed or cursed with long life," said Frank with a chuckle and a smile. "Pretty much everything I've ever wanted came to pass. Sure there were ups and downs. Hard work, sometimes for nought or so it seemed at the time. And yet I cannot complain about my life. If there were no setbacks, no disappointments, there would be no joy in success and good fortune. You can't win and enjoy winning unless you have experienced loss or failure. No matter what, you march on, sometimes scarred, battered and less trusting of fortune, but you march on constantly trying to make your life more ordered, more cohesive while the spin of the world tries to pull it apart. Eventually it succeeds."

"So no matter how successful your life is, you are bound to die and ultimately fail? Isn't that a cheery thought," said Eddie.

"Is a life well lived a failure? I always believed that while most people believe God will stand in judgement of their lives, that the truth is that their peers and society stand in judgement of their lives. And society is ultimately less demanding than God on what constitutes success."

"In the end, most people get what they want, even if they never really articulate what that is. My life is the mirror of my nature, my comfort and my desire. It may seem jumbled and unclear to others who want things more cut and dried, but I cannot really say I regret any decision I made. And I made many. Even if I have a desire to revisit some decisions, to see what would have happened if I'd chosen a different direction, if I had to make one call, in hindsight, I cannot say any call I made was the wrong one."

"That sounds like success to me," said Rodney. "I think Captain Hathaway would likely agree."

"You know I'd like to hear his voice one more time. He was cheerful, happy and to the point all at the same time. The boys really did love him. Even more so when they ran across other CO's who displayed their foibles. Some were loud to cover their fears. Some were standoffish to cover their inexperience and others were sharp to try to maintain command. Cap Hathaway was good to us. Let us be men. Treated us as equals, like he was the conduit through which the official army reached our unit. He was the guy who had to be responsible. Sometimes he just asked us to humor the army's regulations so we wouldn't get him tossed in the stockade. I learned a lot about leadership from him. Used it in my business."

At the end of the day he cast a shadow on all our lives, made us better people I think. Funny that he had his own personal problems. I always thought he had it all figured out and that he lived his life in amused benevolence which he passed on to us."

"I know what you mean. He had a presence. Just like that photo you showed us Rodney. He's in the middle, in more command of the situation than the superior officer, and yet he is still with us. On our side, in control of things."

"That's quite a legacy. And yet, will it survive beyond the two of you or my memories of this conversation," asked Rodney.

"Well son, that's likely up to you in a way. However, I know the things he taught me have been passed on to my family. Even some of his phrasing, mannerisms and the like, his way of sparking people up with a gentle chide, or his love of temporary nicknames, tailored to the situation. We try to be like those we admire. So in a way he lives in all of us. And I guess, do so many more people that we encounter on a regular basis. Our experiences make us and they are translated into our actions which in turn influence those we know."

"So few are remembered for anything specific - for a great act, a great accomplishment or a great feat of engineering. Most of us are remembered in a speech pattern, likes, dislikes and ways of thinking. All of which is virtually untraceable."

"All of us cast a shadow across the future. Some of those shadows are large. Some are barely noticeable. You have to be content with that or your life appears unimportant. But to the large number of people you cross in your lifetime, it is not."

Eddie Fiarona sat quietly. His staff had cleaned up around them and he waved them off for the night. They looked at the restaurant manager for corroboration and received it with a nod and indulgent smile. Old Eddie was revered in this place.

"Please, another bottle of wine and pitcher of water. I have not heard these sentiments expressed out loud before. I often think them in a swirling way - never quite able to put my finger on these ideas. As an old man, I seek the comfort that you two appear to have achieved."

"Nirvana?"

"No, I think it is just peace. An understanding of life, of things, of the world beyond your existence in it."

"No you guys are getting a little too profound," laughed Donna, unsure if she should break the spell.

"It's my life. It doesn't tie up into a nice neat ball," said Tom. "It cannot be quantified or disassembled to determine its ultimate value. And I like it that way."

"Ms Roberts wanted it to tie up nicely. She couldn't accept that there was no finish, no end to her inquiry."

"That's my point. There is no end to it. We may falter, fail and ultimately pass on, but bits of us travel on in ways we can never know. Our existence is unquantifiable. Sure there are things that are easily pointed to as significant but it is the small stuff which influences people for generations that has the most impact, like grains of sand I suppose, each one tiny and insignificant on its own, but taken together help to build a beach or push a life in a specific direction. Sometimes it's like the absence of a thing which can make the difference - like a shadow blocks out the light."

The small group remained chatting; now about yesterday, then about today and eventually about tomorrow. And the shadows remained cast by the light around the table.

Another novel by F. Bradley Reaume

A Picture of Distance

The story of the Stuart family of Toronto and the lives of their six children through the 20th century in war, economic upheaval, and personal struggles.

The girls scurried back to the dormitory, quietly moved through the cellar door and stealthily returned to their own room, dodging a couple of girls on the way. Their coats were sure to give them away if they were caught. Anne fished out a needle and thread from her coat pocket. The girls turned their coats inside out and carried them like they were about to do some repairs with Anne flashing the needle to anyone who they encountered. As long as they weren't touched there was nothing that would give away their short absence.

Once back in the safety of their room they hastened to their tasks to further cover their time tracks. The last of the laundry was completed and hung to dry. The dormitory mother came to check on their progress with the laundry and give them their nightly bed check. They had been gone for less than two hours.

It had all been very exciting and incredibly mundane. However, Kate knew she would not soon forget the frenzy of young men, the large crowd and the happy formality of the evening. Nor would she forget her sister's seeming indifference to the rules that others followed without question and her own willingness to be led.

After a bit of whispered chatter regarding their adventure they stopped talking. Kate tried to think of instances where Anne was inexplicably busy with other tasks and did not join the rest of the girls. She easily identified several and suspected a few more before slipping into dreamless sleep, having gotten away with the harmless jaunt.

The next morning, the girls readied for breakfast before going to class.

Everything was routine and they quickly forgot about their adventure the night before while attending to their usual morning responsibilities.

The day flew by. However that evening, as they took their places at the table for the evening meal it quickly became apparent that the usual routine had been upset. Attributing it to the big news of the day before, the girls paid little attention to the glances being tossed their way.

"The mayor gave a rousing speech at City Hall last night. Kate, did he say he had been informed of the armistice by the Prime Minister?" asked the headmistress.

"I'm afraid I was doing laundry last night, ma'am and didn't hear him speak on the radio," said Kate.

"Anne, did he mention where they new hospital will be located?" asked the headmistress.

"I was with Kate working on the laundry and had no time for the radio."

The headmistress moved to the table and placed the newspaper between Kate and Anne. A photo of the mayor standing on the steps of City Hall was on the front page, and standing behind the mayor, up a small flight of stairs beside a pillar, were Kate and Anne, as plain as day, looking cold and a little wide-eyed.

The headmistress waited a moment to let the gravity of the photo sink in, "As I as saying did he say he had been in touch with the Prime Minister?"

Kate swallowed hard. This was not likely to be a very pleasant few days.

Another novel by F. Bradley Reaume

All Fall Down

New York is destroyed by terrorists but the fallout is not only radioactive.

The country is rocked inside and out by political and economic concerns. Taken together they create a new normal to be understood.

The captain reached for the controls and pressed a button which set the hold cover in motion, once engaged it would open up the cargo bay exposing machinery stored under the deck. The whine of the motors hauling the heavy metal cover away from the large opening in the deck could be heard throughout the ship. Several more minutes passed.

The Sea Merchant had cleared the tip of Manhattan and was passing the North Cove Yacht Harbour.

An explosion on the bow stunned the ship. Small explosions and shrapnel ripped through the bridge followed by a roar of jet engines. Two F18s flared out over head, now visible through the shattered glass of the bridge as they made their way up the Hudson. They made to turn for a second pass.

The captain grabbed the internal radio control. "Fire!"

The F18 pilots had located the ship, their first rocket had hit the bow in an attempt to disable the screw. As they passed they saw the opening in the deck. The fighters fired their first close range volley into the control tower to attempt to kill anyone there and further disable the ship. Two Port Authority speed boats were making their way to the Sea Merchant as the jets passed overhead.

Since Rome and the near miss in London the previous year, western port operations were sensitive to anomalies in procedure. The F18s could be on scene within minutes of getting the call. Other defensive measures were also engaged.

The jets wheeled around to challenge the tanker ship again. Both pilots expected to again pepper the control tower, and then swing around to fire rockets at the screw, just under the waterline in the stern. However, both pilots had seen the open hold and the strange contraption inside.

"Shit, Red Leader what was that?" the question was unnecessary as both pilots knew what they faced.

They had to target ship's command and the hold on their second pass. They made calibration adjustments as they turned to bear down on the Sea Merchant.

The planes took deadly seconds to turn around. As the fighters approached the ship, the large metal cylinder in the hold was flung skyward by the contraption it was resting in. The first F18 pilot couldn't target it as he was locked in on the ship and was too close

304

to recalibrate his target. He fired anyway, as he had no other shot. Two rockets exploded against the bridge and two more entered the hold area.

The rockets hit amidships, into the open hatch and exploded convulsing the deck. A small dingy was nestled under the ship's port side and a few men had jumped aboard. Red Leader had seen the men flee the tanker and wondered for a moment what they were doing.

A Port Authority speedboat approached the Sea Merchant and shots pinged off their boat. They returned fire to the deck edge of the ship and swung around the larger cargo ship to see men boarding the dingy. They squeezed off a few rounds before more shots came their way, causing them to duck and take cover as they rounded the bow.

The second fighter pilot was also targeted on the ship but with more time to react as the cylinder rose he flipped quickly to manual and let off a stream of rounds aimed at the cylinder as it climbed into the air. His desperation, coupled with the speed of his jet and proximity to the new target guaranteed his miss.

The metal cylinder, about seven meters in length, and not quite two meters in diameter, glinted in the sun as it slowed, reaching the height of its upward thrust. It looked like someone had flung a piece of sewer pipe into the air.

Some New Yorkers with a view of the river watched the dance between the jets, the ship and its cargo with only the faintest idea of the drama was occurring. A few knew what they watched and simply held firm, unable to take their eyes off the drama. Most New Yorkers only heard the sounds, which reminded them of the

September 11th airplane attack.

The cylinder hung over the river, pausing briefly as it lost the last of its upward momentum and began to fall back to earth. The second F18 pilot exhaled as he banked his plane over the Statue of Liberty and turned towards the Jersey Shore, now two miles away from the river, then three, then four.

The Red Leader F18 pilot had banked the other way over Brooklyn and had turned back toward Manhattan when a sunburst filled his screen. He was flying at nearly the speed of sound directly into a nuclear fireball. He pulled on his controls in a hopeful but ultimately inconsequential attempt to survive.

The second pilot was moving away from the explosion when he saw the flash of light coming from behind. He continued to fly away from the scene waiting for the inevitable shock wave.

As the cylinder rose against the backdrop of Manhattan, the crew screamed "Allahu Akbar". The captain clicked off a text message . . . "It is done." As he pressed 'send', the bomb exploded.

The presence of fighter jets had alerted many New Yorkers to the drama in the Hudson. Many thousands could see the ship and witnessed the attacks from the fighters. Many saw the cylinder rise from the ship and could feel their chests tighten - not really knowing why, but fearing the worst.

The cylinder had reached just over 400 feet in altitude, falling back about 35 feet before exploding. Watching from the upper floors of many Manhattan skyscrapers the skirmish on the Hudson was small and far away given the vast scope of the city spread out beneath them. The cylinder reached up only as high as some of the smaller skyscrapers in its vicinity.

Millions were vaporized as the air itself burned. With temperatures rivaling the center of the sun, metal and glass melted, the water in concrete and mortar boiled and exploded. The air itself was consumed with the resulting shock wave, first pushing everything outward and then rapidly pulling it back in as the air itself rushed in to replace that which was consumed.

About the Author

F. Bradley Reaume

Brad has written for his
entire career, first as a
sportswriter, then moving
into news and column
writing. He spent many
years writing in politics
and government before
pursuing fiction. Casting
Giant Shadows is his third
novel.

Brad has written several books, including:

All Fall Down (2016) - novel

Other Skylines (2015) - short fiction collection

A Picture of Distance (2014) - novel

The Wonderful World of Wogs (2014)

(children) Illustrated by Nicole Flax